TO KILL A
WARLOCK

TO KILL A WARLOCK

Book 1 of the Dulcie O'Neil series

HP MALLORY

TO KILL A WARLOCK
by
H.P. Mallory

To Kill A Warlock

Copyright © 2010 by H.P. Mallory

For everyone who took a chance on my books and helped me reach the success I have.

Thank you.

Acknowledgements:

To my fabulous mother, thank you for all your help. This book wouldn't be anywhere near as concise without your input.

To my husband, thank you for all your love and support.

To my son, Finn, for all your coos and giggles every morning.

ONE

There was no way in hell I was looking in the mirror.

I knew it was bad when I glanced down. My stomach, if that's what you wanted to call it, was five times its usual size and exploded around me in a mass of jelly-like fat. To make matters worse, it was the color of overcooked peas—that certain jaundiced yellow.

"Wow, Dulce, you look like crap," Sam said.

I tried to give her my best "don't piss me off" look, but I wasn't sure my face complied because I had no clue what my face looked like. If it was anything like my stomach, it had to be canned-pea green and covered with raised bumps. The bumps in question weren't small like what you'd see on a toad—more like the size of dinner plates. Inside each bump, my skin was a darker green. And the texture … it was like running your finger across the tops of your teeth—jagged with valleys and mountains.

"Can you fix it?" I asked, my voice coming out monster-deep. I shouldn't have been surprised—I was a good seven feet tall now. And with the substantial body mass, my voice could only be deep.

"Yeah, I think I can." Sam's voice didn't waver which was a good sign.

I turned to avoid the sun's rays as they broke through the window, the sunlight not feeling too great against my boils.

I glanced at Sam's perfect sitting room, complete with a sofa, love seat and two armchairs all in a soothing beige, the de facto color for inoffensive furniture. Better Homes and

Gardens sat unattended on Sam's coffee table—opened at an article about how beautiful drought resistant plants can be.

"You have nine eyes," Sam said.

At least they focused as one. I couldn't imagine having them all space cadetting out. Talk about a headache.

Turning my attention from her happy sitting room, I forced my nine eyes on her, hoping the extra seven would be all the more penetrating. "Can you focus please?" I snapped.

Sam held her hands up. "Okay, okay. Sheesh, I guess getting changed into a gigantic booger put you into a crappy mood."

"Gee, you think?" My legs ached with the weight of my body. I had no idea if I had two legs or more or maybe a stump—my stomach covered them completely. I groaned and leaned against the wall, waiting for Sam to put on her glasses and figure out how to reverse the spell.

Sam was a witch and a pretty damned good one at that. I'd give her twenty minutes—then I'd be back to my old self. "Was it Fabian who boogered you?" she asked.

The mention of the little bastard set my anger ablaze. I had to count to five before the rage simmered out of me like a water balloon with a leak. I peeled myself off the wall and noticed a long spindle of green slime still stuck to the plaster; it reached out as if afraid to part with me.

"Ew!" Sam said, taking a step back from me. "You are so cleaning that wall."

"Fine. Just get me back to normal. I'm going to murder Fabian when I see him again."

Fabian was a warlock, a master of witchcraft. The little cretin hadn't taken it well when I'd come to his dark arts store to observe his latest truckload delivery. I knew the little rat was importing illegal potions (love potions, revenge potions, lust potions … the list went on) and it was my job to stop it. I'm a Regulator, someone who monitors the creatures of the Netherworld to ensure they're not breaking any rules. Think law enforcement. And Fabian clearly was breaking some rule.

Otherwise, he wouldn't have turned me into a walking phlegm pile.

Sam turned and faced a sheet of chocolate chip cookie mounds. "Hold on a second, I gotta put these in the oven."

She sashayed to the kitchen and I couldn't help but think what an odd picture we made: Sam, looking like the quintessential housewife with her apron, paisley dress and Stepford wife smile, and me, looking like an alien there to abduct her.

She slid the cookies in, shut the oven door and offered me a cheery grin. "Now, where was I? Ah yes, let me just whip something together."

Kneeling down, she opened a cupboard door beneath the kitchen island and grabbed two clay bowls, three glass jars and a metal whisk. One jar was filled with a pink powder, the next with a liquid that looked like molasses, and the third with a sugary-type powder.

"Sam, I don't have time to watch you make more cookies."

"Stop being so cranky! I'm stirring a potion to figure out how the heck I'm going to help you. I have no idea what spell that little creep put on you."

I frowned, or thought I did.

Sam opened a jar and took a pinch of the pink powder between her fingers. She dropped it in the bowl and whisked. Then she spooned one tablespoon of the molasses-looking stuff into the bowl and whisked again. Dumping half the white powder in with the rest, she paused and then dumped in the remainder.

Then she studied me, biting her lip. It was a look I knew too well—one that wouldn't lead to anything good.

"What?" I demanded.

"I need some part of your body. But it doesn't look like you have any hair. Hmm, do you have fingernails?"

I went to move my arm and four came up. But even with four arms, I didn't have a single fingernail—just webbed hands that looked like duck feet. I bet I was a good swimmer.

"Sorry, no fingernails."

"Well, this might hurt then."

She turned around and pulled a butcher knife from the knife block before approaching me like a stealthy cat. Even with my enormous body, I was up and out of her way instantly.

"Hold on a second! Keep that thing away from me!"

"I need something from your body to make the potion work right. I won't take much, just a tiny piece of flesh."

I felt like adding "and not a drop of blood," but was too pre-occupied with protecting myself. I glanced at the wall and eyed the snotty globule, still attached to the plaster as if it had a right to be there. "What about that stuff?"

Sam grimaced but stopped advancing. "I'm not touching that."

"Okay, fine. How about some spit then?"

"Yeah, that might do."

My entire body breathed a sigh of relief which, given the size of me, was a pretty big breath. She put the knife back, and I made my way over to her slowly—not convinced she wasn't going to Sweeney Todd on me again.

She held out the bowl. "Spit."

I wasn't sure if my body was capable of spitting, but I leaned over and gave it a shot. Something slid up my throat, and I watched a blob of yellow land in her bowl.

It was moving. Gross.

It continued to vacillate as it interacted with the mixture, sprawling this way and that like it was having a seizure.

"Yuck," Sam said, holding the bowl as far away from her as possible. She returned it to the counter as the timer went off. Facing the oven, she grabbed a mitt that said "Kiss me, I'm Wiccan," pulled open the oven door and grabbed hold of the cookie sheet, placing them on the counter.

My stomach growled, sounding like an angry wolf, and unable to stop myself, I lumbered toward the cookies. I grabbed the sheet, not feeling the heat of the tin on my webbed hand. Sam watched me, her mouth hanging open as I lifted the sheet of cookies and emptied every last one into my mouth, swallowing them whole.

Sam's brows furrowed with anger, giving her normally angelic face a little attitude. "I was saving those to bring to work on Monday, thank you very much!"

Sam didn't wear angry well. She was too pretty—dark brown shoulder length hair, perfect skin, perfect teeth, and big brown eyes.

"Come on, Sam," I pleaded, my mouth brimming with gooey chocolate. "You know I didn't do it on purpose. I don't even like sweets."

Something slimy and pink escaped my mouth and ran itself over my lips. It took me a second to realize it was my tongue. Rather than curling back into my mouth, it hesitated on my lip as I focused on a stray chocolate chip lounging against the counter. Instantly, my tongue lurched out and grabbed hold of the chip, recoiling into my mouth like a spent cobra.

Sam quirked a less-than-amused brow and ran her palms down her paisley apron, as though composing herself. I have to count to ten, twenty sometimes. Otherwise, my temper is an ugly son of a bitch.

"Besides, none of the guys at work deserve them anyway." I knew because I worked with Sam.

She appeared to be in the process of forgiving me, a slight smile playing with the ends of her lips. I turned to the potion sitting in the bowl. The yellow ball of spit was still shivering. I nearly gagged when Sam stabbed it with the whisk and continued stirring.

I peered over her shoulder and watched the potion change colors—going from a pale brown to red then deepening into flame orange. "What's it doing?"

Sam nodded as if she were watching a movie, knew the ending, and was just dying to tell someone what happens. "Ah, of course, I should've known. The little devil put a *Hemmen* on you."

"A what?"

"It's a short-term shape-shifting charm. You'll be back to normal in about five hours or so."

"Five hours? Look at me! Can't you get rid of it sooner?"

Sam shook her head. "Would take lots of herbs and potions I don't have. I'd probably have to get them at Fabian's." She laughed. "How ironic is that? Just hang tight. It'll go away, I promise."

It figures the little bastard would've put a short-term spell on me. Currently, there weren't any laws against turning someone into a hideous creature if it would wear off after a day. And even if he had turned me into this creature long term, he'd probably only get a slap on the wrists. The Netherworld wasn't exactly good with doling out punishments.

I was working on making it better.

"You're sure?" I asked.

She nodded. "One hundred percent. Let's just watch a couple movies to keep your mind off it."

She hurried to her entertainment center and scanned through the numerous titles, using her index finger to guide her. "Dirty Dancing? Bridget Jones?"

"The first or second Bridget?"

"I have both," she said with a triumphant smile.

"I like the first one better."

With a nod of agreement, Sam pulled the DVD out and gingerly placed it into the player.

6

I wasn't really sure what to do with myself. I couldn't fit on her couch, and with my slime ball still suspended on the wall, sitting was out.

Sam pointed a finger in my general direction. "How did Fabian catch you unaware enough to change you into … that?"

I sighed—which came out as a grunt.

"Well?" she asked while skipping into the kitchen to microwave a packet of popcorn.

I couldn't quite meet her eyes and, instead, focused on drawing slimy lines on her counter top with one of my eight index fingers.

This was the part of the story I was least excited about. Fabian never should've caught me with my guard down. I'm a fairy. We're renowned for being extremely quick, and we've got more magic in our little finger … well, you get it.

"My back was to him," I mumbled. "I know, I know … super dumb."

Sam's eyebrows reached for the ceiling. "That doesn't sound like you at all, Dulce. Why was your back to him?"

If I wasn't excited about that last part of the story, this part excited me even less. "There was someone in his shop—a guy I've never seen before."

Sam laughed and quirked a knowing brow. "So let me make sure I've got this right."

She plopped her hands on her hips and paused for a good three seconds. Maybe she was getting me back for the cookies. "You, one of the strongest fairies around, turned your back on a known dark arts practitioner because he had a hot guy in his store?"

"No, it wasn't that at all. I'd never seen him before, and I couldn't figure out what he was."

As a fairy, I have the innate ability to decipher a creature as soon as I see one. I can tell a warlock from a vampire from a gorgon in seconds. I don't get paid the big bucks for nothing.

7

Sam's face took on a definite look of surprise, her eyes wide, her lips twitching. "You couldn't tell what he was? Wow, that's a first."

I nodded my bulbous head. "Exactly. And if he's here permanently, he never checked in with me or Headquarters."

Any new creature who hoped to settle in Splendor, California, needed to contact Headquarters, otherwise known as the A.N.C (Association for Netherworld Creatures). And more pointedly, they had to register with me. This new stranger had done neither. Maybe he'd gotten lost when coming over. It wasn't rare for a creature to come through the passage from the Netherworld to Earth and somehow get lost along the way. You'll find the directionally challenged everywhere.

"Maybe you should talk to Bram," Sam said. "He always seems to know what's going on."

It wasn't a bad idea, actually. Bram was a vampire (I know, how cliché …) who ran a nightclub called No Regrets. No Regrets was in the middle of the city and was the biggest hangout for creatures of the Netherworld. If something was going down, Bram was always among the first to know.

"Yeah, not a bad idea," I said.

First things first, I'd pay a visit to Fabian and let him know how much I didn't appreciate his little prank. Then, if he couldn't give me any info on his strange visitor, I'd try Bram. My third choice was Dagan, a demon who ran an S&M club called Payne that wasn't far from No Regrets. Dagan was always my last resort—I hated going to Payne. I'd seen things there that had scarred me for life.

So it looked like my plans for the weekend were shot. Not like I had much planned—just editing chapters of my romance novel, *Captain Slade's Bounty*. I'd been looking forward to a quiet weekend, so I could focus on Captain Slade and his ladylove, Clementine. Now, it looked like I'd be working the streets of Splendor instead.

Big goddammit.

###

Six hours later, and with Bridget Jones one and two, Dirty Dancing and four bowls of popcorn under my belt, I was home and back to myself. I felt like hell considering I'd eaten more in one evening than I usually ate in a day.

I headed through my sparse living room and straight to my bathroom. I threw off the clothes Sam had lent me (the mass I'd been turned into had shredded my outfit) and turned on the shower full force. I was back to myself, but still disgusting—covered in a layer of what looked like clear snot, like I'd just dropped out of God's nose.

I tested the water, waiting for it to warm. Then I turned to face myself in the mirror. I'm not a vain person but I was very happy to see my small and slender self reflected back at me. I pulled my mane of honey-gold hair from behind my back and inspected it. If I was narcissistic about anything, it was my hair. It was long—right down to my lower back and it looked like it had fared well in the metamorphosis. Except for the slime.

I keep my hair long because I'm not thrilled with my ears. As a fairy, my ears come to points at the tops. Think Spock. Other than that, I look like a human. And no, I don't have wings.

I checked the water again; it was warm enough. I lived in a pretty crappy apartment and the pipes in the wall screamed every time I turned the hot water on—they'd just pound if I wanted cold. I know I mentioned earlier that I make a good living, and I do. The crap apartment is due to the fact that I'm saving all my money to retire from the A.N.C. Then I can focus on my writing full time.

It might sound strange that one as magical as I would need to work nine-to-five weekdays and some weekends, but there it is. There are strict laws that disallow those of us who can, to create money out of thin air. I guess the powers that be thought about it and realized all creatures who can create

9

something from nothing—fairies, witches and warlocks, just to name a few—certainly would be at the top of the food chain … something bad for the less fortunate creatures and humans, too.

That, and money created from magic turns to dust after a few days anyway.

So I have to work. I've accepted it.

I stepped under the less-than-strong flow of water, which was more like a little boy peeing on my head, and grabbed my gardenia-scented soap, lathering my entire body. I repeated the process four more times before I could actually say I felt any semblance of clean.

After toweling myself off, I plodded into the living room with a towel wrapped around my head and body. Then I noticed the blinking red light on the answering machine beckoning to me. I had three new messages.

I hit play. Bram's alto voice, the pitch reminiscent of his English roots, filled my living room.

"Ah, I've missed you, Sweet. Come by the club. I have information for you."

The arrogant bastard—he never bothered saying, "It's Bram." As to the information he had … that could be meaningless. Bram had been trying to get into my pants since I became a Regulator—about two years ago. And just because he had my home phone number didn't mean he'd succeeded—I used to be listed in the phone book.

I deleted the message. I'd have to pay him a visit tomorrow. The next message was from my dry cleaners—my clothes were ready to be picked up. The third message was from my boss.

"Dulce, it's Quillan, Sam told me what Fabian did to you. Just calling to make sure you're okay. Give me a call when you get in."

I hit delete. Quillan was a good boss; he was the big wig of Headquarters, and an elf.

Elves are nothing like you're imagining them, although they are magical. Whereas I have the innate ability to create something from nothing (all it takes is a little fairy dust), Quillan is magical in his own way. He can cast spells, control his own aging and he's got the strength of a giant. Fairies and elves are like distant cousins—sprung from the same magical family tree but separated by lots of branches.

Quillan is tallish—maybe five-ten or so, slim, and has a certain regality to him. He's got a head of curly blond hair that would make Cupid envious, bronze skin, and eyes the color of amber. And he's also the muse for the hero in my romance novel. But he doesn't know that.

I wasn't in the mood to call Quillan back. I'd add him to my long list of visits for tomorrow. Even though it was Saturday, it looked like I'd be working.

Sometimes working law enforcement for the Netherworld is a real bitch.

TWO

A.N.C. Headquarters is located on Main Street in Splendor. It's a two-story, white concrete building with dark triangular windows—like it shared the same architect as the Amityville house. It was busy when I arrived at nine a.m. Saturday morning. A couple of werewolves were already in custody, a fairy in one holding cell, and a leprechaun in the other.

"Hey, Baby," the fairy called out.

"Hello, Zara. Nice outfit," I grumbled.

She twirled around as if I were a ballerina. Her hot pink halter dress inched up her thighs until I worried she might flash everyone. With her fishnets, she looked every inch the hooker—which was fitting, considering she was one. She smiled as I walked by, her red lipstick screaming out, as if enraged it was paired with orange hair and a pink dress.

I nodded at Elsie, our receptionist, who was busy entering the weres' info.

"Hey, Dulcie," she murmured, her voice barely audible over the crying of the old woman next to her.

"My poor baby! They ate him!" the haggard woman sobbed. Amid a bout of breathlessness, she pointed at the two weres. "Tore him to bits, so there was nothing left but fur! Disgusting, you're disgusting!"

I cringed.

Elsie just bobbed her head while she tried to console the old woman, even as the old woman berated her. Ever since creatures of the Netherworld had decided to go public, over fifty years ago, we were still subject to fear and ignorance from humans. Most humans had learned to accept us, but plenty still believed we should all be dead.

I hightailed it down the hall and poked my head into Quillan's office, only to find it empty. With a shrug, I headed further down the hall to my desk.

Every city with a large enough Netherworld population had its own A.N.C. precinct. Our A.N.C office wasn't a huge unit—Quillan kept about fifteen employees on staff—but it was big enough for Splendor and the three other cities within our jurisdiction—Sanctity, Estuary and Haven. The crux of the Netherworld activity—what activity there was—always centered in Splendor, though.

When I reached my desk, Quillan was sitting on the edge of it, deep in conversation with Trey, our only other Regulator. Quillan flashed me a disarming grin of pearly whites, as I threw my backpack onto my seat.

"Dulcie O'Neil, you decided to grace us with your presence. You okay?" he asked.

Trey laughed, his rumbling chuckles echoing through an immense stomach. "Heard you got turned into somethin' pretty nasty, O'Neil?" he said.

I narrowed my eyes. "Yeah, I did Trey, and when I looked in the mirror, there you were."

Quillan grinned and put a concerned hand on my shoulder. "You didn't call me back last night."

I turned my attention from the heat of his hand to my computer and booted it up. "I was really tired. I got in the shower and went to bed."

"Are you going to see Fabian today?" Quillan asked.

"That's my plan." At the mention of Fabian, I remembered the stranger who'd been in his store. "Before the little bastard turned me into that green thing, I noticed a man in his store. I couldn't tell what he was."

"Really?" Quillan asked.

"Yeah. And he hadn't registered with me. Did anyone register with you yesterday?"

Quillan pulled out his Blackberry and flipped through the bios of recent creatures to our territory. Every bio included the creature's photo, what part of the Netherworld he or she was from, his or her race, reasons for being in our district, and contact names and addresses.

"I thought maybe he'd gotten lost on his way over," I said.

Quillan nodded to Trey. "You see anyone suspicious around?"

Trey managed to shake not only his head but also his three double chins. He was one chubby guy, well, a hobgoblin actually. The only reason he was a Regulator was he had a great knack for seeing the future and the past, something that made him ... useful, though I hated to admit it.

"Nothin' out of the ordinary," he said, the light glinting off his perpetually wet upper lip.

"I'm planning to talk to Fabian about it today," I said. "After I let him know exactly how much I didn't appreciate his stunt yesterday."

Quillan smiled. "I'm coming with you. I don't want him trying anything again."

I had to swallow the annoyance that careened through me like a fat man on a bicycle. "I can handle this on my own."

"Not up for argument," Quillan said.

"Fine," I grumbled, secretly making note of his tight-lipped expression—it would serve me well in my characterization of Captain Slade, the hero of my romance novel.

Quillan quirked a brow but didn't say anything more. Trey returned to his desk which, unfortunately, was right across from mine. Quillan's office had a great view of Splendor Park which was now in bloom with orange poppies.

My desk had a view of Trey.

"I'll just get my jacket," Trey said.

"What is this—a field trip?" I asked.

Quillan met my gaze and shook his head. I frowned and turned my computer off, wondering why I'd booted it up in the first place. Not finding an immediate answer, I stood and started down the hall, ahead of Quillan.

"And what's Trey doing here anyway?" I asked. "Doesn't he have something better to do on a Saturday?"

Quillan shrugged. "Apparently not."

As we hurried down the hall, me hoping we'd lose Trey somewhere along the way, Zara wrapped her hands around the prison bars, running them up and down, trying to be suggestive.

"Hi, Honey," she said, looking at him like he was crack and she, Whitney Houston.

Quillan didn't meet her eye. "Hi, Zara."

She smiled and made me want to hit her. Her attention fell to me, and she smiled even wider.

"When are you two going to give me a visit? You're both so easy on the eyes. We could have us a good time, you know? A little fairy on fairy action …"

"Not anytime soon," I said between stiff lips.

"Who's driving?" Trey asked with a toothy grin, coming up behind us.

"My car is right out front," I said in a less than thrilled voice.

"Shotgun," Trey said.

I shook my head. "You ride with me, you're in the back."

"Jesus, O'Neil, love you too."

Quillan opened the front door for me. "Enough, both of you."

Once outside, I unlocked my yellow Jeep Wrangler and threw open the driver-side door. I jumped in while Quillan folded the passenger seat forward, allowing Trey to catapult into my small back seat.

15

It took us a few minutes to reach Fabian's store—it was just a couple miles east of Headquarters. There was plenty of parking, which was almost never the case, so I sailed into the spot right out front. It always makes my day when I get a good parking spot.

I jumped down from the Wrangler and pulled the seat forward. A look of surprise crossed Trey's wide face, which lit up in a smirk. "Aw, you do love me."

I shook my head. "Just get out, please."

Quillan was already at the front door of Fabian's shop. "Looks like he doesn't open until eleven."

Eleven was over an hour away. I strode past Quillan and headed into the alley that bordered Fabian's. "I know the back way," I said with a self-satisfied grin.

I reached for the back door and froze. It was already ajar.

Something was rotten in the state of Denmark, or Splendor, as the case may be.

"What's the hold up?" Trey asked, his putrid breath rolling down my neck.

I cringed and glared up at him, wishing I could've arrested him for halitosis.

"It's open. Fabian always locks his door."

I pulled my Op 6 pistol from my shoulder holster. Even though it was a small gun, the length just spanning the width of my palm and fingers, it was lethal. The dragon blood bullets would cause instant death to any creature unfortunate enough to get in the way of one.

I nudged open the door to Fabian's store, my pistol ready should the need arise. If the little jerk was brewing an illegal potion, I needed to catch him in the act. And if he was in the middle of an illegal sale to a human, the bust would be a gold star on my upcoming review. Most Netherworld creatures could handle the toxins involved in drinking potions, but the same couldn't be said for humans. With their weak temperaments, just a swallow could do permanent damage.

I turned to Quillan and Trey and brought my index finger to my mouth in the universal sign of *shut the F up*. They both nodded and were good about not making any noise behind me. That is, until Trey kicked something metal and sounded as inconspicuous as a garbage truck in a narrow alley.

"So sorry," he muttered.

'Shhh!" I turned to glare at him then held my gun close to my face as I continued down the long hallway. I couldn't see a damned thing.

My fairy eyesight finally kicked in and I was able to make out the corners of the wall and the mouth of the doorway leading into Fabian's store. When I came to the front of the store, it looked empty. I walked headlong into a piece of mermaid netting hanging from a ledge and pushed the sticky stuff out of my face, hoping it might catch Trey.

Talk about claustrophobia—Fabian's store held entirely too much junk. Boxes piled against the walls so the actual space within the room was reduced to maybe twelve feet by twelve feet. Barely enough room to breathe. I continued forward, wondering where the hell the little bastard could be. I couldn't hear any voices. Maybe they'd heard Trey trip and had already hidden whatever illegal deeds they'd been doing.

Damn Trey.

My foot hit something and made a *thunk* sound. I dropped to my knees and clenched my hand into a fist. I shook it until a mound of fairy dust grew in my palm. Reholstering my pistol, I opened my palm and snapped with the fingers of my other hand. A flame bubbled up between my thumb and middle finger. I blew on the flame and the fairy dust caught fire, lighting the room in an eerie glow.

I glanced down and couldn't stifle my gasp. I'd nearly tripped on a head, Fabian's head. It had been ripped from his body and not in one neat stroke like you might find with a long blade. This looked more like the work of an animal—the flesh at the nape of what was once Fabian's neck was torn and uneven. I lifted my palm of light and spotted a mangled arm with tendons and muscle looped back over it, looking like a red lace doily. A few fingers were scattered in a far corner.

"Hot Hades," Quillan whispered as he came up behind me. "Ugh, what's that smell?"

"That would be Fabian ... or what's left of him," I answered.

Trey stumbled into the room, sounding like a herd of buffalo, and stepped on one of Fabian's dismembered fingers. It made a crunch like biting into a carrot.

"What the hell," he started.

I blew the flame in my palm, and like a thousand fireflies, the lit embers floated on my breath, illuminating the area just around Trey's foot.

"Holy dragon's balls!" he gasped. "What the heck did that?"

Even though I couldn't say I was fond of Fabian and even less so since he'd turned me into a booger, still, this was no way for someone to go.

"No idea. Looks like it could be the work of a were," I said.

Quillan whipped out his cell phone and speed-dialed Headquarters. Well, now I knew what the rest of my Saturday would entail. I'd been hoping to get home and clean the apartment before heading down to Bram and Dagan's. And I'd planned on penning a bit more of *Captain Slade's Bounty*. Guess I'd had a change of plans.

"I need the coroner to Fabian's store. Promptly," Quillan said, then hung up and dropped his phone back into his pocket, facing me. "The intruder might still be here."

He pulled his Op 7 gun from his belt; something most similar to a 9mm Glock. It was also loaded with dragon blood bullets.

I pulled my smaller version from my shoulder holster and followed Quillan's lead as he headed back down the hallway. Fabian's place only consisted of the front room, a hallway and a restroom right off the hall. Quillan paused outside the restroom and signaled me to open the door. I grabbed hold of the doorknob and shook my fist until I had a handful of fairy dust.

Quillan mouthed, "One, two, three."

On the count of three, I yanked the door open and threw the dust into the room while Quillan aimed his gun into the darkness. The fairy dust acted like mini drops of acid once on the person in question, and it would only attach itself to you if you were, in fact, guilty. Sort of like a better version of a lie-detector.

I dropped my gun but didn't re-holster it.

"Clear," I said, my heart still racing.

"Hey, can you get some light in here?" Trey asked from the front of the shop.

Frowning, I turned to the problem of lighting the entire space. Setting a flame to some fairy dust wasn't enough to light the shop, so I'd have to do more. Remembering the mermaid netting hanging in the rafters, I shook my palm until the dust appeared and blew it toward the rafters. Then I focused on the netting and watched as it unraveled. Using just my vision, I pulled on each end, stretching the netting until it spanned the entire width of the ceiling. I shook my palm until another mound of dust appeared. Then I aimed it at the netting, lit a flame between the fingers of my other hand again, and blew the embers toward the mermaid netting. It immediately caught and burned a crisscross design just above our heads. It looked like a checkerboard aflame, kind of pretty.

Well, the netting might have been pretty, but the rest of the situation wasn't. In the light, Fabian was even more hideous. His head was definitely dismembered but half his two-foot spine still ran the length from the base of his skull to where his ribs would've been. He reminded me of a prop someone might use to decorate a haunted house. His tongue hung out of his mouth and rested against the floor, looking like uncooked tuna. He'd never been a good looking guy when alive—about four feet tall, largish nose, wide brow and badgerish eyes—but now, yuck.

"There's no blood," Quillan said as he inspected the corpse.

I glanced at the unfortunate Fabian. There was no blood. Hmm, definitely strange. A gruesome attack like this would warrant blood all over the place.

"No blood—looks like the work of a vampire," I said.

Quillan shook his head. "Vampires leave their corpses dry. This is … a hell of a lot messier."

Trey laughed. "So Dulce, looks like you might've been the last one to see Fabes, here, alive."

I reholstered my gun. "Don't go there, Trey."

He shrugged. "The motive is there. You seemed pretty pissed off that he turned you into that green thing." He paused. "That's all I'm saying."

My breath caught, anger constricting my lungs. Trey and I were going to have it out—I'd known that since he'd started working with us over a year ago. Maybe now was as good a time as ever.

"Right, like I could tear a warlock apart."

"You could be in cahoots with someone else."

"You slimy little ball of gremlin …"

Trey's smile broadened. "Come to think of it, that creature you got turned into had to be pretty strong."

"Enough," Quillan interrupted. "Dulcie, I'm going to need to take your statement. Strictly for the record."

I swallowed the humiliation that crept up my throat. "You're serious?"

Quillan nodded. "Maybe you were the last person to see him alive."

I shook my head against the injustice of the whole damned thing. "The killer was the last person to see him alive and besides, I wasn't the only person in the store. That stranger was there, too."

"That's right," Trey said, trying to subdue a laugh. "Our mysterious stranger. That's one rock solid alibi, Dulce."

I took a step toward him. "Do you have anything else to say?"

Quillan grabbed my arm. "I said … enough. Now Dulce … let's go back to Headquarters. Trey can stay here until the crime scene team arrives."

Without saying a word, I spun on my heels and stomped down the hall, Quillan behind me. Shaking my fist until a mound of dust emerged, I blew in the direction of the burning netting. It immediately went out, leaving the shop in total darkness.

"Thanks, O'Neil," Trey said. "Real professional."

"Fire hazard, Trey," I answered.

"Quillan," Trey called. "How am I supposed to—?"

"Figure it out," Quillan snapped.

I pushed open the door, and the sunlight acted like a blowtorch to my retinas.

"Back to the office then, is it? Or do you trust me enough to drive there?"

I knew it was standard A.N.C protocol to take my statement, but I wanted to make it tough on Quillan since he hadn't told Trey he was full of it for thinking I could do that to Fabian.

I threw open the door to the Wrangler and didn't wait for Quillan to buckle himself in before peeling out of the parking spot.

"I don't think you did it, you know that, right?" Quillan finally asked.

"Yeah, thanks for saying as much to Trey." I shook my head, irritation bleeding through me, and sighed. "Look, I know it's standard procedure, but that doesn't mean I have to like it."

He nodded. "How about I give you Monday off? You've spent plenty of your weekends in the office. Maybe you need a day off."

I snickered. "Aren't you afraid I'd ditch town and head for Mexico?"

"You're not going to let go of this, are you?" he asked with a grin.

I shook my head. "The eight ball says no."

We said nothing for the rest of the drive and even as we walked back into Headquarters. Quillan continued playing mute as he escorted me into the interrogation room.

The interrogation room, for Hades's sake.

I threw my keys onto the table, unholstered my gun and set it beside my keys. Then I took my seat with as much disdain as I could muster.

Quillan didn't sit but leaned his head out the door. "Lottie, I need Saturn please."

Saturn was a logging system that took statements in real time and then logged them into whatever case file they belonged to. It was basically a glorified computer that had been bewitched by Sam, but it didn't look like a computer—it looked like a scroll with a feather pen.

Lottie flew into the room, carrying Saturn with her as her little wings beat madly to keep airborne. She was small, maybe the size of my hand and Saturn was about double her size. Pixies have incredible strength though—think ants—so it wasn't too much of a struggle for her to carry the scroll.

Lottie was dressed in a flowery yellow skirt with a matching blouse, her platinum hair pulled into a severe bun like she thought she was a librarian or something. She smirked at Quillan but regarded me with disinterest. Stupid pixie had never liked me—she'd always been jealous of my close relationship with Quillan. Well, I'm sure she was getting miles out of this one.

She unwound the scroll. As she unrolled it, the feather pen flew out like a dog ready to retrieve a stick. If the damn thing had a tail, it would've been wagging. Then the pen poised itself on the scroll, waiting for direction.

Lottie faced me with a frown. "Dulcie is being interrogated today, is she?"

I narrowed my eyes and turned to Quillan who just smiled. "Not interrogated, Lottie, we just need her statement. So yes, you can enter Dulcie's name into the system."

Lottie tsked at me, and I wished I had a fly swatter.

She glanced at the scroll again. "Name: Dulcie O'Neil." Her eyes sought Quillan. "What case is it?"

"Murder of Fabian Nesbeth, the dark arts warlock."

She nodded and faced the scroll. The pen was already poised and raring to go.

"Murder case of Fabian Nesbeth, the warlock," Lottie finished.

The pen scribbled on the scroll, the writing looked like calligraphy in gold paint. As soon as it entered my name, a red case number bled through the scroll in the upper right corner. I was case number 2,456. That might sound like we had a lot of cases, but Headquarters had had Saturn for over five years.

Lottie turned to us again. "Okay, Dulcie, you can start explaining how you killed Fabian now."

"Don't screw with me, mosquito, or I'll smash you," I spat.

"Thanks, Lottie," Quillan said. "I can take it from here."

She flew from the room in a huff as I turned to the scroll which was apparently recording my little outburst.

Quillan shut the door with a weary sigh. "Watch yourself, Dulce. You know this recording will be sent back to the Netherworld so you'd better be on best behavior."

I frowned. "Or else what?"

"Or else you could be going back to the Netherworld. Understand?"

"Crystal clear," I snapped.

A small, sympathetic smile played on his lips. "Okay, Dulce. Tell me about everything that happened yesterday, starting when you woke up."

THREE

"I woke up yesterday morning," I started.

"What time?" Quillan interrupted.

I shifted in my chair and resisted the urge to sigh. I should've known better—I'd have to give minute details. Hades-be-damned, I so didn't have the patience for this.

"In the late morning, maybe ten a.m."

He nodded. "Go on."

I glanced at Saturn. The quill pen was doing a good job of writing our every word. Time to trip the thing.

"Ten a.m.," I started, my voice a whisper. The quill paused and cocked its feather, as if trying to make out what I was saying.

"Dulcie, don't screw around," Quillan interrupted with an impatient sigh.

I frowned and figured it was fun while it lasted. The pen tapped itself against the scroll. The thing had no sense of humor.

"Okay, okay," I grumbled. "Anyway, I woke up at ten and ate some cereal. Before you ask, it was frosted flakes."

Quillan just shook his head.

"Then I took a shower and tidied up the apartment. I'd planned a visit to Fabian's dark arts store because word on the street was he'd be receiving a delivery soon."

"How did you know it was arriving yesterday?" Quillan interrupted.

"Well, I didn't know for sure it was going to come yesterday. Trey had been getting visions of a truck delivery to

Fabian's sometime last week, so I made sure I patrolled pretty frequently."

"But Trey didn't get any inkling that Fabian would be murdered?" Quillan leaned back in his chair and crossed his long legs at the ankles. Holy Hades, he was one sexy bastard.

I shrugged. "If Trey did, he didn't share that with me." I took a breath. "So when I went to talk to Fabian about his delivery, he looked nervous. He was helping a stranger who I'd never seen before, which threw me off. Otherwise, I would've been prepared for the *Hemmen* spell."

"The stranger," Quillan started. "Can you describe him?"

"Tall, maybe three inches taller than you."

Quillan faced the airborne pen. "I stand five feet eleven inches making this stranger six feet two inches." He faced me again. "What else, Dulce?"

I frowned. Quillan was really five-ten, but if he wanted that little inch, he could have it. "He had dark hair and blue eyes."

"How dark was his hair?"

"Black."

"What type of creature was he?"

I shook my head. "That's the kicker. I couldn't tell."

"Let the record note this stranger didn't register with Headquarters," Quillan added.

Every time he spoke, he faced Saturn as if he were addressing a crowd full of voters who might put him into office.

"Once he bespelled you, then what happened?" he asked.

"Fabian must've known I was paying attention to the stranger because that's when he put the *Hemmen* on me. I left the store immediately because I started to feel pretty sick. It took me a few minutes to realize it was the spell taking shape. I ran all the way to Sam's house, and then the spell took over and turned me into that blob."

Quillan faced the pen again. "For the record, 'Sam' is Samantha White, witch. Employee of Splendor, A.N.C. Headquarters."

"34B bust size," I added.

Quillan just smiled. "How far does Sam live from Fabian's?"

"Half a mile."

"Were you able to see what Fabian had in the truck delivery?" He paused. "Could the stranger have been the delivery driver?"

I shook my head. "No, he wasn't dressed in uniform. And no, I didn't get to see what Fabian had in the delivery. He bespelled me before I got the chance."

Quillan nodded and clapped his hands together before leaning forward. "Okay, Dulce, that's all I needed. You're free to go."

"That's it?"

He threw me a smile. "I believe you're innocent, Dulce. Just have to follow procedure."

I stood up as he opened the door and poked his head out, calling for Lottie to take care of Saturn. When he returned his gaze to me, there was something in his eyes … concern maybe?

"I know I don't need to tell you this," he started with a pause. "Just be careful on this case, okay?"

I nodded and strode out the door, smiling to myself as I thought maybe my day wasn't going to be screwed up after all.

Three hours later, I sat at my computer, typing out the last scene of my romance novel, *Captain Slade's Bounty*. The book was about a pirate captain, Slade Montgomery, and a stowaway named Clementine. Over the course of two months at sea, Clementine and the captain had sex nine times, and I was ending the book with their tenth.

But I was having trouble seeing the scene in my head—typical writer's block. I tapped my fingers against the particleboard of my Ikea desk and watched the cursor blink, taunting me with its restlessness. I just couldn't really get into writing about Slade's engorged manhood as it penetrated Clementine in her naughtiest of places.

Instead, my mind refused to relinquish images of Fabian's severed head. With a frustrated sigh, I closed my eyes and tried to conjure up an image of Quillan wearing only an eye patch. Even though it usually got my writing juices flowing, it did nothing for me now.

Well, when you can't write, you can edit. I clicked on the search and replace option and began replacing Quillan's name with Captain Slade's. It was lots easier to imagine Quillan as my pirate hero if I wrote using his name. Go figure.

The phone rang and I bolted for it.

"Hi, Sam," I said, after catching her name on the caller ID.

"Hi, Dulce. Quillan told me about Fabian. That's crazy."

I plunked down into my sofa and played with my dry cuticles. "Yeah, it was pretty awful. It looked like he'd been ripped apart, but there was no blood."

Sam gasped. "So you think it was vampires?"

At the mention of vampires, I pulled at one dry cuticle too hard, and it began to bleed, the color of liquid gold. "Too soon to tell."

"So what are you doing now?"

I eyed the open document page on my computer screen and noted the cursor still blinking like it was pissed off that I was on the phone. Pretty soon the screen saver would kill it with a calming picture of fish in a tank.

"Well, I was trying to work on my book, but I have writer's block."

"Oh." She paused. "You've been writing a lot. Don't you think maybe you should get out and …"

"Sam, we've been through this," I started, knowing where the conversation was headed. I hadn't dated anyone in a year, not since my last boyfriend had dumped me after a five-year relationship.

"I'm just not ready."

Sam sighed. "I know, Dulce, it's just been a long time since you even went out on a date."

"Sam …"

"I'm just saying I think you have trust issues."

I knew I had trust issues but I really didn't blame myself considering I'd trusted someone for five years only to find out he'd been banging some chick for the last three years of our relationship.

"Anyway," Sam exhaled. "Want to catch a movie and dinner?"

"Can't. I have to go talk to Bram and Dagan about Fabian and that stranger. I want to see if they might have some news about it. You can come along if you want."

Sam's silence was telling. She'd had a fling with Bram for about a month. Only it turned out, he'd been going out with her to get closer to me. Or, so she said.

"You don't have to if you don't want to," I offered, knowing it's never fun to see an ex.

"I'm totally over Bram. I'll go. We should make a night of it since I can't remember the last time we went clubbing together."

It had been a while. I wasn't super crazy about clubbing, but since I'd be going to No Regrets anyway, might as well enjoy myself. And Bram was always good about offering us free drinks.

"Okay, why don't I pick you up at ten?" I asked.

Now, if I could just get over my writer's block.

###

It was nine thirty. I eyed my reflection in the mirror and gave my black miniskirt and red halter top a satisfied smile. Thank God for push up bras—my 32Cs looked more like Ds. Nothing wrong with a little false bravado. I sprayed some Juicy Couture perfume on my neck and wrists and slipped into four-inch black heels. Grabbing my black leather jacket, purse and keys, I locked the door behind me and headed to the Wrangler.

I didn't live in the best part of Splendor. My suburb, Ocacia, was eclectic—some wealthy people trying to turn it into yuppie central, like they'd done with neighboring towns. Then there were the lower income families, the elderly and the single, twenty-somethings like me. But I was as safe as I would be anywhere else. Sam had put a protection spell on my entire apartment building which prohibited anyone who meant me any sort of harm from even stepping foot on our yard.

It even worked on Jehovah's Witnesses.

Sam lives in the suburb just next to Ocacia—Cumquat. Her neighborhood is nicer than mine—the yuppies got to it first.

When I turned onto her street, I pulled out my cell phone and gave her a ring, not wanting to waste time parking and walking up to the door. Hey, it wasn't like I was her date or something. The phone rang twice before she picked up.

"I'll be there in two seconds," I said.

She hung up, and I pulled in front of her white house. The garden's the best part of Sam's place. She's an avid gardener and has every sort of flower blooming out front—azaleas, roses, snapdragons and honeysuckle just to name a few. I've had potted plants over the years, but I don't have much of a green thumb. Kind of ironic considering I'm a

30

fairy, a child of nature, but there you have it. It'd be more apropos to call me a child of concrete and asphalt.

Sam came out wearing her black pants and a blue tube top. She locked her door and jogged down her long entryway, not an easy feat given her high heels. I never understood why tall women wore heels. When you're five-one like me, you need all the help you can get.

I whistled. "Look at you."

She threw open the door and climbed in, giving me the once over as I pulled into the street. "Look at yourself," she said and turned my CD player on. The Chemical Brothers came pounding out in an array of techno beats as Sam settled into her seat.

"What's this?" she asked, leaning down between her feet and grasping a brochure I hadn't wanted her to see.

Heat shot to my face. "Oh, it's … it's nothing. Just some junk mail."

"If you feel self conscious about your ears," she read as I cringed, "call Dr. Goodman for a free consultation to learn how ear augmentation can work for you." She tapped the brochure against her hand. "Dulcie, tell me you aren't thinking about getting your ears done? Come on, that's so not you."

There was no point in lying to her. "Yeah, I've been thinking about it for a while now."

"But that's what makes you a fairy, Dulce."

"Doesn't mean I have to like it."

Sam frowned. "Does this have anything to do with Jack?"

Jack was my ex boyfriend of five years—the jerk who'd cheated on me. He'd always made fun of my ears, calling me *Tinker Bell*.

"No, it has nothing to do with Jack."

"Okay, but isn't it enough that you have beautiful hair and gorgeous green eyes? And you have the best nose in three counties."

I shook my head. "I was just thinking of going in for a consultation. It's free and I don't have to agree to anything."

"Sometimes I just don't get you. If you do go, will you take me with you?"

"Only if you'll be open minded about it."

She nodded. "I will be." She was quiet for a minute. "So are you going to talk to Bram about Fabian?"

I bobbed my head and turned up the heater. "That and I want to ask him about that stranger I saw. Just find out if he's seen or heard anything unusual."

"Are we going to Dagan's too?"

"No, not if I can help it. Ugh, I hate going there."

"Yeah, it's not exactly a charming place."

I turned a corner and No Regrets loomed before us, the place painted black so you couldn't delineate it from the dark night sky. A bright red electric sign screamed from the wall and looked like it was floating. A line was already forming around the building. It was the one place where all the creatures of the Netherworld hung out. You might get a few humans thrown in here and there, but most times Bram kept them out. Most Netherworld creatures weren't crazy about hanging out with humans.

"Crap, look at the line," Sam said.

I pulled up in front and noticed Bram standing outside with Nick, the ogre. Nick was huge—just shy of eight feet, and he was as big as a wall. Nick's face was broad, and his nose was flat and wide, with a bull's ring through the middle. His eyes were too small for his face and his mouth, too big.

Ogres are known for having terrible tempers, and Nick was no exception. I'd seen him bounce a few wily wolves, and it hadn't been pretty. Broken bones had been the result … and not Nick's.

A huge smile lit Bram's handsome face. He was tall—six-five and broad. Standing next to Nick, though, he looked emaciated. When Bram had been turned into a vampire, he'd had a day's or so growth of stubble, so now he permanently looked the rogue. His looks tied with his English accent gave Colin Firth a run for his money (and I mean when Colin was *the* Mr. Darcy).

"Ladies, ladies," he said, materializing directly next to Sam.

She tightened her jaw, but other than that, she looked totally at ease.

"Can I park in the back, Bram?" I asked, noting there wasn't a spot to be had on the street.

He rested his long fingers on the Wrangler's passenger door. "Please. Park next to me. I am pleased to see you both."

Sam rolled her eyes, and I just shook my head. Bram was the quintessential flirt.

"Are you going to let go so I can go park or what?"

He smirked with a great show of fangs and let go of the door as if it'd been scalding hot.

Course, he was dead, so he wouldn't notice cold or heat or anything else.

I pulled into the back of the No Regrets lot. Bram's black Porsche beamed under the lamplight like it was proud of itself. I parked in the space next to it.

"Hopefully, Bram will be too busy tonight to bother us," I said. "After I get my information out of him, that is."

Sam laughed. "He seems to always make time where you're concerned."

I just shook my head and turned the car off as Sam and I jumped out. The back way in was always locked, so we walked around the front. As we passed the long line, I didn't miss the angry yells and insults those still stuck in line threw at us.

"Hey!" Nick yelled down the line. "Take it elsewhere if you don't like it."

"Hi, Nick," I said, always a little intimidated by the gargantuan guy. He was like looking up a redwood tree.

"Dulcie and Sam," he said with a drop of his head. Nick had it something bad for Sam, but she was as scared of him as I was.

"Ah, you got my message, Sweet," Bram said, coming up behind us.

Tension filtered through my shoulders at the mention of "sweet." Bram thought it was cute or something—Dulce meaning sweet in Spanish. So not original and so freaking annoying.

"I have some Regulator business to discuss with you, Bram," I said.

He just smiled and leaned his elbow against Nick's shoulder, who was sitting on a barstool. Bram reached for Sam's hand and brought it to his lips.

"Lovely to see you, Samantha."

She grumbled something unintelligible and started for the door. Nick gazed at her like she was chocolate and he was on a diet. Bram reached for my hand, but I batted his away.

"Just say hello like any normal person would, Bram."

He chuckled and dropped his hand. "Do you have your identification on you, Dulcie, Sweet?"

"My ID?" I repeated while irritation blazed through me. The bastard was going to ID me?

"If you are on business, I need to see your A.N.C. ID, Sweet. It's only standard protocol."

My ID was sitting on my desk looking at the ceiling and doing me absolutely no good. Goddammit. "I don't have it," I said.

"What was that, Sweet?" Bram repeated.

I extended my hand, knowing I'd have to deal with his ministrations if I were to get inside the club and get him to answer even the simplest of questions. He took my hand and rather than kissing it, pulled me into the hard length of his chest. I squeaked in protest as he bent his head, grabbing my neck to hold me in place. Then he kissed me over my jugular.

My heart pounded in my chest, as if it wanted to bust free and punch him in the face.

When he let go, I nearly lost my footing. "You son of a," I started.

Bram's raspy laugh interrupted me. Nick pretended he hadn't seen anything, but his face was too red to deny the fact that he had. If I'd been in the right frame of mind, I might've actually thought an embarrassed ogre was pretty funny.

"Please, Sweet, go inside, and I will join you shortly," Bram said.

I turned on my heel and walked inside.

FOUR

I took a seat next to Sam at a table with a "Reserved" sign. As far as I was concerned, it was reserved for us.

"What do you want to drink?" I asked, practically screaming over the loud techno music. No Regrets was a pretty happening spot—it was maybe ten thirty, and already, the place was packed.

"Vodka tonic please."

I approached the bar, glancing over my shoulder at the throng of dancers on the floor. A black light sporadically spotlighted them, making them look like they were moving in slow motion.

"Hi Dulce, how's it going?" Angela, the bartender, asked. Leaning against the bar, she pushed her long electric blue bangs out of her face. Last time I'd seen her, her hair was bright yellow but still long in the front and butch short in the back.

I smiled. "Hi Angela, it's going. How's business?"

"Good, been real busy lately. What can I get for you?"

"Vodka tonic and a mojito, please."

She nodded and I felt Bram's shadowy presence behind me. "That kiss was totally uncalled for," I whispered.

"Ah, Dulce, I just could not help myself."

I took my Mojito as Bram reached for Sam's vodka tonic. I fished inside my purse, fingered my credit card, and tossed it on the bar. Angela reached for it but paused once Bram shook his head.

"It is on the house, Sweet," he purred.

"Put them on the card, Angela. Thanks. And Bram, don't pull another stunt like that again."

Bram's chuckle was deep. "Excuse me for offering to buy you a drink. If this is how you are with men, it's no wonder I never see you on a date."

"I was talking about the kiss, Bram." I put the glass back on the bar, turning to face him. "And my personal life is none of your business."

He took a step closer until I could smell the mint of his gum. "It is my business if I wish to be in it."

"Ugh, would you get over yourself?" I turned on my heel and started for the table, but Bram's hand on my arm stopped me. I turned around and something in his eyes pulled at me. I could read the desire in his gaze like I was reading a page in a book.

"What the hell was that, Bram?" I demanded through gritted teeth, pulling my arm away from him as if he were contagious. Vampires were notorious for pulling stunts with their eyes—persuading someone to take whatever actions the vampire desired. But Bram wasn't supposed to bewitch me with his eyes—I should've been too powerful to even get an inkling of the feeling he'd just sent me.

"It is my birthday in two months, Sweet."

Great. Every hundred-year birthday would find a vampire stronger in all abilities—more physically powerful, more mentally capable of persuasion, and most got better looking.

"How old will you be?"

Bram grinned. "Three hundred."

Crap, he'd be pretty powerful. Not that I was afraid of him—it just went to show that having Bram on my side was exactly where I wanted him. "Why'd you call me the other day?" I asked.

I scooted into the seat next to Sam and watched Bram gingerly hand her the vodka tonic. She nodded her thanks, and Bram pulled up a chair, sitting across from us.

"I had some news for you," he said with a shrug.

"And what was that?" I asked, knowing information never came free from Bram.

"All in good time, Sweet," Bram gave me a smile that had probably won him his last few bed partners.

The guy was smooth and, okay, hot—I'd give him that. But that was about all I'd give him. "Bram, what in the hell do you want?" I asked, watching him lean his elbows against the table as he grinned at me for a few seconds. "Hello? Earth to the most annoying vampire I've ever met."

"I want some information, Dulcie O'Neil."

"And what type of information would that be?"

He leaned back in the chair and eyed the room around him, as if counting the patrons. "Do you recall that abandoned building on Kiwi Street that has been vacant for two months?"

"The one that used to be the Chinese massage parlor?" Sam asked.

Bram nodded, his attention finally resting on me again. "Yes, that one."

"So what of it?" I asked, wondering what Bram had to do with a Chinese massage parlor. It sounded like the setup to a bad joke.

"Well," he leaned back in his chair and cracked his knuckles. "I have been considering buying it to open a restaurant."

"What does that have to do with me?" I snapped.

Someone had killed Fabian and I needed to find out who before the finger started to point at me. I didn't have time for this crap.

"Patience, fairy. Patience."

I narrowed my eyes and sipped my drink, counting to ten all the while.

"Get on with it," Sam said. "Our Bram BS meter is nearing its limit."

"You two are in a fine mood tonight." He sighed. "I think, but I am not certain, that Dagan is going to try to beat me to the property."

"Because he, a demon, wants a Chinese massage parlor?" I rolled my eyes. "I don't know, Sam, maybe we should get in on it, too. What do you think?"

She shrugged. "I do like massages."

Bram ignored us. "I got into a row the other day with Dagan, and I think he is trying to get even with me by taking the property out from underneath my nose."

I sipped my drink. "So let me repeat myself, what the hell does this have to do with me? Why should I give a crap? Because, in case you didn't notice, I don't."

Bram just smiled. "I want you to find out if Dagan is planning on purchasing it."

"And why do you think he'd tell me? Dagan and I aren't friends by any stretch of the imagination." The truth was that Dagan was usually on the wrong side of the law, but the only reason I cut him any sort of slack was due to the fact that he gave me lots of good leads. Hey, sometimes you've gotta work with the bad guys to get the even worse guys.

Bram continued to smile like his lips were paralyzed. "He has no reason to hide this from you … it is perfectly legal."

"He has no reason to share his business dealings with me either."

"I was thinking that perhaps Samantha might be able to influence him."

Sam slammed her drink on the table, and it sloshed up and over the side of the rim, as if as outraged as she. "You want me to put a truth spell on a demon?"

Bram just nodded. The vampire had balls.

"No way," I interrupted. "You must think we're total idiots."

"He would never know," Bram continued. "And I do not think either one of you is an idiot."

Sam gripped her glass so tight, her knuckles went white. "It's too risky. If he found out, he'd kill us both."

"How would he find out?" Bram continued, acting like he was asking us to figure out Dagan's favorite color.

"How does anyone find anything out? It just happens and I don't want to be on the end of that temper, thank you very much," Sam snapped.

Bram quirked another winning smirk in Sam's direction, no doubt hoping the amorous feelings she'd once harbored for him might serve him well. As her best friend, if I even saw a hint of that happening, I'd curtail it faster than Bram could piss me off again.

"Well, perhaps you wouldn't need the spell. Just make small talk—see what he says," Bram offered.

Small talk was doable. A spell on a demon wasn't. "And if I just ask Dagan some questions, you'll answer all my questions tonight?" I demanded.

"Yes. I trust your word, Dulcie. I know if you agree to something, you will honor it."

Yeah, now I was thinking my great sense of honor was going to work against me. Dagan wasn't someone you wanted to screw around with. Demons are notoriously short-tempered and they don't get mad or even, they just kill you.

"Okay, I'll talk to Dagan and see what I can find out," I said. "Now, I have some questions for you."

Bram grinned again, his fangs reflecting the low light of the room. As soon as his fangs surfaced, Sam immediately dropped her gaze, and I'd bet money she was thinking about the time she'd let him drink from her. She'd told me the day after it happened. Apparently, they'd been getting hot and heavy, and she'd let him take a little nip of her neck. As soon as he'd started drinking her blood, she'd had like four orgasms in a row. And they weren't your normal, "this feels good" vibrator-type orgasm. They were mind-blowing, like nothing she'd ever felt before. I've never been with a vampire so, of course, I was eating her story up. But even if it sounded good, I still had no interest in some corpse feeding off my neck.

"Ask away, my lady," the corpse in question said.

"What do you know about Fabian's death?"

Bram frowned, his brows knotting in the middle of his forehead. "Fabian died?"

"You're a terrible actor, Bram," I said with a sigh. I so didn't have time to deal with this.

He held up his hands as if in submission. I knew better. Trusting Bram would be like trusting a rattlesnake. Fine and good until the thing sinks its fangs into your skin, and you're dead an hour later.

"Ah, yes, now that I think about it, I had heard Fabian died."

"Who told you?" I asked.

"Cannot say for sure. It was a general theme in here all night."

"What did you hear about it?" Sam asked.

"Well, I heard Dulcie was the last to see him, and she was the only suspect."

Hades be damned. Everyone seemed to be forgetting that I wasn't the last to see him—the stranger had seen Fabian the same time I had. Course, all anyone had to go on there was my word.

"Dulcie didn't do it," Sam said, her mouth tight.

Bram grinned. "I did not say she did. I am merely repeating the rumors I have heard … as you requested."

I gritted my teeth. "Go on."

"Apparently Fabian bespelled you and turned you into something vulgar, and you were upset and came back and killed him. I cannot say I blame you. Life is better without Fabian."

"I didn't kill him."

"I am sure you have wanted to over the years, Dulce?" he asked with a wicked grin.

"Not quite as much as some people I can think of."

41

"Ah, Sweet, you and I go way back."

I sighed. "Regardless, I'm not the one being questioned here. Do you want that information about Dagan?" He nodded. "Yeah, then stop pissing me off."

"Apologies," he said, but the smile quirking his lips said he didn't mean it.

"Okay, what do you know about a stranger in Splendor? Have you seen anyone new lately?"

Bram strummed his fingers along the table as if doing so would help him remember. "There was someone who came in the other night; he was asking for you actually."

"What? Who?" I demanded.

Bram's gaze followed a cocktail waitress as she delivered drinks to the table across from ours. Her boobs were hanging so far out of her shirt, they looked like they might fall out. And judging from the expression on Bram's face, he hoped they would.

I cleared my throat, and he faced me, wetting his lips. "I did not get his name. He said he was passing through but did not give the nature of his business."

"What did he look like?" Sam asked.

More fingers strumming along the table, the sound like a dull axe reverberating through my head.

"Dark hair and light eyes. Probably your type—resembled me."

I glanced at Sam. "It was the stranger from Fabian's."

A shiver coursed through me like someone had stepped on my grave.

"Are you sure?" Sam asked.

I shrugged. "Who else would it be?" Then I faced Bram again. "How long was he here?"

"Not long. He came in, had a drink and asked Angela where he could find you."

"And what did Angela tell him?"

"Perhaps you should ask her." Bram steepled his fingers in his lap. Then he brought his index fingers together and held them out before him like two guns butting up against one another. "When you hold your fingers like this and focus on them both, it looks like there is a little sausage between them."

"Bram, for Hades's sake," I started.

He dropped his fingers and faced me with a boyish twinkle in his eyes. It would've been charming if not for the fangs just cresting his lower lip.

"Talk to Angela, Sweet, she can give you the play by play."

"I will. In the meantime, though, I'm sure you must've asked Angela what she told him?"

"I cannot put anything past you, Dulcie." He chuckled. "She said he could find you at Headquarters. Then he paid for his drink and walked out. End of story."

I was quiet as I considered it. If the stranger had been looking for me, why hadn't he just approached me at Fabian's? True, I'd left there in a hurry once the little creep had bespelled me. And maybe the stranger hadn't known what I looked like. But as a fairy, my ears give me away. If he knew I was a fairy, then he would've known me from Fabian's store. It wasn't like there were lots of fairies in Splendor. In fact, there were only two—Zara the hooker and me.

"When was the stranger here?" I demanded.

Bram looked up at the ceiling as if it had an answer for him. "Evening before last."

Before Fabian's death. Interesting.

"Are we done with him yet?" Sam asked, sipping the last of her vodka tonic through the straw until it sounded like the ice cubes were snoring.

Bram turned toward me expectantly, a smile just stealing his lips.

"Mmm, I like the sound of that. Use me then throw me away."

"Yeah, we're done."

Bram stood up so quickly, I didn't see him move. "Very well, I will leave you two as I have things to do and people to see. Samantha, drinks are free if you are interested. Dulcie insists on paying for hers."

He gave a theatrical bow and walked away. I glanced at Sam, who sat as still as a tombstone. "What prompted me to ever date him?" she muttered.

I laughed. "Beats the hell out of me."

She just shook her head, and we both faced the throng of dancers on the floor. Holy Hades, I was so not in the mood to dance. Fabian loomed in the back of my mind like a monster in a kid's closet.

"Do you want to get out of here?" Sam asked.

I frowned. "Why? I thought you wanted to go out partying tonight?"

"I'm not really feeling it at the moment. You?"

"Actually, I was just thinking the same thing."

She stood up. "Brilliant minds think alike."

She started for the door, and I was right behind her. I stopped at the bar and mouthed "credit card" to Angela. She was quick with the receipt. I signed it and dropped the pen back on the bar.

"Thanks, Angela. By the way, did a tall, dark-haired stranger come looking for me?"

"Yeah, maybe two nights ago. I told him he could find you at Headquarters."

"And he didn't say anything else?"

She shook her head. "Nope, that was it."

So Bram hadn't been full of it.

"Great, thanks, Angela. Have a good night."

"Will do, night guys."

I followed Sam outside where Nick gave us a quick smile. Sam didn't even slow down but ran-walked to the car as if she had to pee.

I unlocked the door with my beeper remote.

"Do you want to go somewhere else or call it a night?" I asked.

Sam threw herself into the passenger seat. "I think I just want to go to bed."

I started the Wrangler and pulled out of the driveway.

"Okay, sounds fine to me." Clearly, something was wrong, and I was pretty sure that something happened to have dark hair and a winning smile, even if he was a jerk.

"Are you okay, with seeing Bram and all?"

Nick watched us drive by and waved. I waved back, but I don't think Sam even noticed him. Poor ogre.

She sighed. Yeah, she wasn't okay.

"I thought I was, but I don't know. He's just so cute."

"Yeah, he's cute. It's a shame the cute ones are always jerks or if not jerks, gay."

She nodded. "I mean, I think I'm over him. It just sometimes sucks seeing someone again that you used to have feelings for, you know?"

I knew only too well. I'd moved to Splendor from Estuary to ensure I wouldn't have any run-ins with my ex. And so far so good.

"Well, give it another couple of weeks, and I bet you'll be totally over him. You just need to find his replacement."

"I could say the same to you about Jack," she said and laughed. "You'd think between you and me and our abilities, we could create the perfect guy."

I shook my head, instantly picturing Frankenstein. So not wanting to try that anytime soon. I had enough problems as it was. Still, it was an interesting thought … What was wrong with me? I was so not contemplating creating a man. Ludicrous.

"You're thinking about it, aren't you?" Sam asked with a wide grin.

No point in lying. "Sort of. But not seriously, of course. It would be cool though. Create some totally hot guy and make him clean our houses and do dishes and laundry."

"And watch chick movies with us," Sam added with a sigh.

I laughed and pulled up to her house. Sam undid her seatbelt and opened the door. "Thanks, Dulce. I guess I'll see you Monday."

I nodded. "Well, have a good weekend if I don't talk to you sooner."

She hopped down from the Wrangler and pulled her house keys from her purse. I waited for her to unlock the front door. Before disappearing inside, she turned and waved. I pulled into the street and headed for my house, imagining our invented man wearing nothing but an apron and ironing my clothes.

###

Captain Slade stood before me on the sandy beaches of some foreign place that looked like Tahiti. The beaches were white, the sky dissolving into the ocean on the horizon. The captain's chest was bare, a ragged pair of pants his only clothing. My gaze traveled up his exquisite body until it rested on his face. But it wasn't his face at all, it was Quillan's.

"What are you doing dressed as a pirate?" I asked.

He shrugged. "I've been Captain Slade all along."

I shook my head and couldn't grasp how that could be. Captain Slade was a fictional character, and Quillan was my boss. I glanced at him again and Bram smiled back at me.

"You're the last person I wanted to see," I said, horrified as he started toward me.

Bram threw me a smirk that was so uniquely his, he could patent it.

"Dulce, Sweet, you know you find me attractive …"

"Dulcie, I need to speak with you."

It was a voice I didn't recognize. It reverberated through the sky almost like it belonged to the clouds. But

46

clouds don't talk. I glanced around but couldn't find the perpetrator.

"Who is that?" I asked Bram.

"Who is what?" he said and then shrugged, taking hold of my arms. "Let's talk about us, Dulcie."

I jerked away from him, the sand slipping between my toes and tickling me like thousands of fleas.

"There is no us," I said, my eyes still searching the clouds.

"Dulcie."

It was the voice again. Frustration surged through me as I searched the clouds, spinning around and around, but finding nothing. With a sigh, I stopped, feeling slightly dizzy. As soon as my gaze dropped from the sky, I was in Bram's club. Bram was nowhere to be found. In fact, I was sitting in a booth completely alone—like No Regrets hadn't opened for the night. So what was I doing here?

I glanced at the table and found a drink before me. I brought the straw to my mouth and took a couple sips. Hmm, Vodka Cranberry. Not bad. I glanced up and found the stranger who'd been in Fabian's store sitting across from me.

"You," I said.

He smiled. "Sorry to interrupt your dream."

"I'm dreaming?" I repeated, staring into the crystal blue of his eyes.

"You were." He paused. "You'll wake up thinking this was a dream but you need to convince yourself it's real. We have much to discuss."

I put the drink down, and it disappeared into the surface of the table. "You were in Fabian's store that day. I saw you."

He nodded. "I was there looking for you."

"But I was there. Why didn't you …"

He shook his head. "The situation wasn't right, Dulcie."

"Who are you?"

He smiled and it was beautiful. "When we meet, I'll tell you."

"How do I find you? I don't even know what your name is."

"I'm waiting for you outside. Just come out."

I blinked and found I wasn't in Bram's club anymore but was in my bed. My alarm clock glowed eerily, the only beacon of light in the dark room. I sat up and rubbed my eyes, glancing around myself as if to prove I really was where I thought I was. Talk about a weird dream.

Then I remembered the stranger's words—*You'll wake thinking this was a dream. But you need to convince yourself it's real. We have much to discuss. Just come out.*

Hmm. I rolled onto my side, threw my pillow over my head and went back to sleep.

FIVE

My writer's block was finally gone. It was two a.m. on Monday morning, and I had to go to work in seven hours. I typed the final scene of Captain Slade's Bounty, clicked save and leaned back, my chair squeaking in protest.

I'd done it. Finished. A slow grin spread across my face as my imagination went into overdrive. I could see it … me landing the perfect agent and making loads of cash. I shut the computer down and walked my empty coffee mug back to the kitchen all the while trying to force myself to yawn, knowing I should get to bed. I just wasn't tired. Too much caffeine pounded through my veins.

There was an energy in me that would only be appeased by exercise. I threw on stretch pants and a sports bra, then fished my sneakers out from underneath my bed. A good jog would wear me out. Then I could sleep. Jogging in the near middle of the night might not sound too bright, but who was going to mess with a fairy?

I locked the door behind me and started down the steps of my apartment. The air had a certain chill to it, something cold at the moment, but as soon as my blood started pumping, I'd welcome the coolness.

I picked up my feet and started jogging, enjoying the fact that I seemed to be the only person awake at this hour. There's a certain intimacy to the night when you don't have to share it with anyone. The sound of my feet pounding against the pavement was my own type of meditation; the chirp of crickets overlaid with the shuffling of various night creatures music to my ears.

I started up the base of a large hill, looking forward to cresting the top. The steep incline was making itself known in the burn of my calves. I hadn't gone for a run in over a week. Usually, it didn't sting like this.

"You can do it," I whispered to myself. Hey, even the magical sometimes need a few words of encouragement.

Gritting my teeth, I closed my eyes and pushed my legs into the ground. The asphalt leveled off and my muscles relaxed. I opened my eyes with a grin. My gaze focused and my smile faded.

A man stood directly in front of me—maybe ten feet away.

I gasped and stopped in my tracks. Every nerve in my body was alert and standing at attention. My body was poised, ready to rebuff an attack. It was a built-in response in law enforcement. You never know when some asshole's going to try to make your day.

The man was dressed in black. His hooded sweatshirt hung low over his face, making him look like the Grim Reaper, only without the scythe. He dropped the hood, and in the moonlight, I recognized the stranger from Fabian's store.

I sucked in a breath. He was just as beautiful as I'd first thought. His black hair had the same reflective quality as raven's wings and glowed under the moonbeams. The moonlight heightened the angular planes of his face, throwing shadows beneath his cheeks and the square lines of his jaw.

Even if he was beautiful, that didn't mean he wasn't here to kill me. And as far as I was concerned, he was here to kill me.

"What do you want?" I said, taking a step back, my feet shoulder width apart and my body tuned to lunge into action should this stranger make a wrong move. Then I remembered I'd left my Op 6 with the dragon blood bullets on the floor next to my bed. How convenient. Well, I could nail him with a lightning bolt or maybe make the ground open up and swallow him.

He made the mistake of coming toward me.

I shook my palm until a mound of fairy dust emerged. I blew the particles at him and imagined him frozen. He stopped mid-gait, like he was stuck in freeze frame; the ice surrounding him twinkled like diamonds. I dropped my shoulders, moving my right arm in a circle, trying to get the blood back into my shoulder. I'd held myself so straight, awaiting his attack, I felt a bit frozen myself.

Either way, I'd just taken down the man who'd probably killed Fabian.

No help from anyone. No problem. Dulcie O'Neil: Regulator extraordinaire. Just what I needed for my review.

I neared him carefully, trying to figure out what the hell he'd wanted from me. No sooner did the thought leave my head, then the ice shattered around him and dropped in an ineffectual mound. I jumped back as a bolt of fear shot through me. As if he'd never even been frozen, he strode toward me again, and he didn't appear to be in a forgiving mood.

I backed up and throwing another handful of fairy dust, imagined a circle of fire surrounding him. He walked right through it. Just walked through the flames like they weren't even there. Not good. Really not good.

"Stop screwing around," he said in a deep, harsh voice. "I just want to talk."

"Then stop walking."

He didn't take my advice, so with another thrust of fairy dust, I pictured a lightning bolt. Once I had it sizzling in my hand, I unloaded it on him. He took the bolt right in the chest and fell with the weight of it, landing on his back. It looked like it had not only taken him down, but knocked him completely out. He had to be dead. No one could survive that much energy. Well, maybe a vampire could, but somehow I didn't think this guy was a vamp.

I kicked his foot, and it shifted slightly but it was an involuntary motion. He was out cold. Which meant I was safe. I squatted down on my calves and reached for his neck, intending to check for a pulse. As soon as I touched him, I felt myself fly through the air and land flat on my back, the air completely pushed out of my lungs.

Then the stranger was atop me, holding my arms down with a superhuman strength. Maybe he was a vampire.

Stars exploded behind my eyes like a fireworks show. I closed my eyes and forced myself to see through the stars. If I passed out, I was as good as dead—it was an open invitation for this jerk to rape or kill me or something worse. I opened my eyes again and could clearly focus on his face as it loomed above me. He wore no expression—just stoic placidity.

"Behave yourself and I'll let you up."

I just nodded, the wheezing in my chest admitting its own kind of defeat. "What do you want?"

"To talk. I tried to reach you in your dreams but you ignored me."

"Who are you?" I managed to choke out.

"Can we go somewhere more private? I don't want the neighbors to wake up."

I narrowed my eyes. It was just as it had been in Fabian's store. There was absolutely no hint of anything—not the smell of a werewolf, nor the pounding in my blood that usually hinted at a vampire. Zip, zilch, nada, nothing.

"There's a park up the street. Should be empty and there aren't any houses nearby," I managed. "That means you'll have to get off me."

He stood, but watched me as if ready to pounce. "Lead the way."

I got to my feet, rubbing the pain out of my hands. I met his eyes and immediately started forward, keeping a sizable gap between us.

"How'd you get into my dream?"

He smiled, and his teeth reflected the moonlight. But I was more concerned with the fact that I couldn't detect any fangs.

"I have that capability. The power of persuasion. I persuaded you to let me in."

Eerie. "What are you?"

He stopped walking. I stopped walking.

"How about introductions first? I'm Knight and you're Dulcie. Nice to meet you."

He extended his hand, but I didn't take it—I had no clue what he wanted. Best to keep my defenses up. He dropped his hand, and we started walking again.

"How do you know my name?"

"I'm from the A.N.C. Relations Office in the Netherworld."

He reached into his pocket and pulled out a slate tablet about the width of my palm. He handed it to me. I noted his image that appeared on the tablet—the stone turning into what looked like a screen. It was a three-dimensional photo—three dimensional to make it difficult to forge. I searched for the indentation on the back that would prove it was an original. I'd met a handful of people from the A.N.C. Relations Office and knew what their badges looked like. I found the indentation on the back and slipped my thumb into the slit.

"Dulcie O'Neil, Regulator, Splendor," a computerized voice read out from the screen. So far, so good.

"I wish to know if you have a … Knight among the Relations Office employees," I said, eyeing the subject all the while.

The tablet was quiet as it searched its profiles. "Knightley Vander, Association of Netherworld Creatures, Relations Officer, third precinct."

So he wasn't lying. I handed the slate tablet back.

"Believe me now?" he asked.

It was impossible for someone to fake a Netherworld badge to this extent. It had to be real. "Yeah, okay. What are you?"

We reached the park, and Knight took a seat on one of the swings. He looked ridiculous but, okay, sexy. Ahem, really sexy.

"You haven't come across my species before. There aren't any of us on Earth."

That explained why I couldn't tell what kind of creature he was.

"So you're from the Netherworld?"

"Yes, I'm a Loki. We were born from the fires of Hades."

A Loki. Weird. I'd always thought Hades was just a fable.

"So what can you do?" I asked, sounding like a kid comparing video games.

"I can withstand fire for one thing," he said and laughed, thinking himself funny. I didn't.

"What do you do for the Relations Office?"

He shifted back and forth in the swing, shuffling his feet. "I'm a detective."

I leaned against the trunk of a nearby tree, crossing one foot over the other. I was trying to look relaxed but finding it difficult.

"What brought you here?"

Knight stopped swinging. "Someone called a creature from the Netherworld to Splendor, and the same creature killed the warlock."

"Fabian?" I gulped. So Knight was involved, but only so far as he was investigating. Damn. The finger was still pointing at me. "I had nothing to do with it."

He started swinging again, a smile tugging at the corners of his mouth. "I didn't think you did. I'm here to find out where the creature is and who summoned it."

"What does that have to do with me?"

He shrugged. "You're a Regulator and this is your territory. I thought I should pay you the courtesy of informing you I was here so we could ... work together."

"But you never registered at Headquarters. If you're so interested in working with us, why not register and why not come to Headquarters to find me? Why talk to Angela about me?"

He arched a brow, and that same slow smile slid over his lips like a snake. "You did your homework. It's confidential as to why I didn't register."

I frowned. "Confidential? I'm law enforcement, too, in case you forgot."

He nodded. "I didn't forget. But confidential is confidential. It doesn't matter who you are."

I pushed away from the tree, annoyed. "Quillan gives me my jobs, not you. Talk to him."

"This goes over his head. If you want me to report back to the Relations Office that you were less than willing to comply, I can do that."

I stopped in my tracks. He was threatening me now? Great, I was stuck. Whatever the Netherworld wanted, it got. Otherwise, I could be deported for failing to do my job. Especially when it appeared that job was now coming from a higher power than Quillan.

"No, don't do that," I said, annoyed. "So going back to this creature, you think someone called it?"

Knight smirked, knowing he had me. "I know someone called it."

His cockiness really irked me. "Do you know what the creature is? I think it's a werewolf."

"No, it's a *Kragengen* shifter."

"Oh, really?" I said, pretending to know what the hell that was.

"You don't have *Kragengens* here," he said with a smile, as if he knew what I was thinking. "They only exist in the Netherworld."

"Great, how in the hell are we going to find a shape-shifter?" I asked. "Talk about a needle in a haystack.

"*Kragengens* are not true shifters. They can only assume one form aside from their animal forms. If we find it in its human form, we've got it."

I was quiet as I considered it. "What about the fact that there wasn't any blood?"

"*Kragengens* are blood suckers though not vampires. Distantly related," Knight finished, looking as pleased with himself as an A student.

I threw my hands on my hips. "Since you have this all figured out, what do you need my help for?"

He nodded. "Two heads are better than one."

"Aren't macho guys like you supposed to insist they work alone?"

He shrugged. "Whoever said I'm macho? Truth of it is, I do prefer to work alone. But orders are orders."

"You have orders from higher up to work with me?" He nodded. "Why me and not Quillan?"

"Confidential."

I glared at him. This "confidential" stuff was getting old. "So back to you—you said you were a lichen?"

He laughed again, this time deeper. "A Loki. Lichen is algae."

Heat shot to my cheeks. Lichen? Ugh. "Whatever, a Loki. What's so great about you?"

"I have the strength of a vampire and I can influence dreams."

"That's it?" I asked, not meaning to sound so rude. "I mean, you can't do magic?"

He shook his head. "No magic. I'm immune to it, though."

"So I noticed," I grumbled, remembering the ice and fire episodes. "Okay, smart-guy, any ideas on how we nab this shape-shifting creature?"

"Based on the fact that it tore Fabian to pieces, it probably enjoys causing pain. So I ask you—where would a supernatural creature who enjoys inflicting pain want to spend its free time, here in Splendor?"

I felt a chill. "Dagan's S&M club, Payne."

He slid off the swing and nodded. "Bingo."

SIX

I pulled into the alley bordering Dagan's club, Payne. Marilyn Manson's *The Beautiful People* blared through the open doors, punctuated with a few rounds of raucous laughter.

"Hey, hottie," a short guy with frizzy blond hair called out, pursing his lips and kissing the air.

I shook my head, watching him take a drag of his cigarette as he motioned to his crotch. His companion laughed. I ignored them and coaxed the Wrangler into a spot by the back door.

I turned the car off and exhaled, pulling the keys from the ignition. Opening the door, I slid down the seat onto the asphalt below. The heels of my thigh-high stiletto boots tapped the pavement and echoed the frenetic beating of my heart.

A dark form stepped out from behind a dumpster. I steadied myself for an attack, even as I recognized Knight.

"Damn it," I snapped. "Do you always have to jump out at me?"

He wore blue jeans and a white T-shirt that stuck out against the dark night like a goblin in heaven. The white T-shirt didn't do much to hide his ample biceps, and was visibly straining around his pecs.

Show off.

"Evening," he said.

"Night," I grumbled, forcing my attention from his healthy body.

He chuckled. "Meaning my name or a greeting?"

"Greeting," I muttered, smoothing down the non-existent creases in my black vinyl miniskirt.

"Are you carrying a gun?" he asked, his gaze starting at my eyes and traveling the length of me. With my black miniskirt, bra top and boots, there wasn't room for a gun.

"I've got magic, remember?"

"Yes, I remember," he said, quirking a brow like my magic wasn't very impressive. "Well, at least one of us is armed."

I glanced at him, and he pulled up his shirt revealing the butt of a gun sticking out of his pants. It also revealed what looked like a six pack of abdomen. I looked away.

"Glad you're prepared," I said, then feigned interest in my skirt again.

"What should I wear? I imagine jeans and a T-shirt aren't exactly dress code?"

"No," I said. "They aren't."

"Maybe something not quite as revealing as what you've got on?"

"Hey, I'm dressing the part," I started, my hands on my hips. "Wait until you see some of the women in there—I'll ..."

"Sorry," he interrupted, eyeing me again. "You look … incredible. I'm just less thrilled with baring all my assets."

I frowned but didn't respond as my thoughts turned to getting the show on the road. First, Knight's costume. "You might want to take your gun out of your pants."

"Is that what you say to all the guys?"

I just shook my head.

He removed the gun. Closing my eyes, I shook my hand until a mound of fairy dust appeared. Then I imagined him in black leather pants and tossed the dust into the air. I opened my eyes and watched the dust circle him in a cloud of what looked like glitter. Once it disappeared, I found him before me, chest completely bare. He was nothing short of glorious

59

in shiny leather that clutched his muscular thighs like a second skin.

"I thought you were immune to magic?" I asked.

Knight lifted his legs up as he inspected the boots. "I am. My clothes aren't."

I tried not to notice the thick white scar running from his collarbone, across the muscular landscape of his pecs and ending at his waist. It was like someone had taken a knife to a beautiful work of art.

"It's from a battle with a werewolf," he said.

I shrugged, pretending indifference. "None of my business."

He nodded but didn't drop his attention from my face. I blushed and could've hit myself. Hades be damned, blushing was just so … obvious.

"Can I have a shirt?" he asked.

"Most guys inside won't be wearing one, but if you're self-conscious about …"

"I'm not self-conscious about anything," he snapped.

I hadn't meant to offend him. I hadn't even been talking about his scar. Dulcie O'Neil, always putting her foot in her mouth. "I didn't mean to insinuate you were, I was just saying …"

Knight's eyes were piercing. "Never mind. Shouldn't I have something on to disguise this?" he asked, holding up his gun.

I'd forgotten about the weapon. As he shoved it back into the band of his leather pants, I tossed a fistful of fairy dust at him and imagined a red satiny shirt. It covered the gun perfectly. Knight glanced down and shrugged.

"I'm not thrilled with red."

"Get used to it," I said with a smile.

"I have a feeling these pants are going to chafe after a while … if you know what I mean."

Holy hell, I'd forgotten to give him underwear! "Boxers or briefs?" I demanded, hoping the blood would drain from my flushed face.

He chuckled. "I'm a boxer man, myself."

I shut my eyes, though I didn't really have to. But it made the task easier when not confronted with his amused gaze. Producing some fairy dust, I imagined a pair of red satin boxers underneath the leather and opened my eyes, blowing the ethereal particles at him.

Knight glanced down and pulled the band of his pants forward, inspecting the boxers below. "Thanks, not really a satin guy, but I guess these will do," he said, a smile dancing in his eyes. "Ready?"

I didn't say anything but headed for the back entrance of Payne. I pushed a button on the intercom.

"Yeah?" A voice echoed through the alley.

"I'm here to see Dagan. It's Dulcie from Headquarters." Silence.

"Hello?" I demanded.

"Do you have an appointment?" the speaker box asked.

"I don't need an appointment. Just tell Dagan I'm here. He'll see me."

There was more silence on the other end. I turned to face Knight who just grinned as if he were enjoying every minute of my disquiet. The door buzzed, and I pushed against it. Knight rested his hand on my lower back, and his touch brought me some sense of ease as I approached the long, dark hallway. I never knew what would happen at Dagan's.

The insistent thudding of what I hesitated to call music met my ears and rattled around in my head like marbles spilling on a floor. The sound pounded against the walls, the beat almost too fast for even the song to keep up with.

"Prepare yourself for some kinky stuff," I said.

"To watch or to partake of?"

"To watch," I snapped.

Dagan appeared at the end of the hall. He was wearing a pair of black boxer shorts, nothing else. Both his nipples wore hoops. He leaned against the wall, crossing his arms over his chest and making his muscles bulge until they looked like they might explode.

Dagan wasn't that bad to look at—a very large guy ... not quite as big as Nick the ogre, but getting close. Tattoos ran the length of his arms and most of his chest. The tattoo on his chest was a wolf fornicating with an angel. Really tasteful. My eyes met his. They were literally black. Not a dark shade of brown, but black. Like vapid pools of nothing.

He glared down a thrice broken nose. "Dulcie, what do you want?"

"I need to talk with you. We have a few questions."

"Who's your friend?" Dagan asked, looking Knight up and down like he was Dagan's own personal sexual fantasy. Dagan wasn't just gay—he was into it all—women, men, whatever. As long as the sex was painful, he was into it.

"I work with the A.N.C. office in the Netherworld," Knight said.

"Another cop. Great." Dagan dropped his attention back to me, his gaze traveling the length of my body as if undressing me with his eyes. "Am I being deported?"

"No, Dagan, you aren't," I snapped.

Dagan approached me, and I wished I had my gun. He ran his finger down my shoulder and arm, then grabbed hold of my hand. I held my breath the entire time. My skin burned at the touch of his fingertips, and I didn't need to glance at my arm to know his touch had left my skin red. A demon's touch is like instant sunburn to a fairy.

I pulled my hand from his.

"Come in," Dagan said as he started down the hall.

"Are you alright?" Knight whispered and ran his hand along my arm. I shivered against his touch and glanced down my shoulder, finding the redness completely gone. I faced him in shock, but he just winked.

I turned to Dagan again and followed him to his office. It was in the back of the building and set apart from the hideous things going on in the belly of the monster, that monster being his club. Dagan's office suited me just fine.

"Have a seat," Dagan said and closed the door behind us, shutting out the pounding music. His office was black with a few red bulbs fighting against the otherwise pitch darkness. If the devil had an office, this is what it would look like. I took a seat across from Dagan, who piled his legs up on the desk before me. Knight stood in the corner.

It was the four monitors set up against his desk that caught my attention—each one monitoring the four rooms of his establishment. Every room was occupied. The monitors were too far away to detect exactly what was going on within them—something I had no argument with. In this case, ignorance was most definitely bliss.

"Tell your friend to make himself comfortable," Dagan said as his gaze settled on Knight.

"I'll stand, thanks," Knight answered, and I could hear the annoyance in his deep voice.

"Dagan, no more screwing around. I'm sure you're interested in why we came here?" I asked.

Dagan faced me again with his lazy gaze. "Yes, Dulcie, enlighten me. I didn't imagine you came for a threesome?"

I couldn't help my cringe. "No, we didn't," I snapped. "And the only reason we dressed the part was because I knew you wouldn't let us in otherwise."

Dagan nodded and clasped his hands in his lap, looking like a professor about to scold a less than impressive student. "Right, we've been through this before, haven't we?"

"Yeah, we have," I said, wishing we could cut through the crap. "We're here because we need to know if you've seen any strangers in the last couple weeks. Anyone you didn't recognize?"

Dagan laughed, but it wasn't a happy sound—fraught with acerbic undertones. "Dulcie, darling Dulcie." He dropped his feet to the floor, the thud vibrating through the small room like thunder. "I get people in here I don't recognize all the time. Sadomasochism draws crowds from all over. We serve a vast clientele."

Ugh, my question had been pretty dumb. I should've known that. Damn.

"This particular stranger would've had a zestier appetite than most," Knight said eloquently, coming to my aid.

Dagan smiled, his gaze holding Knight again. "What kind of zesty appetite?"

I half-turned in my seat, wanting to give my eyes a break from Dagan. Knight was much more pleasant to look at.

He shrugged. "I'd say the creature would enjoy extreme pain—possibly receiving but definitely giving. Have you had any instances that are … out of the ordinary?"

Dagan's gaze landed on me again, his eyes traveling up my legs until I wanted to cover them. But I didn't even flinch. I'd trained myself.

"No, nothing I can think of. Now drop the charade, and tell me what's going on."

"A.N.C. business," Knight started.

I shook my head. "He won't tell us anything until we tell him what he wants to know."

Dagan released another acid laugh. "Dulce, you know me so well."

"Something killed Fabian. It was called from the Netherworld and we're trying to find out who called it. The bigger thing at stake now, though, is finding the creature," I said.

"I can't help you, Dulcie. There hasn't been anything out of the ordinary here in a while. Been boring, actually," Dagan said.

I started to scoff but Knight's hand on my shoulder shut me up. "Can we take a look around?" he asked.

Dagan leaned forward, his face suddenly all seriousness. "You can take a look around, but don't even breathe you're A.N.C. If my clients suspect any cop, anything, coming out of you, neither of you will be welcome here again. I do a lot to ensure my clientele are comfortable."

"Understood," Knight said, gritting his teeth.

Dagan stood. "Then please go ahead. Look around, but don't call any attention to yourselves. I'll be around to make sure."

I stood up, dread pounding through me. Now, I had to drop the cop persona and face whatever horrible things were going on in the belly of the beast.

Dagan stood next to me, so close I could feel the heat of his breath across my cheeks. "Just remember, Dulce, everyone is here of their own accord. Nothing is illegal if they enjoy it."

"That's not …"

"Shh," Knight interrupted and grabbed my arm.

Dagan opened the door. "After you."

This was so not going to be fun. At least it wasn't a huge place. Once we did a walk through, we could leave. That's what I promised myself, anyway.

Dagan watched us walk down the hall and retired back into his office. He'd stay true to his word. If he said he'd keep an eye on us, he would. I'm sure the monitors in his office would help.

I noticed a group of about four or so people standing outside the first room on our little tour. Here's where the "fun" started.

I stepped beside a woman dressed in what amounted to tape—a piece of duct tape across her breasts and across her … lower area. Later on, it would probably give someone a great amount of pleasure … sadistic pleasure … to rip the tape right off her. And I imagined she'd enjoy it too. I winced involuntarily.

The woman smiled, her gaze roving over me and then Knight who stood directly behind me. She was tall—nearly as tall as Knight and attractive with long red hair.

"What's going on in there?" I whispered.

The woman leaned down, desire so thick in her eyes, I could've cut it. "A woman with three vamps."

Egad.

She trailed an index finger down my collarbone, stopping just above my breasts. I gulped, trying to swallow the disgust wedging itself in my throat. Knight must've noticed because he took a step closer to me and slid his arms around my waist.

"Do you want to get a better look?" he asked and grinned down at me, his eyes sparkling. I could've shot him.

So Knight was playing with me? He was going to milk this just as Dagan had. I couldn't very well say no—talk about destroying my alibi. I turned my attention to the hall as Dagan approached us. Goddammit.

"Yeah, that sounds great," I managed.

The woman stepped aside and gave Knight a knowing grin and an equally knowing pat on the ass.

"She's new," he said.

The woman smiled at me again. "Welcome. If you want to … play later, find me."

"Thanks," I managed then moved through the open door. There wasn't a wall or anything separating the room from the hall, so we all just stood along the sidelines and watched.

Well, I didn't. I'm not sure how I managed, but I stared at the carpeting the entire time.

"Like it?" I looked up at Dagan who grinned, looking like a shark.

I was about to give him a piece of my mind when I noticed the expression of the woman behind him, the tall red head wearing the duct tape. She watched me inquisitively.

Her hands ran the length of Dagan's naked back, and he leaned into her.

"Yeah, it's great," I managed.

Knight pulled me against him and dropped his head into my neck like he was going to bite me. I tried to push away from him, but he held me in an iron grasp.

"Don't blow our cover," he whispered.

Then he kissed my neck and ran his hands down my stomach. Shivers raced over my skin. My blood was boiling and not with lust. With anger the likes of which I hadn't felt in a very long time. Well, okay, and maybe a little lust. Either way, Knight was going to get an earful later.

My gaze drifted to Dagan who'd changed places with the woman and now stood behind her. He kissed the woman's neck, and she melted into him. He started to pull against the duct tape on her breasts. As if he could read my mind, Dagan faced me, his eyes full of sinister deliberation. The woman moaned against him, and before I could take another breath, he ripped the tape.

"Get me out of here now," I whispered to Knight.

Knight didn't respond but lifted me up, newlywed style, and took a few steps away from the room. He dropped me and pushed me against the wall, forcing his lips on mine. As soon as his head shielded my face from the onlookers, I exploded.

"What the hell are you doing!"

"Go with it," he whispered. "I'm getting us out of here."

He pushed himself against me and I retreated as far as I could into the unforgiving wall. The concrete scratched my naked back, forcing me into Knight's kiss. Knight glanced at Dagan, smacked my ass, and then started for the door.

Once outside, I slapped him hard against the face. "What the hell was that?"

It had been the first time someone had kissed me since Jack, over a year ago.

Knight gritted his teeth, his cheek red where my palm had let him know exactly what I thought of him. "If not for me, you would've blown our cover. Jesus, Dulcie, you were like a schoolgirl in there."

"You didn't have to kiss me and take advantage of the situation. Groping me like that was uncalled for."

Knight chuckled. "You're a Regulator, Dulcie. You should know the job isn't always smooth sailing."

I frowned and started for my car, my legs weak. "Either way, don't ever touch me again."

"Look, it had to be believable."

"Whatever." I unlocked the door and hopped into the car. I wasn't sure how he'd gotten here, but I wasn't about to leave him in leather pants in a dark alley. "How did you get here?"

He shrugged. "I took a cab. I didn't know how long I'd be here so I neglected to get a rental. I'll probably get one tomorrow."

"Get in," I said with a sigh.

"You're offering me a ride?" he asked with a bashful grin.

"Get in before I change my mind."

Knight started for the passenger seat. "I'm staying at the Marriott on Evergreen Street."

I nodded and pulled out of the lot when I remembered I hadn't brought up Bram's Chinese massage parlor with Dagan. Damn. Well, now I'd have to make another trip. Double damn.

"Well, that was basically a waste of time," I said, wanting to break the monotony of silence.

Knight shrugged. "Maybe. Maybe not. It's all part of the job."

So he had a good perspective on it. Guess I was impatient.

"What's your phone number?" Knight asked.

I threw him a frown. "I'm not giving you my phone number."

"I need to be able to get in touch with you." He shrugged. "It's that or I interrupt your pirate dreams again."

Heat washed over my face like a wave. I dropped my gaze and tightened my hands on the wheel. How freaking embarrassing could this night get?

I gave him my phone number.

SEVEN

The he creature had struck again.

In a matter of two days, there had been two more killings. The first, Guy Riley, had been a well-known illegal potions importer who'd been contributing to the delinquencies lining Splendor streets for years. I couldn't say his death brought me any level of sorrow.

Now, as Trey and I had been called onto the scene of the second killing, I didn't know what to expect. Guy had been torn up like Fabian had. And like Fabian, his head had been left. Apparently, the creature didn't have a taste for brains.

Trey handed me a pair of latex gloves and stepped aside, motioning with his arms that I should go ahead of him. Such the gentleman. I stepped over the yellow crime scene tape and blinked against the glare of the portable floodlights shining down the alleyway.

Guy had been killed inside his dark arts store, much like Fabian had been. But this second murder had taken place in an alley behind Guy's; almost like the victim had witnessed something he shouldn't have.

"Do they have any idea who the victim is?" I asked Trey, who'd managed to get on the scene a few minutes before me.

He shook his head. "No, I waited for you."

I nodded and followed the white hazmat-suited A.N.C. forensics team down the alley where they gathered around what I could only assume was the body. At our approach, they separated like bowling pins.

I glanced down at what was left of the body. As with Fabian and Guy, there was no blood. Just a head and a fleshy mound sitting beside the head. The fleshy mound was about the length of my forearm with the white of various bones peeking through the flesh. I squatted down and reached for the pulpy mass before noting the numbered markers set beside the head and rib cage, used for crime scene photos.

I glanced up at the forensics team who were still surrounding the body.

"Am I good to shift stuff around now?"

A man with beady eyes gave me a salute. "It's all yours."

I lifted the fleshy mass. "Rib cage," I said to Trey.

"That's what I was thinking too."

"Bag it," I said and handed the rib cage to the closest hazmat man. He regarded it with disinterest so I waved my hand a bit, acting the charade of "take this damn thing already."

"Looks like there are some teeth marks on the bones but other than that, it isn't going to tell us much more than what we already know about the killer," I said.

A short man with blond hair and a blonder handlebar moustache opened a clear plastic bag as Mr. Reluctant dropped the rib cage in, sealing it away. It would then go to our crime scene lab to be placed in a cryogenic chamber that would ensure we could return to study it.

One rib cage down, one head left to go.

I sighed and turned to the fun task of rotating the head so we could get an idea of who our John Doe was. In the heat of the lights, I could feel beads of perspiration skiing down the small of my back. No one ever said this job was a glamorous one.

I grabbed a handful of black hair which felt cold against my gloved hand. I rotated the head until the eyes fixed their sightless gaze on me, an expression of wide-eyed shock still resident in them.

I couldn't help my gasp.

"Tad," I said in a breathless voice.

Trey groaned and shifted his extreme weight from one leg to the other. "Damn."

If Guy and Fabian's deaths hadn't bothered me much, Tad Jones was a different story. Though Tad had definitely had his dealings with the law and he'd spent many a night in our holding cells, he was someone you wanted to bring under your wing. There was a flawed, but innate goodness about him.

He'd been addicted to marsh root, an illegal potion that worked like speed, since I'd first met him five years ago. He was young—maybe in his late teens and he'd had a hard, short life. He was a werewolf without a pack—he'd been ousted as soon as he'd gotten addicted to marsh. Wolves weren't the most forgiving of creatures.

"I always liked the kid. Thought he'd clean up eventually," Trey said as he chewed his lip.

I nodded. "He was a good kid."

Even though I didn't say much, that didn't mean I wasn't reeling inside. I'd spent lots of time with Tad, talking about his future and trying to help him. As a Regulator, it was my job to bust the bad guys but I also tried to keep everyone on the straight and narrow. I couldn't help but think I'd failed Tad and it brought stinging tears to my eyes.

"So you think Guy's murder is related?" Trey asked.

I could tell he was trying to change the subject, trying to get my mind off the fact that I'd failed Tad and because of that, he was now dead before me. I had to give it to Trey for trying.

I cleared my throat, forcing the tears back. I would not cry.

"Yeah," I said with a sniffle that I turned into a cough.

Trey nodded. "They were both torn up like Fabian," he said and flicked up one finger.

"They all had something to do with the illegal potion industry." Finger two.

"Yes," I said, forcing guilty thoughts of Tad to the back of my mind. I couldn't save him, but I could damn well find out who killed him and see them pay.

"So whoever did this was trying to cover something up. All the deaths were related to street potions," I said.

"Fabian was a dealer and so was Guy, but Tad wasn't," Trey pointed out.

I nodded. "So why kill him?"

Trey shrugged. "Maybe Tad saw something or knew something?"

"Maybe. I can't help but think if he'd known something was up, he would have come to me."

"Yeah, the kid did have a crush on you," Trey said with a sad smile.

"Whatever it was, he trusted me."

And I failed him … the silent words clung to my tongue.

"Well, do you think we got enough here?" Trey asked and we both glanced around the alley again, almost waiting for another clue to rear its head. Of course nothing did.

Yeah, I was ready to go.

###

I was tired. Tired, depressed and really not in the mood to go to work but hey, sometimes you have to do things you don't want to, right? I opened the double glass doors to Headquarters and stifled a sigh.

"You look like something the cat dragged in," Elsie said with a compassionate smile.

I frowned and bobbed my head—it was all I could manage. Luckily, today didn't look like much of a busy day—no one in our holding cells and no phones ringing. Thank you, Hades. Now I just needed coffee and lots of it before I started writing up the notes on Tad's murder.

I walked to my desk and threw myself into the seat.

"Dulce." I didn't need to turn around to recognize Quillan's rich baritone. But I did anyway.

"Morning," I muttered.

He avoided my gaze. That's when I knew something was up. "Can I chat with you for a minute?"

Words that no employee ever wants to hear from her boss. I so didn't want to deal with this today. I stood up with a sigh and followed him into his office.

"Have a seat. Do you want some coffee?"

I took the chair. "Yeah, please."

Shutting the door, he turned to his Mr. Coffee, and poured me a cup, using a mug I'd gotten him for Christmas. It had a picture of the Blues Brothers—his all-time favorite movie. He plopped one sugar cube and a bit of Coffee-Mate into the cup, then stirred—just how I liked it.

"Here you go." He handed me the cup. "You and Trey were on the murder case last night?" he started.

"Yeah, it was Tad Jones."

Quillan shook his head. "Damn shame—he was a good kid."

I didn't want to think about exactly what a damn shame it was ... shame wasn't even the word for it. Instead, I turned my attention to the warm cup in my hands and thought about the information I needed to share with Knight. But I had no way to reach him. Guess it would have to wait.

"What did you make of it?" Quillan asked.

I shrugged. "Guy, Fabian and Tad all had something to do with the illegal potion trade. I'm not sure what the link is between them yet, but I intend to find out."

Quillan nodded. "Next steps?"

"We should put some guys out to monitor the comings and goings of other creatures dealing street potions. Not only for their own good but also to see if we can get any leads." I paused and tapped my fingers against the ceramic cup. "I don't think it's a coincidence that all the deaths have to do

74

with street potions and if I had to guess, I'd say the creature will kill again."

Quillan smiled with a nod of his curly-locked head. "I'll get a list going of all creatures we've suspected of being involved with illegal potions."

"I don't mind doing a little reconnaissance, myself."

Quillan immediately shook his head. "I'll take care of it."

I just gave him a small smile of thanks—he knew I didn't exactly enjoy stakeouts.

"So Dulce ..." Quillan started, looking at me anxiously. "What's up?"

He rested his tightly packed ass against the edge of the desk, one leg curling over the side, the other stationed on the ground. I leaned back in my chair, a mere six inches from him—so close I could smell his Tommy Bahama aftershave.

"I received word from the Relations Office this morning ..."

Great, here it came. He was pissed off I'd withheld information about Knight. Well, what choice did I have? Knight was higher up on the Netherworld totem pole than Quillan, and he'd given me none-too-subtle orders not to breathe a whisper of the case to anyone. This was so not my fault, but I couldn't even defend myself.

He took a deep breath. "You're off all future cases."

I felt like I'd been blindsided by an elephant. "What? What the hell are you talking about? What did I do to deserve this?"

Quillan put a hand on my shoulder, but I coldly shrugged it off. There was no way in hell he was going to make me feel any better about getting ... fired.

"This has nothing to do with you," he said, and it was as dumb a line as when a guy breaks up with you and says it isn't you, it's him. It's you—it's always you.

"What the hell did I do?"

"The Relations Office seems to think you might be in danger. That's all they'd tell me. Apparently this is very hush-hush."

I narrowed my eyes. "What a load! I'm starting to wonder if I'm off the squad because I'm a suspect in Fabian's murder!"

Quillan shook his head. "You aren't off the squad. I received word from the Relations Office this morning that you aren't considered a suspect. I don't think you ever were." He paused. "And you know I never thought you were."

I swallowed a retort. "What kind of danger do they think I'm in?"

"They wouldn't tell me. They just said to give you a break for a little while. Think of it as a little downtime—a mini vacation."

I leaned back in my chair. At least I wasn't fired. But this whole danger business? It made no sense. Somehow Knight had to be involved, and the bummer of the whole thing was that I couldn't ask a damned question without somehow bringing Knight into it.

"For how long?" I asked.

"Until I hear back from Relations and they tell me."

I dropped his gaze. "This sucks."

"I know you're angry, Dulce, but it's for your own good. Fabian's killer is still out there and now with the other murders … this way you'll be protected."

"Protected?" I scoffed. "How will I be protected? By staying home?" Well, there was Sam's protection spell on my house, but somehow I didn't think Quillan was referring to that. And Sam's spell could be broken.

"That's not the end of the story. We're … setting up some other protection for you."

"What does that mean?"

"A few gremlins to patrol your house."

I started shaking my head. "But …"

Quillan interrupted me. "You won't see them. They'll be out back in the woods but close enough to keep an eye on the place."

"Gremlins, Quillan? You should be more afraid of them attacking me!" Gremlins had the unfortunate reputation of attacking anything that moved. "And what about my neighbors? They're all human and wouldn't survive a gremlin attack. That is the worst freaking idea …"

"The Netherworld is sending a species of evolved gremlins. They're smarter and stronger than your average … gremlin."

I was so pissed off, I didn't even get to ponder the fact that I'd warranted Netherworld gremlins. "This bites the big one, Quillan."

He shook his head, like he didn't think it bit the big one at all. Yeah, well he wasn't about to have gremlins pooping in his yard and killing neighbors' animals if not the neighbors themselves.

I was so going to be evicted.

"You won't even see them. They have strict orders to stay on the perimeter of the property. The only thing you have to do is feed them once a day."

"Feed them?" I stood up. "What the hell am I supposed to feed them?"

Quillan laughed. "Dog food. Two scoops a day."

"Okay, you do realize I've killed every houseplant I've ever owned?"

A smirk played with his lips. "Dulce, I'm sure you'll be fine. This will be good for you."

"I never planned on having a dog or a cat or anything else. I'm not a pet person."

The smile didn't vanish from his lips. "Well, now you have gremlins."

"I'm so glad you're enjoying this."

Quillan crossed his arms above his chest. "It might be slightly entertaining but I'm more worried about you than anything else." He paused. "I'm going to check on you every day after work."

I sat down again and sighed until it felt like all the air was escaping my lungs. "You don't have to do that. With freaking gremlins around, I'm sure I'll be fine."

Quillan touched my shoulder again. "I want to. You know I don't want anything bad happening to you, Dulce."

I dropped my gaze as heat rushed to my cheeks. "Yeah, yeah," I waved away his concern with an indifferent hand. "I'm your favorite, blah blah blah."

Quillan laughed but it didn't make me feel any better.

"How many gremlins do I have to feed?"

"Just two."

I nodded, feeling slightly guilty that I was still keeping the fact that Knight and I were working together from Quillan. Quillan was a good boss and my friend.

"So am I free to go now?" I asked.

"Yes, and just so you know, the gremlins are arriving tonight."

Holy Hades, it was like a bad horror movie. "Great, then I need to go to the store and get some Purina." I shook my head. "Goddammit."

Quillan chuckled. "I already took care of that for you, Dulce. I've got it in my truck."

I forced myself to smile. It wasn't his fault. He was trying to make this as easy on me as he could. "Thanks, Quill. What time are you coming over?"

"How about six thirty? I'll bring dinner."

"Don't get any ideas."

He laughed. "I'll try not to."

When six p.m. rolled around, I'd managed to e-mail my Captain Slade queries to nearly every agency on my list. I stood up, stretched, and caught my reflection in the mirror.

78

An oversized T-shirt and boxers weren't the greatest thing to wear when company's expected.

I neared the door of my bedroom and eyed my jeans draped over my armchair. They'd do. I threw them on along with a black tank top and considered myself dressed. I mean, I didn't want to give Quillan the wrong impression.

A knock sounded on the front door.

After checking the peephole, I pulled it open and found Quillan with a bag of Alpo on one shoulder and dog dishes in both hands.

I reached for the dishes, but Quillan just grinned and showed himself into my unremarkable apartment.

"Where should I put this?" he asked and lifted his shoulder as if he needed to draw attention to the enormous bag of dog food.

"How about outside?"

He frowned. "It'll get wet outside or animals will get into it. You need to embrace the gremlins, Dulce."

I'm sure he couldn't help his smile. "Funny. I guess in the kitchen."

Quillan dropped the mammoth bag of Alpo onto my linoleum floor and headed for the back door that led into the woods bordering my apartment building. I watched him open the door and drop both bowls onto the weed-ridden "yard."

"And what do I do if any of my neighbors sees one of the ugly things and freaks out?" I asked.

Quillan slapped his hands together as if his job here was done and closed the door behind him. "They won't. I cast an illusion, so to the unknowing eye, they look just like dogs—a Labrador and a Dalmatian, to be exact."

"I'm not allowed to have dogs here."

"Then don't let anyone see you feed them. They'll stay in the woods and won't cause you any trouble. No one will even notice they're here." Quillan started for the front door. "I left the food in the truck. Got Chinese."

Of course, that immediately made me think of the massage parlor. Dammit, I still needed to pay a visit to Dagan.

"That sounds great, thanks Quill."

I watched his large frame as he walked through the door, then I started for the kitchen. Pulling out my best silverware, I held a fork up to the light and used the hem of my shirt to wipe away the water spots.

Quillan walked back in, the smell of sweet and sour something wooing my nose. My stomach growled, and I could feel my cheeks instantly coloring. Quillan didn't seem to notice or was polite enough not to comment. He started dishing us up, as I searched for a place for us to sit. I only had two chairs and one was currently residing at my desk. Quillan handed me a plate and motioned for me to sit at the table while he assumed my computer chair.

"So when are the gremlins coming?" I asked.

"Not sure. The delivery guy is supposed to call me when they're close."

"Thanks," I managed and watched him take a few bites. He accidentally nudged my mouse and *Captain Slade's Bounty* jumped onto the screen, causing a bite of Chinese food to get lodged in my throat.

"What are you going to do with your free time?" Quillan asked as he glanced at the word document.

I shrugged, trying to swallow my panic and a lump of sweet and sour pork. I had done all my search and replaces of Quillan's name, hadn't I?

"Nothing really," I answered.

Quillan nodded and turned his attention to the computer again. "What's this?"

I jumped from my seat and raced to the computer, hoping and praying Captain Slade's name would greet me. "It's a book."

Quillan took a bite of rice. "What's it about?"

I blushed and reached the desk, scanning the page. "Um, pirates."

He glanced at the screen again. "Cool, I like pirates. May I?"

I nodded before I could stop myself and peered over his shoulder as he read the page and clicked to the next. And there, highlighted in blue was Quillan's name with the prompt: *replace?* staring at me like it was having the last laugh.

"What?" he started, sounding completely confused.

Heat like liquid lava attacked my neck and face as I tried to grab the mouse but he shifted it away and continued reading.

"I, um … I was using you as the inspiration for one of my characters," I said, my heart pounding in my head.

"You were?" He actually sounded flattered. "*Captain Quillan reached out to Clementine and grabbed her by the bodice*," he read as I cringed. "*Pulling her to him, he grabbed her head and tilting it back, brought his lips to her throat as she moaned in ecstasy.*"

I lurched for the mouse and closed the document. "Okay, that's enough."

Quillan swiveled around in his chair and gave me a huge smile. "Wow."

"Don't look so pleased with yourself," I said, searching for a reasonable excuse as to why my boss's name happened to be in my sex scene. "I just wanted Captain Slade to be … a blond and um … you were the first person who came to mind."

Okay, that didn't totally suck.

"Oh," Quillan said and dropped his smile.

"Yeah, it just makes it easier for me to write when I can think about the people I know." I paused. "Trey and Sam are in it too."

Okay, getting better.

His phone went off before he could ask me any more questions, and I inwardly sighed.

"Hi," Quillan said into the receiver. "Yeah, we're here. Ten minutes? Great."

He hung up and faced me again, delving back into his Chinese food. I was already full.

"You're finished?" he asked and eyed me like he didn't trust me.

"Yeah, I don't eat much. Want the rest?" I offered my plate. He nodded, still mid chew, and took the plate.

When he was halfway through my dinner, the sound of the doorbell interrupted us. I got up, but Quillan was quick to subdue me. "Don't know who it is, better that I get it."

I jumped in front of him. "Give me a break. This is my house, and Sam's spell keeps anything bad away."

"Sam's spell is breakable, Dulce," Quillan said, looking fatigued.

"I know that," I snapped.

The doorbell dinged again. Quillan sighed. "You're so stubborn," he said as I pulled open the door, and we both faced a short and rotund man. Well, actually, goblin.

"Delivery for a Dulcie O'Neil," the goblin said. "Got them in the truck."

Quillan started after him. I decided to clean up the Chinese food. Glancing out my kitchen window, which overlooked the yard, I watched as Quillan and the goblin struggled with a large wooden crate. Finding the Chinese food less than interesting, I started for the living room window, which would offer a better view.

Luckily, it didn't seem like any of my neighbors were home. Quillan had probably cast a spell to keep them away. Whatever worked, I guess.

Thinking I should pay more attention to my new companions, I started for the front door and closing it behind me, followed the curse words into the back yard. Quillan had a crow bar up against the crate, and the goblin had one on the opposite side. They pulled together, and the front popped open.

Neither man moved, but something inside the crate did. It poked its head out and continued advancing, looking like some sort of pig dog. Labrador or Dalmatian? Yeah, no. Its enormous head looked like a bulbous circular mound with two red eyes and tusks as long as my forearms.

Quillan neared the opening of the crate, bending down as if to make friends with the hideous thing. The gremlin approached him, and sniffed at his hand. Its skin was pasty white and completely devoid of fur. It looked like an albino dog with mange. It wasn't a small creature. Seated, it came up to my waist, and its head was easily bigger than any St. Bernard's. But this creature had nothing endearing about him, even if you wrapped a little first aid kit around its neck.

"Dulce, come say hello," Quillan said, before turning to face me.

Reluctantly, I started toward the crate, noticing the other gremlin cautiously making its way out of the enclosure. I stood beside Quillan, and he drew my hand forward. The strange little creature sniffed it with little interest. Apparently finding me less than appetizing, it trotted off into the woods, its friend following.

"So which one's the Lab, and which one's the Dalmatian?" I asked.

Quillan smiled down at me. "Very funny, Dulce."

An hour later, I had two gremlins who were happily scouting out the environment of the woods alongside my apartment. I was doing dishes, and Quillan was en route back to his place.

The shrill ring of the phone cut right through the calmness of the moment. I answered it and heard the unmistakable sound of panting on the other end.

"Dulce, it's Trey. I gotta come over."

"What?" I was less than polite but still, Trey needing to come over was definitely on the weird side. We weren't exactly friends and we'd never been to one another's houses, which was totally and completely fine by me.

"I had a vision, Dulce. I had a vision of the creature killing Fabian."

My heart about dropped out of my chest.

EIGHT

T rey was shaking, but he assured me it wasn't unusual after he had a vision. Not blessed with second sight, I had nothing to go on but his word.

"Do you want a glass of water?" I asked as I showed him into my living room.

He shook his head, sweat sailing from his forehead onto my floor. I tried not to gag and instead, motioned him toward the couch. "Have a seat."

Trey threw himself onto the sofa, the cushions and springs groaning under his weight. His gaze rested on the TV until it looked like he was hypnotized. But the TV wasn't on, so it couldn't have been that enthralling.

"I know I'm not supposed to be here—Quillan said you were off the squad for a while. But, Dulce, I thought you'd want to know anyway."

I got the gist of it. Trey was scared but didn't want to go to Quillan in his current unsettled state. And he probably didn't want to stay home either, with visions of a creature tearing Fabian apart dancing in his head.

"Do you want to take the couch tonight?" I asked.

"Yeah, if I could. I'm usually not like this after a vision, but this one was pretty bad." He glanced away, and I knew there was more. I just hoped he wouldn't start crying—his lower lip was trembling like a three-year-old before a tantrum.

"I'm afraid if anyone knows I had the vision, they'll come after me. There's a lot of incriminating stuff in it."

That was something I hadn't considered. "How would they find out?"

"When I have visions, sometimes whoever is involved knows I'm having them."

"That's happened before?"

"Yep, if whomever I see is sensitive enough, they can pick up on it."

"If that's the case, you need to tell Quillan. You should be protected."

Trey just nodded, but it was a nod that said he probably wouldn't. That was one of the things I didn't get about men—the whole machismo thing—that if Trey told Quillan he was scared, he'd look like a wuss.

"Why don't you tell me about it?" I started.

Trey exhaled. "Here goes. I was eating dinner tonight, and it hit me out of nowhere. I saw Fabian in his store. It was late, and he was there by himself. Then I remember seeing him trying to get away from something. I got the impression that whatever it was, it was female. And there was someone else in the background. He was dressed all in black and had his head down so I couldn't see his face. But he was there, watching the whole thing."

"Okay, you think the creature is female. That's good to know. Did you catch anything about the size of it or what it looked like?"

He shook his head. "No, nothing. I might've been seeing the situation through the creature's eyes. I could see everything about … Fabian."

Trey shivered and dropped his attention to his fidgeting hands. "I can't be alone, Dulce. Not after seeing that."

"You can stay here tonight. I've got Sam's protection spell on the place, and Quillan dropped off two gremlins earlier this evening so I'm about as safe as can be." I laughed, trying to lighten Trey's mood, but he barely managed a half smile. I'd never seen him like this, and it freaked me out.

Usually he was the annoying sidekick—the perpetual thorn in my side. I wasn't prepared for a role change.

"Thanks, Dulce."

"You know you have to tell Quillan tomorrow?" I asked. "I'm off the case, remember?"

How I was going to get this information to Knight was another question. I'd given him my phone number, but I didn't have his. I'd have to wait until he called me or showed up in my dreams again. Hopefully I'd get the call.

"Yeah, I'll tell him tomorrow."

I stood up and started for the hall closet, pulling two blue blankets from the top shelf and tossed them to Trey. "I'm going to get some shuteye. It's been a long day," I said.

A sad smile twisted his lips. "Yeah, me too."

"Help yourself to anything—there's some left over Chinese and juice and beers in the fridge."

Trey threw me a half-hearted smile. "Thanks, Dulce. This means a lot to me. I owe you one."

"No worries," I said and started for my bedroom. "Night, Trey."

###

I woke up to the sound of the shower running. Trey had literally made himself at home. Not that it bothered me. I sat up and sighed, pushing my feet into my dog slippers. I plodded into the living room and noticed Trey had folded the blankets neatly in a corner of the couch.

I started for the kitchen to put the coffee on. The shower stopped and moments later, Trey walked into the kitchen wearing his clothes from last night.

"What's for breakfast?" he asked and I suddenly had the very strange image of waking up to him every morning. Egad.

"Just the leftover Chinese food. Want some coffee?"

"No, no coffee, but do you mind if I help myself to the Chinese?"

I shook my head and handed him a fork. "Go for it. Are you driving to Headquarters now?"

"Yeah," he said as he pulled a box of Chinese from the fridge. He started in on the cold fried rice right away, not even pausing to take a seat. The dude was serious about eating.

"Do you need to stay here tonight?" I asked, trying to sound ... friendly. It wasn't that I'm a bitch or anything. I'm just not really used to having company. Maybe I'm a little on the antisocial side. But considering Trey's current state, he needed a friend.

He shook his head. "No, I think I'll be alright. I've got to get over it anyway—it's not like I'm going to move in with you."

He actually looked hopeful.

"Exactly. Will you do me a favor, and talk to Sam? She'll put a protection spell on your place."

"Yep, I'll do that," he said.

"I'll call you tonight to see how you are."

"What are you up to today?" he asked.

My thoughts returned to his question and my face flushed. Sam was meeting me in about an hour to go to my ear augmentation consultation. Not like I wanted to admit that to Trey anytime soon. "Oh, Sam and I are meeting for lunch." It was sort of the truth, we were planning on getting lunch—afterwards.

Trey finished his rice, threw the container in the trash, and then faced me with a big grin. He started for the door, looking one hundred times better than he had last night. "Well, I guess I better get to work. Thanks, Dulce."

"Sure, Trey, I'll see you later."

###

Thirty minutes later, Sam and I were sitting in the waiting room of Dr. Goodman's. I hadn't been able to shake my intense feelings of anxiety, guilt and excitement—anxiety because I was eager to hear what the doctor would say; guilt because it was like I was failing some part of me just by considering this; and excitement because I've always hated my ears. Now, they all warred with each other until I felt nauseous.

"Trey came to my place last night," I whispered. Sam dropped the magazine she'd been reading back on the side table.

"What for?" she asked and wiggled her eyebrows. "I didn't think he was your type."

An image of his shiny forehead sweating bullets littered my mind. "Come on, Sam. You don't think I slept with Trey, do you?"

She started to laugh. "No, I guess that would be totally weird."

"I haven't had a date in a while, but I'm not desperate."

"Okay, point taken. Why did he come over?"

"He saw a vision of Fabian's murder."

Her eyes went wide. "Did he see who did it?"

"No, not exactly. Just that the creature was female. He was super freaked out, though, and stayed the night. I'm worried about him."

And honestly, as much as he annoyed me, I was worried. If what Trey said about the creature sensing him was true, he could be in serious trouble.

I faced Sam again. "Can you put a protection spell on his place?"

"Yeah, sure. Why was he so scared?"

"He was worried the thing might come after him."

"Do you think it will?"

"I don't know."

She was silent as she considered it. "You know Quillan is going to be pissed off if he finds out you're still working on this case?"

"Yeah, I know. That's why he isn't going to find out." I considered telling her about Knight. Part of me knew I shouldn't—that it was top secret, but the other part of me wanted to gab. That part won.

"You're never going to believe this, Sam, but …"

"Dulcie O'Neil?" the receptionist interrupted and gave me an expression that said I'd better hurry.

I guess Dr. Goodman didn't like waiting for his patients. Wasn't that the pot calling the kettle black? I stood up and started forward, Sam behind me. The receptionist led us to the first room down the hall and told us to take a seat. She closed the door behind us, and we were alone again.

"What won't I believe?" Sam started, her eyes sparkling.

"Some detective from the Netherworld was sent over here to find out about Fabian's murder. He said that someone summoned the creature from the Netherworld."

Sam's eyes went wider. "That's an automatic death sentence for whoever called it."

"I know. Anyway, this detective said he had orders from the Relations Office to work with me."

"Wow, Quillan is going to be uber pissed. Or does he already know? Is that why you're off the case now?"

"No, Quillan doesn't know. The order to put me under protection came from the Relations Office. Quillan had nothing to do with it. No one is supposed to know I'm working with the Relations team on the case."

Sam crossed her arms against her chest. "My lips are sealed. You know me."

"Yeah, that's why I told you. So the kicker in this whole thing is that the detective is that guy from Fabian's shop. The stranger."

Sam gasped. "Dulce, you need to be careful. What if he's involved?"

I waved away her worry like an errant fly. "He's not. I checked out his badge. He's legit."

"What's his name?"

"Knight."

"Wow, sexy name. Is he as hot as you first thought?"

I paused. Was Knight as hot as I'd first thought? Hmm. An image of him in tight black leather pants erupted in my mind. That broad, muscular chest. Sparkling blue eyes and black hair. "Hotter."

Then the door opened, putting a halt to our conversation. The doctor was tall and his forehead so high, he must've had a big brain. He smiled at both of us, but I couldn't really say he saw us. It was one of those polite but completely impersonal smiles. He closed the door behind him, and in perfectly upright posture, took the leather chair in front of us, swinging around until he looked like a corpse going through rigor mortis.

He glanced at what I presumed was my file, flipping through the pages with ennui. "Which of you is Dulcie?" he asked in a high-pitched and nasally voice.

"That's me."

He didn't glance up but continued shuffling through the library of papers. "You're here to find out about ear augmentation?"

"Yeah, I don't like the points at the top of my ears."

He still hadn't acknowledged me. "Are you a fairy?"

"What else would I be, a Vulcan?"

Sam laughed, the doctor didn't. I dropped the smile from my lips and nodded. "Yeah, I'm a fairy."

He sighed. "That makes it a little more difficult."

"Why's that?" Sam asked, her voice wary.

The doctor eyed her down his ski-slope nose. "And who might you be?"

"I'm Sam, Dulcie's best friend."

He faced me again, ignoring Sam. She glanced at me, anger etching her features. "It's difficult because the properties in your blood and tissue are different than a human's. The operation requires some extra equipment and possibly more anesthesia," the doctor concluded.

Extra equipment?

"Okay," I said, not really sure what else to say.

He stood up and towered over me. He motioned with his long fingers that I should stand. I handed Sam my purse and got to my feet. Then he turned me so I was facing the wall and shifted my hair behind my right ear. He ran a cold finger down the length of my ear, and I shuddered involuntarily.

"They certainly are pointed, aren't they?"

"She's a fairy," Sam snapped. "I don't see anything wrong with them."

I gave her a discouraging look.

"Yes, that's a matter of opinion, I suppose," the doctor said, and a wave of resentment wafted through me. Why did doctors have to be such jerks?

He turned me to face him again. "Other than those ears, you are beautiful." It was the same thing Jack had told me for five years. "An ear augmentation would make you perfect."

I sat down again, feeling like I was selling my soul to the devil. I glanced at Sam, who was feigning interest in her shoes. A fierce pink had taken over her cheeks.

"How long would the surgery take?" I asked, trying to draw Sam's attention away from her irritation.

"Maybe two hours. Depends on how much you bleed."

I disregarded that statement. "What would it cost?"

He shrugged, and that meant it would cost more than I wanted to spend. I had a lot of money in savings—granted it was so I could retire from law enforcement and focus on writing full time. I guess I could work a little longer.

"Normally ear augmentation runs around six thousand dollars for both ears. But since you're a fairy, which

92

complicates it, I'd say you could expect to pay around ten thousand."

Sam's mouth dropped open. "You've gotta be kidding,"

The doctor's stern expression said he wasn't kidding—not by a long shot.

"Okay, great, let me take some time to think about it," I said and stood. Sam was quick behind me.

The doctor didn't stand but gave us another frozen smile in compensation. "Hope to see you again soon," he said.

We showed ourselves out.

"Have you lost your mind, Dulce?" Sam asked as we left the building. "You can't have that cretin operating on you. What a jerk! Ten thousand dollars?"

I unlocked my car. "Yeah, he was a creep, wasn't he?"

"I'd say so. Please tell me you aren't considering it."

I shrugged. "I can't lie, Sam. I've been thinking about this for so long now."

She narrowed her eyes. "Even though you won't admit it, I think this has everything to do with Jack."

"Well, let's agree to disagree."

Two hours later, I was back at home, replaying the events of the day in my head as I turned on my computer. Yeah, the doctor hadn't been especially friendly, but I really wanted the surgery. I'd wanted it for years now and though Sam was convinced it had everything to do with my jerk ex-boyfriend, I wasn't convinced. I mean, I'd disliked my ears before Jack was ever in the picture. But Jack being the reason—or not—didn't take away from the fact that the doctor was a jerk. Of course, there weren't any other ear augmentation specialists in a hundred mile radius of me. So I was stuck between a Doc and a hard place.

I logged into my e-mail, excited to see if any agents or publishers had responded to my query. As for the surgery, I pushed it to the back of my mind. There wasn't a rush. I could decide later.

I had eighteen new e-mails in my inbox. My heartbeat raced. Upon further inspection, they were all agents and publishers. Wow. That had to be good, right? I opened the first one.

Dear Ms. O'Neil,

Thank you for your interest in Jones & Jones representing Captain Slade's Bounty. Unfortunately, we don't feel strongly enough about the work to offer you representation, but we wish you the best of luck.

Okay, so that was just one. There were seventeen more.

After getting to the fifteenth, I started recognizing a pattern—rejection. I opened the last e-mail and sighed. Another rejection. At least this agent had ended the e-mail by telling me historicals were out and the market was really looking for paranormals.

Un-flippin'-believable.

The phone rang. "Hello?"

"Hi, Dulce." It was Sam. "Thought any more about the ear thing?"

"No, haven't made up my mind."

"You sound bummed out."

"I just got rejected by every agent and publisher I queried. One of them said historicals aren't popular right now but paranormals are. Paranormals, I mean, come on. Who the hell reads those?"

"Sorry to hear it. Don't lose faith though." She paused. "Maybe you should write a paranormal."

"I'm done. I put everything I had into that book and not one agent wanted to look at it. Maybe I'm just not cut out to be a writer."

"Don't feel sorry for yourself, Dulce. Maybe you just have to give the market what it's looking for and it sounds like that would be a paranormal."

"I have no interest in that. What would I write about anyway?"

Sam was quiet for a minute. "I know." I could hear the smile in her voice. "Write a book about Bram. Everyone loves vampires, right?"

Hmm, if you want to succeed you have to be flexible, right? Maybe it would do me good to try another genre. "Yeah, that's an idea," I started, considering it. "He'd eat it up, I'm sure. His ego is already big enough as it is. Any bigger and it could take out a small family."

Sam laughed. "Okay, well I gotta run. Quillan wants something. Just wanted to check in on you."

I could hear Quillan talking with her.

"Quillan says hi, and he's stopping by after work tonight," she finished.

"Okay, tell him hi back and I'll see him later. Thanks, Sam."

I hung up, pondering a book about Bram. Maybe it was worth a shot.

NINE

I didn't think it was Quillan's responsibility to buy dinner again, so I ordered a pizza.

"Ham and pineapple, my favorite," he said, sinking his teeth into a slice.

I smiled—his stopping by every day after work was becoming comfortable. Today had only been the third time, but somehow it felt … right. The thought scared the crap out of me. What was I thinking? I was Quillan's employee. And nothing more.

"How are the gremlins working out?" Quillan asked between bites.

I pulled my attention from the wall, where I'd been zoning out into space and daydreaming about all the things that could and would never be.

"So far so good. I haven't seen them. Well, other than feeding them every morning."

Quillan nodded, but his attention was glued to the floor. He took another bite, chewing slowly. There was something definitely bothering him. If he'd had laser vision, I'd have a sizable hole burned into my carpet right about now.

"What's up, Quill?" I asked, half wondering if I really wanted to know.

He dropped the crust of pizza onto the plate. "I wanted to talk to you about something."

"Hmm?"

"I overheard you and Sam talking on the phone the other day about a doctor's appointment you had."

Mortification, embarrassment and shame all took turns attacking my pride until I felt like a pile of self-consciousness.

"That's really none of your business."

He nodded, but by the steel set to his lips, he wasn't giving up. "I know. It's not, Dulce, but I care about you and I thought I should tell you … you don't need surgery."

My face had to be bright red—the blaze of complete and total humiliation flooding my cheeks like red dye dropped in water. I wasn't sure if it was anger or embarrassment.

"Well, I wish you hadn't overheard our conversation, since it *was* private."

"Have you made up your mind about it yet?"

"No." I paused, pretending extreme interest in removing the lint from my sweatshirt. "And I really don't want to talk about it." I picked up my pizza, which suddenly seemed to weigh twenty pounds, and brought it to my mouth. I chewed but couldn't taste anything, the aftertaste of shame still polluting my mouth.

Quillan took another bite of his pizza, and the silence in the room was telling. I put my slice back on the plate, feeling completely stuffed and more so … sick.

"You know the anesthesia could kill you or screw up your brain, right?" he finally said. "We can't handle that sort of stuff, Dulce. We're not like humans."

I sighed. "Quill …"

"Just indulge me for a minute, Dulcie, please."

No, I'd indulged him long enough. The subject was closed. It was my decision and damn anyone who wanted to change my mind. "The anesthesia will be fine."

Even though I spoke with assurance, I wasn't convinced. The risks of complication had always been the foremost reason I hadn't gone through with the surgery. But Quillan's doubts didn't need company.

97

He shook his head. "Our bodies aren't meant to handle harsh human sedatives. It's a huge risk."

I stood up and dropped my pizza slice into the trashcan, wishing I could dump the conversation as easily. My eyes fell to the view outside my window as I searched for the gremlins, hoping to focus on something else.

"Is that all you have to say?"

"Why are you doing it?"

Quillan's voice came from behind me. I wrapped my arms around myself, trying not to think about the fact that he was standing so close. His crisp aftershave hit me like a truck and I closed my eyes. After a second or two, I forced my eyes open and turned around. He stood maybe two inches from me, the heat of his breath searing my neck. I took a step back.

"Why do you think I'm doing, er, thinking of doing it?" I quipped, but he didn't respond. "Because obviously I don't like my ears."

Quillan's jaw tightened. "It's not because some guy wants you to do it?"

Leaning against the kitchen counter, I turned my back to him and gazed outside the window again, much preferring the view to the stubbornness in Quillan's eyes.

"I'm doing it for myself. I just happen not to like my pointed ears, and I think if they were … normal looking …"

"You'd be prettier? Maybe happier?" The sarcasm in his voice fueled my anger like kerosene on a fire.

"Yes, I think I'd be prettier and maybe happier!"

"I think you'll be disappointed."

I turned around to face him again but losing my mojo, I dropped my eyes back to the floor, hating the fact that I was so mortified, I couldn't hold his gaze. "Regardless of what you think, I'd be happier with how I look."

He was silent for a second. "You're one of the most beautiful women I've ever seen."

I searched for any indication of teasing in his expression. But his face reflected mine—not a smile, not a sign of playful repartee, just an earnest, searching look as though we were both trying to read each other's thoughts. "I … I um, I don't know what to say," I managed. Quillan grabbed my hand forcing my attention back to him again.

"Not only do I think that, but you're the best person on my team."

"Quill …" I started, not wanting a "you're so money and you don't even know it" conversation.

"You're the smartest on the team, Dulce. You're the best employee I have."

Heat crawled up my neck. "Thanks, Quill, but I really don't need to hear all this."

His eyes narrowed. "Not only that, but I've had to talk myself out of asking you out on a date since you joined my team."

My eyes went wide. It was like I was in a movie, maybe a dream. I'd always imagined I was just Quillan's cohort, one of the guys, his favorite employee maybe. "So is this my review?" I asked with a flippant laugh, trying to make light of the situation.

"No, Dulce, it's not."

I looked down again, wishing the ground would open and swallow me. After another hopeless silence, I glanced up at Quillan—almost to make sure he was still there. He didn't say anything and neither did I. We just stared at each other. Before I could blink, Quillan leaned into me, his face inches from mine.

"Can I kiss you, Dulce?"

I nodded dumbly as he ran his hands through my hair and he brought his lips to mine. His lips were soft and full. I closed my eyes and reveled in the taste and smell of him. He pulled me closer and I wrapped my arms around his chest, allowing myself to sink into him. Surprise flashed through me when I felt his tongue in my mouth.

A wave of unease blew through me and I pulled away. He was my boss, and as such, I shouldn't be kissing him. He didn't drop his arms from around my waist.

"Are you okay?" he asked, flashing an embarrassed smile.

I nodded. "I, um, I'm just a little surprised, that's all."

He laughed. "Good surprised or bad surprised?"

"Good surprised." I glanced away, trying to calm my frantic heart. "I just never thought you felt this way about me."

"I've wanted to do that for years."

I was spared the need to respond when the shrill ring of the phone interrupted. I lunged for it, breaking from Quillan's embrace. "Huh-Hello?"

"Dulce, it's Sam. You've gotta get to Trey's house now. I haven't been able to reach Quillan ..."

"Trey?" Shock jolted me like a splash of cold water.

"Quillan's here," I said.

"Good. He needs to come too."

"Why, what's going on?"

She sighed as if it was too long a story to get into over the phone. "Just come over as fast as you can. I'll explain when you get here."

"Okay, but tell me—is Trey ... okay?"

"Yes, just hurry."

I hung up and faced a puzzled Quillan. "Something's wrong with Trey. Sam said we should go over there now."

"What's wrong with him?"

"I don't know. She just said we need to hurry."

He shook his head. "You're off any cases, Dulce."

My mouth dropped open. "That's not fair. What am I supposed to do, Quill?"

"Wait here. I'll take care of Trey."

"But—"

"Relations Office orders, Dulce."

I narrowed my eyes. "And what if the creature comes here while you're gone? How will you feel then?"

He looked like he was going to fight me about it but ended up laughing and shook his head. Then he pulled his keys from his pocket and started for the door. "How do you to talk me into these things?"

I followed him outside to his black Ford F-150 and got in before he changed his mind. Not that I thought he would—he never had in the past. But then, we'd never kissed in the past either. This kissing thing was really going to screw things up—I could see it already.

"You look pissed off," Quillan said and pulled into the street.

I glanced out the window. "I'm just wondering where we … stand now."

"Where do you want us to stand?"

Hmm, I wasn't sure. I'd imagined kissing Quillan so many times but my daydreams hadn't ever progressed past the kissing stage. "I don't know."

"Tell me you don't regret it."

I threw him a consoling smile, even though the verdict was still out over whether or not I regretted it. "Not at all, Boss."

He glanced at me and put his hand on my knee. "We'll figure it out, Dulce."

Five minutes later, he pulled in front of a white stucco building with an unkempt front yard. Turning off the engine, he offered me a consoling smile before opening the door and jumping down. He started for the apartment building, me in tow.

As soon as we reached the top step, a worried Sam burst from the door of the first apartment down the hall. "Good, you're here."

Quillan disappeared inside Trey's apartment. Sam held the door for me, distress evident in her frown lines.

"What's wrong with Trey?" I asked as she closed the door behind me. Trey's apartment was dark—the thick curtains barring any sunlight. The furniture was mismatched and old—stuff even Good Will would throw away. The place smelled of stale beer and trash lined the floor like it had a right to be there. I glanced at the other side of the room and made out the shape of Trey lying prone atop a filthy sofa.

Sam took a deep breath like she was about to recite the Pledge of Allegiance. "He's under a sleeping spell." Then she took another breath. "I called him on the way home from work today to see how he was since he was still freaked out about that vision he had. But when I called, he didn't answer. I decided to swing by and found him like this."

"He looks dead," I started.

"What vision?" Quillan asked.

"Trey called me the other night because he'd seen a vision of Fabian's murder. He knew it was a female creature and someone else was involved," I said.

"Why didn't he tell me?" Quillan snapped.

I shook my head. "I told him to, but he was really upset at the time. I guess he didn't want you to think he was a wuss."

"I don't care about that," Quillan said, running an agitated hand through his hair. "I should've been told. It's part of the case details. Dulcie, you should've told me."

I held up my hands. "Hey, I'm off the case, remember?"

He frowned. "What else?"

"He was worried that whoever was involved in Fabian's murder would know he'd had the vision and would come after him."

Quillan nodded, like he was letting it all sink in. Then he turned to Sam. "Are you sure it isn't worse than a sleeping spell?"

Sam brushed her hair back from her face. "I did a couple divination spells on him. I know it's a Sleeper; it'll take me a while more to figure out what strain. Whoever did it is well-versed in magic."

"Do you think it's a witch?" Quillan asked.

Sam shook her head. "I have no way of knowing. But I'd guess it was a witch, fairy, elf, warlock … someone with ready access to magic."

"None of that matters now, though," I interrupted. "Can you break the spell?"

"I'm going to need some supplies. Since Fabian's is closed, I have to drive to Harmony tomorrow to get what I need, Quillan." Even though it was a statement, there was a question in her tone.

He nodded. "Go ahead."

"So you can't break it until tomorrow?" I asked.

"No way I can do it tonight. I'm not even sure I'll be able to break it tomorrow—depends on what I can find in Harmony."

"Will he be safe until then?" I asked, trying not to look at Trey. It was uncanny how dead he looked—it was like we were at his funeral and taking turns looking at the body. Only this funeral parlor reeked of old beer.

"He's fine. Think of him as Sleeping Beauty," Sam said with a forced laugh. "But he shouldn't stay here tonight. Who knows if the person or thing who did this might come back?"

"He should stay with me," I said. "Between Sam's spell and the gremlins, my place would be like trying to bust into a military base."

"Wow, Dulce, you trying out for the Girl Scouts?" Sam asked.

I shrugged. "Just trying to do my part."

Quillan nodded. "It's a good idea, Dulce. I'll get the big guy to your apartment." Then he faced Sam. "As soon as we get Trey situated, I need to take your statement."

"Say hi to Lottie for me," I said with a wink.

###

Sam and Quillan took off twenty minutes later, leaving me alone with my comatose guest. We'd set Trey up on my couch and now he lay there with my blue blanket stretched out over him. I felt like I was living *Weekend at Bernie's* or something.

I glanced at Trey and not finding him in need of anything, returned my attention to my e-mail inbox where I'd just opened three more rejection letters for Captain Slade. Big goddammit.

The phone rang and I picked it up mindlessly, not even glancing at the caller ID. "Hello?"

"Dulcie."

It was Knight.

I narrowed my eyes. "Ah, just the person I wanted to talk to."

He chuckled flirtatiously. "Is that so?"

I stood up and rubbed the back of my neck. "Yeah, jerkoff, I didn't appreciate that stunt you pulled at the Relations Office to get me off the squad."

Total silence. "Hello? Are you still there?"

"Too bad."

I sputtered. "You arrogant …"

"It was for your own good."

"So now I have nothing to do all day, I'm not getting paid and I have two ugly gremlins running amok in my yard. I really got the short end of the stick on this one."

"Sorry about the pay thing, but it was necessary. And I didn't order the gremlins, so I have no idea what that's about."

"Oh, you didn't order the gremlins? So what, I have like a secret admirer who sends me monsters instead of candies?"

Knight laughed, pissing me off more. "I don't know what to tell you. Maybe the Relations Office thought you needed them. I'll check into it."

I sat down again and faced my inbox, the rejection notices staring back at me like they were laughing. Well, screw them. "Where the hell have you been?" I asked, wondering why I hadn't heard from him in the last four days or so. I checked the caller ID, but the number wasn't listed.

"Before you answer, what's your number?"

He gave me the number and then added, "I've been running background reports on all the creatures in Splendor."

I sank back against my chair. Yeah, that would probably take a good three to four days. "Let me guess; was I in that batch of reports?" Knight chuckled again, and even though it annoyed me to admit it, it was damned sexy.

"I ran a report on you before we ever met."

Great, that was comforting. "Well, I have news for you."

"Do tell."

I explained the Tad Jones and Guy Riley murders, how they each had something to do with the illegal potions trade and finally, the Trey situation.

"Is your friend a good enough witch to break the spell?" Knight asked.

"Yes, she is," I snapped.

"If she can't, I could. She's meeting you tomorrow?"

"Yes," I answered, rolling my eyes. Holy Hades, the man was arrogant.

"Okay, I'll meet you both at your place, then."

"Aren't you afraid of involving Headquarters in your little secret case?" I asked, my tone thick.

"If your friend is trustworthy, I'll swear her to secrecy."

"Fine, I'll see you tomorrow."

I didn't wait for a response before I hung up.

TEN

Sam came to my apartment around midday, loaded with two shopping bags full of herbs, potions and other less appealing things like freeze dried bat wings, newt legs and sheep intestine. I watched her dump the contents of both bags onto my kitchen table and made a mental note to disinfect the area once she finished.

"Dulce, can you get some bowls and spoons? We're going to need to mix up a few different concoctions."

I nodded and threw open the cupboard doors. I gathered up three bowls—one small and orange, one Tupperware and one large blue one. All covered in a fine layer of dust.

Just as I finished rinsing them off, the doorbell rang, announcing Knight's arrival. "Can you get that, Sam?" I asked, holding up the orange bowl as if to say my hands were occupied. "Check the peephole first," I added.

She threw me a smile. "A little paranoid?"

"Better to be paranoid than taken by surprise."

"Who is it?" she called and peered through the peephole. "Hello tall, dark and handsome."

"Knight Vander," he answered.

"Happy?" she asked as her hand rested on the knob.

I just nodded.

Sam threw open the door with a large smile. "Hi, I'm Sam."

I craned my neck as far as I could without actually moving from my position against the kitchen counter and watched Knight as he walked into the living room. He was dressed in dark jeans and a long sleeved black T-shirt. His hair looked freshly cut—the ends no longer curled up. His dark golden tan seemed to emit a light of its own.

He extended his hand toward Sam. "Pleased to meet you, Sam."

Sam smiled and accepted his offered hand. "Nice to meet you," she said in a soft voice.

Knight turned and caught me staring at him like a lovesick schoolgirl. "Dulcie," he said, a grin breaking across his handsome face.

I muttered an unenthusiastic "hi" and busied myself with drying the bowls, which I'd already dried. I then retrieved two spoons and placed everything neatly on the kitchen table next to the hideous ingredients Sam had pulled from the shopping bags.

Knight neared the table and examined everything as if he were a health inspector. Apparently satisfied, he turned his attention to Trey who still slept on the couch. Knight approached him and picked up his hand, checking his pulse.

"He's not dead," I started but was interrupted by Sam, who turned toward me and mouthed: "he's hot."

I just shook my head.

"Should we get started?" Knight asked.

Sam clapped her hands together like a cheerleader excited for the big game and took a step closer to him. "Well, I went to Harmony and got everything I could to break the spell." She paused. "Are you a … witch too?"

Knight shook his head. "No …"

"He isn't magical like us," I blurted, then immediately wished I hadn't sounded all of thirteen. Knight grinned, apparently taking no offense to my Tourette's syndrome moment.

"No, I'm not magical but I can tell whether something might break the spell on your friend. I thought I might be able to help you pick the right anti-potion."

"Okay, sure. If you don't mind my asking, what are you?" Sam asked.

"I'm a Loki."

Sam's confusion was evident by her vacant expression.

"He's from the Netherworld," I said. "They don't have Lokis here."

Was Lokis even the plural? Lokae? Knight didn't correct me, so I just went with it.

"Oh," Sam said, trying to quell her surprise. I knew she was bursting to ask him a million questions but knowing Sam, she wanted to be polite. That, or she was intimidated by Knight. Probably the latter.

"What have you got?" Knight asked, facing the table with his arms crossed against his broad chest.

"I've got every herb you can think of. And I picked up a white tincture, an erasing potion and a PH 3 potion."

Knight nodded like he understood what she was talking about. I couldn't help but scoff—as if he knew! Although my magic allows me to create stuff with my fairy dust, I don't know the first thing about potions. Unless you're a witch or warlock, one who relies on creating magic rather than possessing magic, there's really no reason to study potions. And Knight wasn't a witch or warlock—he was a bullshitter.

And I was going to call him on it. "What do those potions do?" I asked, then noticed Sam about to respond. "Knight?"

He nodded at the challenge in my tone. "A white tincture will combat any colored potions and pull the strength from them; an erasing potion will erase whatever charm was put on your friend; and a PH 3 potion will negate any spells put on him by means of acid."

Sam smiled; I didn't. "Well done. You know your witchcraft," she said, beaming at him like he was her star pupil.

I frowned and brought the bowls to Sam. She took them and handed one to Knight. "What do you think we should try first?" she asked him. "Maybe the tincture?"

It didn't go unnoticed that she didn't ask me. But, hey, I didn't feel sorry for myself.

"You know this better than I do, Sam," Knight responded, giving me a grin. Bastard.

Sam laughed and started reaching for ingredients. Damn Knight for winning over my best friend.

"Well, I'm thinking that maybe the white tincture might work best. That way we can find out if any colored spells were used on Trey. From there, we can probably just use the erasing potion to break down the potency of whatever's left," Sam said.

"Sounds good to me," Knight concurred.

"Yeah, me too," I added, though they might as well have spoken Aramaic.

I leaned against the kitchen counter, thinking maybe I should go work on something else since I clearly wasn't needed. Let the Bobsey Twins figure it out for themselves. Just as I was about to make my escape, Sam stopped me.

"Dulce, can you boil some water please?"

I nodded and watched her dump a quarter of the white tincture into the bowl. Then she broke off a piece of the bat's wing, snapping it like a dried leaf. Yuck. She paused and glanced at me.

"Here, take this." She handed me a lemon.

"What, are we making lemonade?"

"Cut it in half and once the water comes to a boil, squeeze the lemon into the water. Make sure you don't get any seeds in it, though."

I pulled out a knife and sliced the lemon in half. Then I pulled out the seeds. "What's the lemon juice for?"

"It pulls all the impurities from the water and air so they don't taint my spell," Sam answered. I'd been half hoping her star pupil would answer. I just liked the sound of his voice—like deep, rumbling thunder.

"Oh," I said and turned to watch the water boil.

Meanwhile, Sam and Knight continued to work together on the spell, laughing and comparing spell notes as if they were in a college biology class and about to dissect a frog.

The water started bubbling and grabbed my attention. I reached for the lemon half and squeezed it over the hissing water. The sharp scent of citrus wafted up in the steam. Is there a better smell than freshly squeezed lemon?

"Okay, the water's boiling and I squeezed the lemon. Now what?"

Sam turned toward me, propping her hands on her hips. "Can you bring it here and carefully pour it in the bowl?" Then she faced Knight. "Would you get some of Trey's hair?"

"Sure. Dulcie, where are your scissors?"

I reached into my knife block and considered throwing them at him. Instead, I handed him the scissors. In return, he winked. Actually winked!

The smug jerk walked over to Trey and cut off a good tuft of hair. Knight then handed the tuft of hair to Sam, who set it on the table.

"Water, Dulce," she said, and I realized I'd abandoned my post.

"Sorry," I answered and approached them, the pot roiling and spitting. "Do you want me to start pouring now?" I asked, looking into the bowl. The white tincture looked like sand, and with the pieces of bat wing and frog guts, it looked like some weird foreign dish.

"Yeah, slowly," Sam answered.

I poured. As soon as the water hit the tincture, it began bubbling and let off a huge puff of white smoke. The bat wing started bouncing, but the frog guts did nothing at all.

"Knight, could you add the hair, please?" Sam asked.

He nodded and dropped the tress of hair into the mixture. As soon as it hit the white stuff, the tincture turned blood red. Sam started stirring. The puff of smoke went from white to light pink to a deeper pink and finally turned into a fire engine red.

"Ah, they used a scarlet potion, did they?" Sam asked.

I felt like saying "yes," but I said nothing at all. Better not to be thought a smart ass … or a dumb ass.

She continued to watch the potion, as if expecting it to do something else. After another ten seconds or so, she straightened her back and turned toward Knight and me with a triumphant smile.

"What is it?" I asked.

"They've just used a scarlet on him. That's easy enough to break. Knight, would you mind handing me the erasing vial, please?"

He handed it to her, and she pulled the cork from the bottle. "Dulce, do you have a measuring spoon?"

I opened a drawer and sorted through it until I found a rusted teaspoon. "All I have is a teaspoon—sorry."

Sam frowned. "That'll do. Can you soak it in lemon juice?"

I nodded and pulled a small saucer from the cupboard. I squeezed the remaining lemon half and then basted both sides of the old teaspoon. "Okay, now what?"

"Hand it to Knight, please."

I did so and he held it over the bowl as Sam poured an exact teaspoon of the erasing potion into the spoon. It bubbled against the lemon juice and turned mint green.

"Dump it in," Sam said.

Knight rotated his hand, and the mint green met up with the scarlet red. That's when all hell broke loose. The scarlet liquid pulled up against the side of the bowl as if afraid to touch the tiny teaspoon of green.

"Dulcie!" Sam yelled. "Plastic wrap, quick!"

I lunged for the Saran wrap in the bottom drawer and threw it at her. Knight caught it and ripped off a piece of plastic while the potion in the bowl sloshed against the sides angrily. Knight wrapped the plastic on top of the bowl, and

111

Sam sighed a breath of relief. The potion threw itself against the plastic and no longer afraid of being showered in Hades knew what, I leaned in to get a closer look.

The mint green erasing potion had left the scarlet white in its wake. Now it looked like a one-man army going to slay the river of red. It inched slowly toward the red, which had now completely thrown itself up against the opposite side of the bowl. The white liquid behind the green was placid, just sitting there happily. The green attacked the red, and in about four more seconds, the whole bowl was white and sitting patiently as if it had been lobotomized.

"Hmm," Sam said as she chewed her lip.

"Hmm?" I asked. "Why doesn't that sound good?"

She shook her head. "I did everything I was supposed to. Now it should turn deep blue, but it's still white."

Knight and I leaned over the potion to inspect it, hoping to see a blue tint take over the pearly white. Nothing happened. Sam pulled off the plastic wrap and reached inside her bag again. She pulled a small piece of litmus paper out, which she plopped into the bowl. The color of the litmus didn't change.

"Something's not right," she said.

Knight reached inside his pocket and produced a vial of beige powder.

"What's that?" I asked, wondering if I was the weird one because I didn't happen to carry around random vials of potions.

"Another test—to see if the reason Sam's spell didn't work is because something illegal was used on Trey."

I nodded, mentally kicking myself. An illegal spell made perfect sense. All the facts in this case were revolving around the illegal potion trade, so why wouldn't the bastards have used something not available on the market?

Knight dropped a pinch of the beige powder into the bowl and long, white wisps of smoke circled up from the tincture like ghosts only to dissolve into the air.

"It is an illegal," Sam said in awe. "Am I right in thinking it's a Sleeping Beauty?"

Knight chuckled. "You're right on the money, Sam."

"How are we going to break that?" I asked.

Sam smiled. "The only place they keep the anti-potion is at Headquarters. And you're the only one with clearance to get in after hours, Dulce."

I frowned. "If my clearance hasn't already been revoked. And even if I can get through the front doors, you know I can't access the vault."

The vault was where all confiscated illegal potions evidence was stored until the Netherworld sent us potion-destroying cauldrons. Our cauldron shipment happened once a week.

"I can get you in anywhere," Knight said and handed me a white key-card.

"If you have access, then why don't you do it?" I asked archly.

Knight shook his head. "Because I don't want to alert anyone to my presence. You can come and go unsuspected."

I glanced down at the card and thought about what they were asking me to do. "You do realize if I get caught, Quillan is going to be furious. This could mean I'm off the team for good. No one gets access to the vault; I don't even think Quillan has access."

Sam chewed her lip. "Maybe we should just call Quillan then?"

"No," Knight interrupted. "This is still top secret. Dulcie, you have my permission to go after the anti-potion. If you have any issues, I'll take it up with the Relations Office."

###

When I showed up at Headquarters, the only person around was Elsie, who was tasked with watching our prisoner, a drunk goblin named Ehling who wasn't a stranger

113

to Headquarters. At the moment, he was passed out on a wooden bench. Elsie glanced at me and didn't seem too surprised to see me; sometimes I had to work late evenings so maybe she didn't think it was anything out of the ordinary.

"Hi, Dulce, what brings you here?" she asked and settled the book she'd been reading on her lap.

I swallowed my palpitating heart and forced a smile. "I came to clear out some stuff from my desk."

She nodded. "I think this whole situation is a load, if you ask me. You're the best agent we've got. They're shooting themselves in the foot."

I smiled. "Thanks, Elsie, I appreciate that." And the Hades honest truth was I did appreciate it. At least someone recognized the fact that I was good at what I did. Which only made me feel worse about lying to her.

I started down the hallway, pleased the vault was as far from Elsie as could be. As long as no one else was out and about, I'd be fine.

"If you need any help, just holler," she called after me.

"Will do!"

I found my desk and shuffled around it, thinking I should pack some things so my being here didn't look suspicious. Finding a small box on Trey's desk, I emptied out his rubber band ball collection and started packing up my business card holder, a few pens and three coffee mugs. I left the box on my seat so I could grab it on my way out.

Then, eyeing my surroundings, I moved toward the vault, which was behind Quillan's office and at the end of the hall. Grabbing a piece of blank paper, I scrunched it up and started for the vault, thinking maybe I could say I was looking for a wastebasket in which to toss the paper in case anyone noticed me. Course, why I wouldn't have used my own trashcan was a good question, but one I didn't want to bother with.

No one was around. Thank Hades.

The vault ran the length and height of one wall and now glared down at me, as though knowing I had no right to enter. I eyed the card scanner that would grant me access and pulled Knight's key card from my pocket. Then I slipped it in with a silent prayer. The doors slid open and I grabbed the card, walking inside before the doors closed behind me.

I was in.

Once inside though, I didn't know where to go. With a sigh, I glanced around, taking in the rows of unlabeled, white boxes sitting atop pine shelves. But I wasn't about to start digging through those. Hoping my anti-potion would be easier to find, I headed for the back of the vault where I noticed multicolored vials sitting on the top shelf, contrasting against the dull steel of the vault wall.

Upon closer inspection, these vials were labeled and all were anti-potions—a good fifty or so. Great. Sam had told me the potion I was looking for was purple and called *Dragonroot*. I scanned the numerous titles: *Whisker Remover, Au de Wort, Crabapple* ... finally I settled on a small, cylindrical vial holding what looked like grape juice. Grabbing a nearby bucket, I turned it over and standing on it, grabbed the vial. Even though the label was peeling off and difficult to read even up close, I could faintly make it out. *Dragonroot*—I was in business. I threw it in my pocket before turning around.

A loud thump came from behind me. My heart leapt into my throat. As I scurried off the bucket, one foot tripped over the other and I careened onto the floor. I pulled myself up and glanced around, looking for whatever had made the noise.

No one was in the room.

Even if no one was in the room, I'd made enough of a clatter when I'd fallen that Elsie would come investigating.

Then the noise sounded again and I jumped around. The row of anti-potions innocently stared back at me. I shook my head, when one of the potions, a bright pink powder in a test tube, jumped up and pounded itself against the steel wall. And there was my culprit—*Megane,* an anti-potion that reacted to body heat. I must have been letting off a high temp when I'd been after the *Dragonroot.*

I fingered the *Dragonroot* in my pocket and started for the vault door. From the corner of my eye, I noticed a small closet-like room off the main hall of the vault; inside were more of those white boxes but beside the boxes were hundreds of clear bottles with long cylindrical necks and wide bottoms, like an *I Dream of Jeanie* bottle. It wasn't so much the bottles that grabbed my interest as what was in them. A fluorescent green liquid, and fluorescent green liquid could only mean one thing—*Arsonflower*. We'd busted a dealer with a house full of A*rsonflower* months ago and now the very same bust was sitting on the shelf like it was having the last laugh. I'd thought the Netherworld was better at getting rid of illegal potions than this! No wonder no one had access to the vault.

I turned on my heel, slipped the card in the reader, and hurried outside the doors as soon as they opened. Running to my desk, I grabbed Trey's box.

"Did you hear a noise?" Elsie asked.

I glanced up and said a silent prayer of thanks that Elsie hadn't found me leaving the vault. "No, I didn't hear a thing."

She frowned but seconds later, a smile took control of her lips. "Hmm, oh well. Must be hearing things!"

I started for the front door. "Night, Elsie."

She waved. "See you soon, I hope."

Back at my apartment, Sam took the *Dragonroot* anti-potion and with an eye dropper, sucked up the liquid and released exactly three drops into the bowl of potion that was supposed to break Trey's spell. As soon as the anti-potion interacted with the white substance, the white immediately

116

turned into a sapphire blue and Sam beamed at me. I guess I'd done a good job.

She removed the plastic wrap and shook the bowl a bit. "Okay, we're good to go. The spell should be broken."

I glanced at Trey, who still looked as dead as he had before. "Are you sure?"

"We need to put a dollop of this on the strongest of his pulse points," Sam answered.

"On his neck and wrists?" I asked.

Knight nodded. "That should do."

Sam picked up the bowl and neared the comatose Trey. "Dulce, can you shift his head so I can get to his neck?"

I wasn't exactly thrilled with touching Trey but I took hold of his neck and shifted it to the side while Sam reached her hand into the concoction and piled it atop his neck, getting his pulse point as well as his hair and the pillow below him.

My pillow, I might add.

"Why so much?" I asked.

"Too much is better than not enough."

Knight reached for Trey's wrists and placed them palm up alongside his still body. Sam reached into her bowl for another scoop of white stuff and pasted. As soon as she finished whiting out both of his wrists, Trey's eyes popped open like someone had flipped on his life switch.

"You did it!" I said.

"Sam," Trey started, his eyes dilating. "What's going on?"

Sam took a seat next to him. "You were under a sleeping spell, Trey. I just managed to crack it."

He started to sit up, but Knight pushed him back into the couch. "You need to relax," Knight said.

Trey's eyes traveled slowly to Knight. "Who are you?" he asked, his brow furrowing.

"Dulcie's cousin, Todd," Knight said before anyone else could respond.

My cousin? Todd?

"I didn't know Dulcie had a cousin," Trey said, and sighed as if it took all his energy.

"Do you know who did this to you?" Knight asked, apparently not thrilled with perpetuating his lie.

"Try to remember, Trey," Sam added.

Trey shook his head. "I don't know. I just remember being at my place, and then I heard something and went to the living room to investigate … I can't remember anything else."

"Well, someone was trying to silence you," I said, hoping that might trigger something.

Sam sighed. "We should probably call Quillan. He was working another important case today, otherwise he would've been here, Trey," she finished.

"I think Trey should still stay here with me," I said. I guess I was feeling magnanimous again. Who knew how long it would last …

Trey looked up at me, his expression quizzical. "You let me stay with you again?"

I nodded. "Yeah. You've been here a couple of days."

"Wow. Thanks, Dulce, I didn't know you actually liked me."

I shrugged. "You're okay for a hobgoblin. Even if—"

Suddenly, Trey's eyes rolled back into his head. He trembled violently as if a seven point earthquake was originating from his chest.

"What the hell?" I started, panic seizing me.

Sam grabbed his hand. "Trey! I think he's having a vision."

As soon as the words left her mouth, Knight grabbed hold of Trey's shoulder and closed his eyes. "Knight, what the hell are you …?"

Knight took hold of my upper arm in an iron grasp. As soon as he touched me, I was flooded with emotions that weren't my own.

118

I tried to pull against him, not understanding what the hell was going on. Before I could make any headway, my brain erupted into a fit of images, all flowing through my mind like a stack of pictures in the wind. I closed my eyes. The images stopped flying about and the more I focused, the more they fell into place, until I could actually piece together the scene before me.

It was Fabian's store. And Fabian was still alive. It was like watching a home video—he was whistling as he unloaded a box full of potions. I tried to decipher if they were illegal potions but couldn't get close enough to find out. Out of the darkness, something swooshed by. Fabian brought his head up, having seen it as well.

After finding nothing, he dropped his head and went back to unloading the inventory. Just like that, the something was on him. It moved light speed fast. Fabian fell against the floor and clawed at his assailant. A feeling of intense agony ricocheted up my body, starting at my legs and ending in my gut, the feeling of something tearing at my insides. I ignored the painful throbbing, knowing it wasn't happening to me. It had happened to Fabian, and it was his pain I was feeling. Still, my knees went weak, and I collapsed against Knight, who held me up against him but wouldn't release me—he wanted me to see this.

An image of a woman loomed before me, before Fabian. Her mouth was full of sharply pointed teeth—like a shark. Blood trailed down her mouth and contrasted against the pale flesh caught in her teeth. I felt my stomach turn. It was Fabian's flesh. She'd eaten him! She'd eaten him while he was still alive. Just as she'd no doubt eaten Guy and Tad as well.

She laughed and wiped her mouth with the back of her hand. Then I recognized her. She was the tall redhead from Dagan's club! The one wearing the tape. The one Dagan had seemed to be enjoying.

Holy Hades! Did Dagan know about her? Was Dagan even still alive?

The vision ended, and the room came into view. Knight released me. I tried to right myself, but I couldn't move. He maneuvered me to the sofa next to Trey and sat me down.

"What the hell was that?" I whispered.

"I channeled Trey's vision," Knight responded. "Did you recognize her?"

I nodded weakly.

"Who?" Sam interrupted. "What the heck just happened?"

I took in a deep breath and focused on her pale face. "We know who the creature is."

ELEVEN

I was alone.

It seemed like the first time in a long time, and I relished my privacy; relished the fact that I didn't have to look at Trey's bloated and sweaty face, verbally spar with Knight, or wonder if Quillan was going to bring up our kiss. Men were in a word … exhausting.

I sank into the couch, propping my feet up on the coffee table, still reeling from the events of the week. We knew who the creature was—it was an exhilarating feeling. I had to keep myself from taking action—there wasn't anything I could do until I questioned Dagan about the redhead's whereabouts and that wouldn't be until tonight … with Knight.

That, and Quillan was on his way over to drop off Trey. Quillan had decided that Trey could and should still be working, but because of the whole protection thing, he wanted to make sure someone was with Trey twenty-four-seven. So that meant my watch at night and Quillan's during the day. How was I going to keep an eye on Trey and go to Dagan's? Yeah, I hadn't quite figured that one out yet.

I faced my computer screen and clicked on the last of my Captain Slade query replies. Yep, this one was also a rejection. I deleted the e-mail immediately and leaned back in my chair with a heart-felt sigh.

Maybe writing a paranormal book wasn't such a bad idea? Course, I didn't want to go through the agony of spilling my heart into something for months only to find that no one else liked it. But Sam was convinced I was a good writer and I needed to believe in myself. And Bram seemed an interesting enough subject to carry a book. Hmm, maybe I'd arrange a little detour after our meeting with Dagan, so we could visit Bram. Then I could see what he thought about the book idea …

I laughed and shook my head. Who was I kidding? A narcissist like Bram would love it. That was the part about the whole thing I didn't exactly like—the fact that I'd be stroking an ego that was already the size of Nick the ogre. But sometimes you've gotta do what you've gotta do. And, hey, I still needed to ask Dagan about his Chinese massage parlor thing, so I owed Bram a visit anyway.

But what about Trey? I couldn't just leave him. Then the figurative light bulb went off over my head. I'd leave him with Bram. That would allow Knight and me to question Dagan. And Quillan would never know any of it. Ah, perfect.

The sound of scratching interrupted my daydreaming. I stood up, cocking my head to the side. The apartment was completely silent. I padded over toward the kitchen in my bare feet when I heard the scratching again. It seemed to come from the kitchen door that led out into the yard. My heart pounded as if wanting to burst from my chest.

Then it dawned on me—the gremlins. I hadn't fed them yet today. Bad me. My heart stopped freaking out, and I went to the back door, pulling it wide. The gremlins weren't outside, but their bowls were overturned as if they'd been pawing at them. I reached down and grabbed both bowls and made my way back into the kitchen.

Pulling open the half-full bag of Alpo, I scooped two mug-fulls of the smelly stuff and filled each bowl. How the hell did dogs—or gremlins—eat this stuff? Shaking my head, I poured some hot water over the top of both bowls which made an even fouler smelling gravy. Then I plodded back outside and searched, in vain, for my gremlins. I thought about just leaving the bowls by the kitchen door, but I was paranoid about feeding the "dogs" and being caught by my

neighbors. So I slipped into my flip flops and after making
sure no neighbors were around, started for the woods.

The cold air hit me like an arresting officer, and I
shivered. I bolstered myself against the frigid air and started
forward, hoping the little bastards weren't far. I didn't have
the patience or the interest, really, to chase after them.

Hey, I wasn't the one who was hungry.

As soon as I hit the shelter of the trees, I shook the food
in the metal bowls, hoping the sound would lure them out.
Nothing. Wasn't that the norm when calling a hungry dog? I
shook the food again but they didn't come out. Instead, a few
drops of the gelatinous gravy sloshed over the side of one
bowl and spilled over my hand. Ugh.

Four more steps, and then I was over it. Let the dumb
things go hungry. The sound of something moving behind me
stopped me. I dropped both bowls of food, and one landed
upside-down on my foot, the gravy sliding between my toes. I
pivoted, bracing myself for whatever was behind me.

Nothing.

No sign of the gremlins; no sign of anything. Just the
shadows of pine trees against the blue-black of the night. A
chilly breeze flowed through the pine boughs and lashed my
face, as if trying to pull my attention away from whatever
creature was lurking in the woods, waiting for me. The
sudden still of the woods practically shouted it—something
was stalking me. And I had a feeling that something happened
to have fire-red hair.

With a deep breath, I launched myself in the direction
of my open kitchen door. No sooner did I take two steps,
when I felt myself go airborne, the cold night air freezing as I
sailed through it. I smacked against the ground, bouncing
once and landing on my back. My abrupt landing knocked the
air from my lungs and left me feeling as flat as a Swedish
pancake.

Bright flashes burst behind my eyes, pain radiating
through the back of my head. I lay there, stunned for a

moment, before I realized I had to get up—fast. Whatever had sent me flying was big.

I forced myself to my feet, determined to ignore the dull ache in my head. Another swoosh of air rang out behind me. I spun around toward the trees, seeing nothing but their skeletal outlines. I heard panting, and it was close. The image of Sigourney Weaver with the alien breathing into her ear came to mind and I had to push it away.

If I tried to run, it would kill me. I leaned against the nearest tree and focused on the crude outline of the pines against the dark. I shook my palm until a mound of fairy dust appeared. Blowing the dust, I envisioned a duplicate image of myself. No sooner did the thought leave my mind than a projection of myself stood there—a me hologram.

I nodded toward the projection and thought the word "run." Watching the clone me take off toward the east side of the apartment, I went west. The clone was maybe one hundred yards to my kitchen door. Hopefully whatever was in the forest had fallen for the bait.

I ran full bore for the kitchen when I heard a sound behind me—something running through a pile of dried twigs. I couldn't help it—I glanced over my shoulder but saw nothing. Was the damned thing invisible?

"Dulcie!"

I whipped my face forward again, but it was too late. I ran headlong into Quillan. If he hadn't been bracing himself for the impact, I would've doubled us both over.

He wrapped his arms around me. "What happened?"

I swallowed the lump of fear in my throat. "Some … something was in the woods, Quill. It was after me."

He focused on the woods. "Let's get you inside. I'll tell Trey to make you some coffee."

Coffee?! "Did you hear what I said?"

"Yeah, come on, Dulce."

He opened the back door, and I wasted no time in taking shelter in my house. I collapsed against the table,

124

watching Quillan shut and lock the door behind him. As if a lock would keep whatever was out there … out.

"What the hell, you don't believe me?" I insisted.

"I believe you," he said. "I just didn't want to make a scene out there. No reason for the neighbors to get concerned."

Was he freaking serious? "Yeah, no reason for them to get concerned when whatever is out there could eat them!"

Quillan shook his head and took a seat next to me. "We've discovered the creature was called from the Netherworld. Whoever called it has complete control over it. It will only go after whoever they tell it to."

"So someone told it to go after me?"

"Probably so. Well, if that was the creature who killed Fabian."

So now he even doubted it was the creature? WTF? "What else could it have been?" I scoffed. "And great job your little gremlins did protecting me, by the way."

Quillan dropped his eyes. "We found them dead right outside your back door."

I nearly choked. "They weren't dead five minutes ago. I went out to feed them and thought they were screwing around in the woods. That thing killed them?" I dropped my forehead into the palm of my hand.

"Trey is taking care of them now."

The sound of the door opening grabbed my attention, and Trey walked in, wiping Hades-only-knew-what on his thighs. And he was sleeping on my couch?

"Hi Dulce, you okay?" he asked, wiping the sweat from his forehead.

"Yeah, I'm fine." But I wasn't fine. Far from it.

"Trey, will you put on some coffee?" Quillan asked.

"I don't want any coffee," I snapped.

"Okay, nix the coffee," Quillan said.

Trey took a seat next to both of us. "So what was out there?"

I shook my head. "Quillan doesn't seem to think it was much of anything even though it killed the gremlins."

"That's not true. We haven't figured out exactly what it is yet, and I don't want to make any decisions until we do."

I held my tongue—I really wanted to tell him I knew what it was—that it was a *Kragengen* shape-shifter, and I knew what it looked like in human form but Knight had sworn me to secrecy and did I really want to go against a big wig from the Netherworld? In short: no.

"Well, maybe I should stay with you both tonight?" Quillan said.

Talk about screwing up my Dagan and Bram plans. "No," I said too quickly, then smiled as if to make up for it. "That won't be necessary."

"Dulce, something killed both gremlins and tried to kill you," Quillan said like I was a slow kid.

"We don't know that," I started, thinking it ridiculous that Quillan and I had basically changed places—me feigning nonchalance and him making a big deal out of it. Irony anyone?

He frowned. "It wasn't stopping by for a social call."

I swallowed. There wasn't any other way. "I have a ..." What the hell had Knight said he was? I remember him using the name Todd but that was about it. "I have a ... friend coming over to stay with me."

Quillan's expression was entirely too curious. "A friend?"

Yeah, Knight had said he was my friend, right? "Um, a friend from before I moved here ... named Todd."

It was Trey's turn to frown, and his bottom lip puffed out as if to emphasize his confusion. I tried to give him the look of death, but he was too concerned with whether or not Knight was really my friend to notice. Have I mentioned hobgoblins aren't particularly smart?

"Wasn't he your cousin?" Einstein asked.

Big goddammit. "No, he's an old friend."

Trey shook his head, the pain in the ass. "I thought he said he was your cousin … yeah, I'm pretty sure he's your cousin."

"I think I'd know my own cousin," I snapped. "Anyway, you were completely out of it, Trey, maybe that's what you thought you heard." The doorbell chimed, and I bolted from the chair, relieved to break free from the both of them. "That's probably him now."

I pulled open the door, and Knight gave me a slow smile.

"Dulce."

"Hi, Todd," I said, hoping he'd get the clue that I had company. He straightened and nodded. Thank Hades, someone had some sense.

"You remember Trey?" I said as Knight walked into the house. He smiled at Trey.

Quillan stood at the sight of Knight and lumbered over, extending his hand. "Dulcie tells me you're old friends. Pleased to meet you, I'm Quillan, her boss."

Knight didn't hesitate, but took Quillan's hand and shook it. Neither one let go. I was just waiting for them to sniff each other's asses.

"Hiya, Todd," Trey called from the table. His voice interrupted the handshake, and both men retreated to opposite sides of the kitchen.

"Trey, good to see you feeling better," Todd, my friendly cousin said.

Quillan faced me, an angry set to his features. "Was Todd here when Trey was … sick?"

I gulped, knowing he'd be pissed that someone he thought wasn't law enforcement was now privy to information he shouldn't be. But no use in lying on this count. The cat was already miles away from the bag.

"Um, yeah, he happened to stop by, and he's good with magic so he helped Sam out a bit." I cringed. Ergh, I really wasn't good at this lying stuff.

Quillan held his tongue but I could tell he was pissed by the tightness of his jaw and the fact that his eyes looked as fierce as Drew Barrymore's in *Firestarter*.

"Well, I guess I can get going then," he said in an icy voice, his face a facade of reserve. "Dulce, want to walk me to the door?"

Great, he wanted to yell at me in pseudo privacy. "Sure," I said sheepishly.

Trey started a conversation with Knight, who took a seat at the table across from him. When Quillan and I reached the front door, he pushed it open and inclined his head toward the front stoop. Apparently, it wasn't private enough inside.

"Why the hell is your boyfriend here, Dulcie?" he asked when I'd closed the door behind us.

Hades be damned, how many times was someone going to accuse Knight of being my boyfriend? I gritted my teeth. "He's not my boyfriend."

"Your friend, whatever. What's he doing here?"

"I thought it'd be good to have extra protection."

Quillan's eyes narrowed. "That's what the gremlins are for. That's why Trey is staying with you and that's why I come by every day after work."

My personal life was none of his business. "The gremlins are dead, I'm more protecting Trey than he is me and you stopping by after work is all fine and good, but it doesn't amount to much."

"Instead of coming to me, you call Mr. Bodybuilder shit-for-brains?"

"Don't talk about him like that. He's not dumb."

"He shouldn't be involved in police business. None of this concerns him."

If only he knew exactly how involved Knight was and that he'd basically called his boss's boss a shit-for-brains.

"He doesn't know anything about it."

"Other than the fact that Trey was put under by something and now needs to stay with you. That's more than enough for him to know, Dulcie." He paused. "You really botched this one up."

"Is that it?" I asked impatiently, coming close to botching the frown off his face.

He sighed and leaned against the wrought iron railing. "No, I want you to tell him to go home. I can stay with you and Trey."

"Not gonna happen. Todd's not staying with me and neither are you. Trey and I are fine. Now, why don't you go home, and do whatever it was you were planning on doing this evening."

He crossed his arms against his chest and stared down the length of his nose like I was all of three feet tall. "Is all of this because I kissed you?"

"What?" I shot out. "What does that have to do ..."

"I thought things were fine between us, Dulce."

"Things are fine. Now, before you make yourself sound any stupider, why don't you be on your way?" I pushed at his lower back, but he didn't budge.

"Alright, but we need to talk, you and I."

"Fine. Good. Wonderful. Now go."

He turned and started for his truck. I walked back inside and slammed the door shut behind me.

"Everything okay?" Knight asked.

"Yeah, fine. Uh, Todd, can I chat with you for a second, please?"

He nodded and Trey stood up.

"I'll just watch the tube," Trey said and collapsed into the sofa, grabbing the remote from the valley between the cushions. Then he faced us again. "No mushy stuff when I'm in the same room."

"We'll take it into Dulcie's bedroom," Knight said and I felt like slapping him. "Lead the way."

Not having much choice, I headed for my room, Knight on my tail. I closed the door behind us, propping my hands on my hips. "That was totally uncalled for."

"Have to keep up appearances, right? And by the way, I thought I was your cousin?"

I scowled. "I forgot how you said you knew me." I shook my head as Knight took a seat on my bed. "None of that matters right now."

He smiled up at me. "And what does matter, Dulce?"

"Stop flirting with me."

He chuckled. "Go on."

"Both the gremlins that were watching me are dead."

He wore his surprise. "What killed them?"

"I think it was the *Kragengen*. It came after me when I was in the woods earlier."

He nodded and was quiet for a second. "Someone ordered it to come after you."

"That's what Quillan said." He pulled his attention to me at the mention of Quillan.

"Did you tell him anything about ..."

I shook my head and paced the room. "No, I didn't tell him anything. He thinks you're an old boyfriend of mine."

Knight smiled, nodding. "Okay, good. Dinner and we head to Dagan's?"

"Yeah, but what about Trey?"

Knight shook his head. "He can't come with us. Relations Office orders that no one else is to be involved. It's bad enough Sam got involved."

"I can't leave Trey here alone. Not after what the creature did to the gremlins and tried to do to me. He comes with us."

His lips were tight. "No."

My lips were tighter. "Yes."

"I can pull rank on you, Dulce."

"Don't call me Dulce. My name is Dulcie and I don't care what you pull on me. I'm not leaving Trey alone here."

"Then he can stay in the car."

Okay, we were getting somewhere. "I have a better idea."

He crossed his arms over his chest. "Which is?"

"I have some business with Bram. We go there first, leave Trey with Bram, then go to Dagan's and question him about the shape-shifter. After Dagan's, you and Trey can have a drink while I take care of my business with Bram."

"What's the nature of this business with the vampire?"

"It's personal."

Knight narrowed his eyes. "Are you dating him too?"

"That's none of your or anybody's business."

"Fine." His eyes narrowed. "I'm staying with you and Trey until all this boils over."

My mouth dropped open. "To hell you are."

"You aren't safe now. The creature has clearly made it known it's after you. I'm making it my responsibility to see that you're okay."

"I don't have room for you. The couch is taken in case you didn't notice the hobgoblin in my living room."

He smiled, long and languid. "Then I guess I'll be in here with you."

TWELVE

"So why are we going to Bram's, Dulce?" Trey asked as he leaned over the driver's seat and breathed heavily down my neck.

"Are you buckled in?" I asked. "The last thing I want is a ticket for your sorry ass not being buckled."

Knight chuckled. Trey resumed his position of breathing down my neck—a smell that oddly reminded me of the Alpo I'd been feeding the gremlins.

"Are we going drinking?" Trey started in again. "I haven't been out partying for a long time ... this is going to be so cool. You know, Dulce, you and me have never been out together."

More sweltering breath on my neck. I came to a red light and tested the brakes. I glanced back at Trey in the rear view mirror and watched him knock his head against the back of my seat.

"Jeez, watch your driving," he said, rubbing his forehead.

"No, we aren't going partying. I have some business I need to take care of, and Bram is going to take care of you."

I caught Trey's grimace in the rearview mirror. His shoulders sagged, and his bottom lip stuck out like he was about to cry. "I don't need Bram to babysit me."

"Yes, you do," I said. Not wanting a forty-year-old hobgoblin crying in my backseat, I softened my tone. "Just do me a favor, and don't argue with me. Angela will keep you company. You can stare at her boobs all night."

Trey started to deny the fact that he was a fan of Angela's boobs, but at Knight's chuckle, I guess he thought he'd take the manly way out. A smirk replaced the grimace on his lips.

Trey nodded to Knight. "They're nice, man."

"Holy Hades," I said. "Can we change the subject please?"

The light went green, and I accelerated again. No Regrets was just at the end of the street—the fluorescent sign promising separation from Trey soon enough. And giving the slip to the albatross around my neck was as appealing as a Slurpee on a super hot day.

I threw a wave to Nick as I pulled into the lot behind No Regrets. Putting the Wrangler into park, I faced Trey who was beaming like a kid at the gates to Disneyland.

"Trey, hang out at the bar with either Bram or Angela all night. Make like your ass is stapled to the chair and wait for us to get back, okay?"

He bobbed his head but there was a day-dreamy gaze in his eyes, and I would've bet money he'd paid absolutely no attention to me. "Yeah, yeah," he said, waving his hand in dismissal. Then he seemed to glom onto the fact that I hadn't included Knight in the Angela-babysitting-Trey paradigm. "Hey, why does Todd get to go with you?"

Knight gave me a quick discouraging glance, as if I were such a moron I couldn't remember I'd been sworn to secrecy. "Don't worry about that," I said and glared at Knight.

I opened the door and hopped down, my spine tight with anger. Dropping my attention to my jeans and tank top, I sighed as I thought of the horrible getup I'd have to invent for myself prior to going to Dagan's. I didn't want to give Trey even the slightest inkling that we were headed to Dagan's, so I'd have to use my magic to dress Knight and myself up later.

I started forward with Trey and Knight on my heels. Bram met us at the back door, giving me a lascivious smile. This was going to be a long night.

"Sweet, looking lovely as always."

A snide response buried itself on my tongue when I remembered Bram was doing me a favor.

"Hi, Bram, thanks for watching Trey. I appreciate it."

Bram didn't show his surprise at the first friendly words I'd ever said to him. Instead, he inclined his head toward Trey in greeting. His eyes narrowed when they fell on Knight. "And who is this?" he asked with all the pretense of propriety but anyone with half a brain would realize he was less than thrilled to make Knight's acquaintance. Men of the Netherworld were a macho bunch.

Knight extended his hand. "Todd, an old friend of Dulce's."

Bram pasted on a grin that was as fake as a politician's and shook Knight's extended hand. Even though his lips were smiling, his eyes held a warning. Knight's eyes echoed the sentiment.

Bram stepped aside for us as he opened the door. I lingered near Bram as Knight and Trey walked inside. Knight gave me a quizzical look, as though wondering why I wasn't following them. I ignored him, needing some private time with Bram. "Todd, can you take Trey to the bar? You can put drinks on my tab. Angela's cool with it. And don't worry, I won't be gone long."

"And where are you going, Sweet?" Bram asked as he pulled the door shut behind him and locked it. The Notorious BIG's "Hypnotize" launched me into a drunken flashback to college.

"To Dagan's to talk to him about the creature that killed Fabian," I paused. "You don't happen to know anymore about that, do you?" Might as well try.

Bram shook his head, throwing me another smile laced with desire, and the promise of pleasure. I frowned.

He dropped the smile. "I know nothing, Sweet."

Knight gave me a questioning glance as Trey droned on about how the French judge a perfect breast by using a champagne glass. I breathed a sigh of relief as they disappeared around the corner.

I turned back to Bram. "I'm looking for a woman …"

Bram chuckled. "Aren't we all, Sweet?"

"Ha ha. She's tall with long red hair. Ring any bells?"

Bram tapped his slender fingers against his chin, patronizing me. "No tall redheads have come to the club lately that I can think of. I will ask around for you though."

He smiled again, and I knew something I didn't want to hear was about to come out of his mouth. "Have you decided to try your own sex, Dulcie Sweet? I would hope you'd give me a chance first?"

I just glared at him. "This is police business, and I can't tell you any more about it. I want you to call me if anyone matching that description even walks by your club. I'll give you my cell number."

Okay, not something I actually wanted Bram to have, but this was important.

He grinned like a little kid on Christmas morning.

I propped my hands on my hips. "You only have permission to call me if you see a woman matching that description. No calling because you're bored, or want to talk, or you're horny, got it?"

Bram pursed his lips as if he were offended. I knew better. "And do you have news for me on the Chinese parlor?"

I swallowed, hoping he wouldn't be angry I'd left it so long. "That's my first question for Dagan tonight."

Bram nodded. "Please do not forget."

"I won't. It shouldn't take long. Just make sure you keep a watch out for Trey, okay?"

"Is he mentally lacking? Why all the fuss about him?"

I couldn't help my laugh. "No, all I can say is that we're afraid the creature might be after him, so he can't be left alone."

"Very well."

I paused, not sure if I should tell him about my book now or later. "And after I get back from Dagan's, I … I uh need some private time with you."

That hadn't come out right. And I knew it hadn't come out right by the huge smirk that lit Bram's face.

"Ah, Dulce, finally you reveal your feelings for me?"

"No," I snapped. "I just need to talk with you about … something."

The smile dropped a bit—now it was more of an amused grin.

"I shall wait on pins and needles."

Dagan was dressed in tight red leather pants and nothing else. Well, unless you considered his many tattoos some form of clothing. With his ridiculous pants, he looked like a member of Kiss minus the bad hair and makeup. Now, as he leaned against the chair behind his desk, he eyed me like a starving man handed a Big Mac.

I glanced down at the black rubber dress, fishnets and stiletto heels I'd magicked for myself. I looked more like the fairy hooker, Zara, than I wanted to admit.

"We have some questions for you," I started, mentally checking off my list the fact that Dagan was still alive and the red-headed shape-shifter hadn't gotten to him … yet.

"Go on," Dagan said, his eyes resting on Knight again for at least the tenth time. Like last time, Knight stood in the corner of the room, directly behind me, looking like an impervious bodyguard … in black jeans and black leather chaps. Okay, he looked more like one of *The Village People.*

136

"Do you remember the woman with the duct tape? The tall redhead the night we were here?" I asked, pulling Dagan's gaze from Knight. His eyes continued to twinkle as they met mine.

Dagan chuckled and dropped his feet from the top of the desk. His toenails were painted black. It reminded me of something a young Goth guy with no friends would do. "Yes, I remember," he purred.

"Have you seen her here since?" I asked.

Dagan clasped his hands behind his head and leaned back, giving me a view of his large chest and the hair that ran down his abs, only to disappear into the line of his Van Halenesque pants. "Did she kill Fabian?" he asked.

"That's A.N.C. business," Knight said, his lips tight.

Dagan glanced at him and smiled wolfishly. "If you weren't such a delight to my eyes, I'd take offense to that."

As Knight grumbled something unintelligible, Dagan faced me again. "I haven't seen the woman since that night."

"Did you get any information from her? Like where she lives or what her name is?" I asked, sounding desperate.

"Yes, her name is Allison and she works at Starbucks, she lost her virginity to a boy named Danny when she was nineteen and chick flicks are her favorite type of movie."

"That's about as funny as your pants," I snapped.

Knight chuckled behind me, and Dagan refused to look at either of us.

"Let's try this again," I started. "What do you know about that woman?"

"I avoid questions. Better to get what I want and leave. As far as I was concerned, she was a good lay."

Holy Hades. Dagan had slept with a creature that had eaten Fabian, Guy and Tad alive.

Dagan smirked. "Don't look so shocked, Dulcie. You can't be that innocent."

"If she comes back here, call me," I said, then paused. "If I find out she came back here and you didn't call me, I'm going to be very pissed off. You and I have a good thing here, so don't screw it up."

"I don't have your number."

Great, now I'd have to give my cell number to a demon. With a sigh, I rattled off the number, feeling like I was giving away my bank account info. So now a demon and a vampire could reach me whenever they pleased. Mental Note: *after this case closes, change your number.*

"You might want to avoid that woman," I added. "I'd consider her dangerous."

Dagan laughed, and it was a sound you might hear someone make before they cut out your heart. "I'm a demon, nothing frightens me."

I shrugged. "Don't say I didn't warn you."

I started to get up, but then remembered the other reason I was here. I settled back into my seat. "Dagan, I have one other question for you … just out of curiosity …"

"And what would that be, Dulcie?" He sounded less than amused. I hated hearing my name on his tongue. It made it seem … dirty somehow.

"Word on the street is you're thinking of buying that old Chinese parlor?" I tried to make it sound off the cuff and uninterested, but I wasn't a good liar.

His face was expressionless as he shook his head. "Bram is good. You can go back to the bloodsucker, Dulcie, and tell him I have no interest in his damned parlor. Great that he has you doing his dirty work. Now, both of you can leave. I'm a busy man, and you've wasted enough of your night."

I didn't waste any time in jumping to my feet, just as eager to leave as he was to be rid of us. Well, I had an answer for Bram that would, no doubt, please him greatly. And hopefully, Dagan would play by the rules and call me if the creature resurfaced in his club.

"You think he's going to call?" Knight asked when we were on our way back to the Wrangler.

"If he knows what's good for him, he will. He doesn't want me as his enemy—I'm sure of that. Much better for him if he's on good terms with the A.N.C."

"I thought you said you weren't friends?"

"He's a demon," I said, unlocking the car. "How 'friendly' can you be with one of them?"

Before hopping inside, I shook my hand until I had a mound of fairy dust, then dumped it on myself, imagining a pair of jeans and a tank top.

"What about me?" Knight asked.

I did the same for him, conjuring up a pair of khakis and a black shirt. He settled into the passenger seat as I started the engine and peeled into the street.

"What now?" Knight asked.

"Back to No Regrets. I need you to chill with Trey for a bit while I talk with Bram."

"If it's anything about this case, I need to be there."

"It's not about the case."

"Then what is it?"

"None of your business."

"You tell me that a lot."

"Maybe you should start listening."

I pulled into the No Regrets parking lot and turned the car off, facing Knight. "I'll just be a little while. Maybe thirty minutes."

Knight nodded and stepped out of the Wrangler, shutting the door behind him. "Thanks for leaving me with Trey, by the way. He's not exactly thrilling company."

I laughed and started for the back door. "I'm sure lots of people would say the same about you."

He glowered as I knocked on the back door. A small, attractive vampire woman opened it and ushered us inside. Walking toward the bar, I found Trey exactly where I knew he'd be—sitting at the bar and slobbering over his straw as he stared at Angela's boobs.

139

"Hi, Angela," I said and took the barstool next to Trey. "How's it going, Trey?"

He didn't even turn to face me, but kept staring at Angela as if he was afraid she'd disappear. Course, he was probably used to women disappearing the first chance they got.

"Hi, Dulce, did you and Todd get your business taken care of?" Trey asked Angela's cleavage.

"Yeah. Angela, could I get a rum and diet, please?" I glanced at Knight. "Todd, what are you drinking?"

"Guinness."

Angela took one look at Knight and meandered toward us, suddenly interested in our company. She looked him up and down, nothing shy in her gaze. Knight just grinned.

"You here again?" she asked and confused me. Then I remembered Knight had come to Bram's looking for me before we'd ever met.

"Good to see you," Knight answered. "Angela, right?"

"Yep," she smiled. It was the first time I'd ever seen her smile.

"Dulcie, Sweet."

I'd never been happier to hear Bram's voice. I turned on him so quickly, I nearly made myself dizzy. Then I jumped to my toes and gave him a big smile. His eyes widened. I guess he wasn't used to me being anything but surly.

"Bram, can we talk in your office?"

He nodded to Trey and Knight before he led me down the long hallway into an office that had more of a sitting room feel to it. The carpet was thick white, and I had no idea how he kept it so immaculate. Two red velvet armchairs bookended a dark mahogany coffee table. The only business-like thing about the room was the laptop that stood unattended on the coffee table. With the black of the walls and ceiling, the white curtains, and the red chairs, I felt like I was in a newspaper with a nosebleed.

Bram pulled out the plush velvet chair for me as he took the one opposite. "Did you question Dagan about my massage …"

"It's all yours," I interrupted. "He said he has no interest in it."

"Very good news, although I am not convinced I believe him."

"That's between you and him."

He laughed and eyed me curiously. "I am intrigued, Sweet. Tell me why you are here."

I cleared my throat, not exactly sure where to start or how. "I um, I'm interested in writing a book about you."

Bram leaned forward, his eyes wide with surprise. "I must say, I was definitely not expecting that! I did not know you fancied yourself a writer."

I shrugged. "I wrote a … historical novel. When I sent it out, the feedback I got was that paranormals were in demand. Especially about vampires, if you can believe it."

He leaned back against the red velvet of the chair. With his black hair and light skin, he looked like part of the room's scenery. "I see. Will this be a biography?"

"No, more a … a romance."

I swallowed the humiliation that was choking me and wanted to shoot myself for even considering the ridiculous notion in the first place.

He bobbed his head enthusiastically. "A romance? I like that even better."

"But it will be biographical, too. I bet in your nearly three hundred years, you must've seen a lot?"

"Yes, of course." He paused. "I would be honored to be your muse, Sweet."

"Great, thanks."

"Who will be my love interest?"

"I don't know. That part I can just make up."

He smiled. "Perhaps a fairy?"

"Oh, Hades," I grumbled and stood up. "I've gotta get going, Bram, but thanks. Can we make some time to get together this week? I'd like to start interviewing you."

He laughed. "I am available whenever you are."

I bit my lip. "There's just one other thing …"

"Anything, Sweet."

"Would you mind coming to my apartment?" Since I was stuck watching Trey for a while, it would be easier if Bram came to me.

"Of course. Shall I see you tomorrow evening?"

"That would be great. Thanks, Bram."

Bram opened the door for me. Trey and Knight were in deep conversation with Angela, and the surge of jealousy that warred through me gave me pause. Why the hell did I give even the slightest of craps that Angela was flirting with Trey and Knight? Hmm, better rephrase the question: why did I give even the slightest of craps that Angela was flirting with Knight? It was an answer I didn't want to know.

"We can go now," I said. "Angela, what do I owe you for the drinks?"

She glanced at Knight. "Nothing, on the house."

I just shook my head.

THIRTEEN

Two hours later, Trey was passed out on the couch, and Knight was trying to find something on TV. He surfed the channels, stopping periodically to watch something seemingly intriguing, only to change the station yet again. I'd been working on the intro to my new Bram book, and the background noise was becoming an issue. With a sigh, I focused on my first page and read the opening paragraph again:

Raven was a vampire, and like most vampires, he was tall, dark and handsome with curly locks and caramel eyes. But he was one man you didn't want to rub the wrong way. With his superhuman strength and bewitching eyes, his wish was my command. And now, as I realized the vampire was about to sink his fangs into my carotid artery, deep inside, I was scared.

Okay, so I was using myself as the narrator and yes, the love interest—so what? It wasn't like I had the hots for Bram.

I didn't realize I'd been softly reading out loud until Knight glanced up. He scrutinized me like an old woman squinting at an eye chart. "What are you working on?" he called from the couch.

"Just a ... book, that's all," I grumbled, not pulling my eyes from the monitor.

"About what?"

Goddammit. I'd brought this on myself—working on it when he was here in the room with me. But even with privacy at a premium, I had to get my writing in somehow.

"I, uh, I'm working on a paranormal book."

He sat up and dropped the volume of the television to a gentle drone. "I didn't know you were a writer."

"I'm really not much of one," I said, shaking my head.

As I refocused on the page, I glimpsed Knight still watching me. Okay, so he found me more interesting than the TV—that was a compliment. I swiveled around in my chair, so I could face him, and thought maybe a break was just what I needed.

"Is this your first book?" he asked.

"No, I wrote another book and tried to get an agent but no one was interested."

"Sorry to hear that." He nodded toward the computer. "What's this one about?"

I blushed, not entirely sure why I was so embarrassed. A writer shouldn't be self-conscious about her own work, right? "It's a paranormal."

His brows drew together in what appeared to be confusion.

I sighed. "My first book was historical, but I was advised that historicals are out and paranormals are in."

"You still haven't said what it's about."

I dropped my gaze. "It's about a vampire."

Knight's eyebrows arched in surprise. "Was that the business you had with Bram, then?"

Well, if nothing else, he was astute. I bobbed my head, and Knight's eyes narrowed in what appeared to be resentment. "He hardly warrants a book," he said. "He's … unimpressive."

"Well, that's your opinion."

Knight chuckled. "Why write about vampires? Why not something more … unusual?"

"What, like a Loki?" I laughed as Knight shrugged. "One agent told me everyone likes vampire stories."

"Can't say I'm a fan, myself."

I picked up a pen and tapped the tip against my lips. "I can't say I am either."

We both fell silent as I debated whether or not to continue working on the book. It was already getting late and I'd lost my inspiration, what little I had anyway. Besides, I had all the time in the world to get it done.

"So if you're from the Netherworld, why do you sound like you're American?"

Knight laughed a deep and rumbling sound. A nice sound if I had to judge. "You've never been to the Netherworld, I take it?" He leaned back against the tiny section of couch Trey wasn't occupying and folded his hands behind his head, revealing the great width of his chest. I gulped and feigned interest in the sleeping Trey. Holy Hades, Trey was unsightly, but it was damned easier looking at him than Knight.

Then I remembered Knight had asked me a question. "No. I was born here."

"Are your parents still here, then?"

I shook my head and dropped my attention to the floor as I thought about my parents, something I hadn't done in the last six months, at least. "No, my father's still in the Netherworld … as far as I know."

"But you've never been?"

I picked at a loose thread in my shorts, only managing to weaken the seam. "No. My mother came to California from the Netherworld when she was pregnant with me. I was born in Southern California. I moved to Splendor after Mom died and … some other things happened."

"Other things?"

I cleared my throat. "A bad relationship."

"I'm sorry to bring up a painful subject," Knight said and finally dropped his arms. "And your mother?"

"My mom died a long time ago." Even now, eight years after my mother's death, the words still rang through me empty and hollow.

"Dulcie, you don't have to talk about if you don't want to."

He leaned forward, his elbows on his thighs and glanced up at me, a lock of black hair obscuring his left eye. He pushed it aside, but I couldn't tear my focus away from it. It was as if that little wavy lock of jet black hair would help me get through the memory of my mother's untimely demise.

"I haven't talked about it in a very long time," I said, amazed by the upwelling of emotions within me. "She was killed by a goblin. That's why I became a Regulator."

He nodded. "I'm sorry to hear that. Your mother would be proud of you. You're smart and very perceptive."

I smiled and thought he sounded like Quillan. And thoughts of Quillan led to thoughts of that one kiss. Suddenly I wondered what kissing Knight would be like. Yeah, we'd kissed in Dagan's club, but it wasn't like a real kiss. I glanced at Knight again, at his full, pouting lips which looked like they'd been made for kissing. I sighed, trying to force the thoughts from my mind, as I expelled the air from my lungs.

"So tell me about the Netherworld."

Knight shrugged. "What would you like to know?"

I felt the stitch in my gut relax. I'd learned long ago when memories became too painful, you just had to shelve them and move on. "First, what's with the American accent? Last I checked, the Netherworld wasn't part of the US."

He chuckled. "Actually, it is."

"What?" I felt my eyebrows furrow. "I did pretty well in geography, Knight."

Knight laughed again, and I wondered if he found me attractive, and if he was at all aware of how attractive I found him.

"The Netherworld isn't a single place, Dulcie. It parallels Earth. It's just another level to what you already know here."

"What are you talking about?" I asked, my voice sounding a little too caustic.

"Just as there's a Splendor in California, there's a Splendor in the Netherworld. Think of it like this—it's like a

146

cake—you have your cake layer and then a frosting layer. The cake layer is the earth you know—the frosting is the Netherworld. It exists in the same place but on a different level."

"So you really are from the States?"

"Yes, from the region where your Montana is. In the Netherworld, we don't call it Montana, though. We call it *Crannag*."

I nodded although I found it hard to fathom, the image of Knight as a cowboy from Montana flashing through my head. "Interesting. So is *Crannag* like Montana, looks wise?"

Knight stood up and lumbered toward me, making my heart palpitate as I felt a rush of adrenaline. What was it about this man that always had me on edge? And better yet, why in hell was he coming so close? I automatically leaned back in my chair to put some space between us.

He extended his hand. "See for yourself."

I grasped his hand and closed my eyes.

It was like a movie screen dropped before my eyes. I wasn't in my apartment any longer. Sort of like the same thing that had happened when Knight channeled Trey's vision of the creature. Only now I wasn't witnessing the creature eating Fabian … I think I was in Montana.

"That's *Crannag*," Knight said, his voice gentle.

His breath wafted across my cheek like a thousand pixie kisses. I couldn't help my gasp as a blush feathered over my neck and continued to rise until it stained my face.

"It's incredible," I whispered, half remarking on the feel of his breath. Then I refocused my attention to the virtual reality of *Crannag*. Verdant hills tumbled carelessly around a cornflower blue lake that reflected the azure of the sky. The lake was so clear, the reflection of the hills and sky in the pristine water looked like a mirror.

"Yes," Knight said.

He squeezed my hand and his hand felt large and overpowering, just like the man. Granted, I considered myself

147

petite, but Knight felt enormous. He must've been at least six-feet-four, if I had to guess. The feel of his hand caressing mine pulled my attention from his height as I swallowed.

This was so not good.

Dropping my defenses was something I'd always hoped to avoid—to avoid the uncontrolled feelings of helplessness; now I felt as if every last one of my defenses was burning up in an incendiary of lust. And Knight was planning on living with me until all this creature business was settled? Holy Hades, I didn't know if I could make it.

I yanked myself from my longings and reinspected the landscape of *Crannag*. There weren't any structures—just a row of large boulders jutting from the top of a hill. The boulders looked like a sculpture but didn't appear to be man-made. Nothing looked as if it were touched by man, just wild and untainted. My attention shifted to the sky as it was invaded by something black soaring through a cloud, like an arrow piercing the billowy white sails.

"What's that?" I asked.

"You call them dragons."

I caught my breath and watched the dragon as it soared, its long neck as graceful as a swan's. But unlike my fairy tale image of a dragon, this one looked more like a giant lizard with bat-like wings. The body didn't look intimidating by any accounts. Not unless you're intimidated by a flying newt.

"What do you call them?" I asked.

"*Dorneags*."

I nodded, thinking this one of the strangest moments of my life. To think I'd never set foot in the Netherworld, and yet I could see it as clearly as if I were there.

"Do all of them look like that?"

"Yes, and in a variety of colors."

"Am I seeing this in real time?" I asked, sounding like an Internet nerd.

Knight chuckled. "Yes, you are."

I shook my head, completely amazed. Okay, so Knight wasn't magic, but he did have some pretty cool tricks up his sleeve.

"They don't look like what humans seem to think dragons are."

"You'll find that most creatures aren't quite what humans make them out to be."

The dragon swooped down to the lake and opening its mouth wide, lapped up a gulp of water and then started back up toward the sky, disappearing over the horizon.

"Wow," I said, incredulously.

Knight dropped my hand, and the vision faded. When I reopened my eyes, all I could see was Trey snoring on my couch. My hand felt cold, and I put it in my pocket, hoping to warm it up again. I brought my attention back to Knight, who was watching me with a curious expression—one I couldn't read.

"That was amazing," I said, feeling slightly uncomfortable under his rigid stare.

He pulled up a chair and sat next to me. "You'd like the Netherworld."

I nodded. "Maybe. How were you able to show me that and Trey's vision?"

Knight shrugged. "One of my Loki abilities."

My eyes narrowed. "You never told me you could do that."

He laughed, and his knee bumped against mine, the touch bolting up my leg and into my angst-filled gut.

"You never asked."

I shook my head, feeling so out of sorts, I couldn't even think of a retort. All I knew was that I most definitely had asked him what his abilities were. He'd just chosen not to tell me.

"So about living in *Crannag* ..."

"What would you like to know?"

"Are you married?" I blurted and snapped my mouth shut as quickly as an angler fish. I'm not sure why Knight's marital status was the first mystery I needed to solve, but as soon as the words left my mouth, I was mortified. "I mean, if they have that sort of thing in the Netherworld …"

Knight chuckled. "Yes, we have similar unions." He held up his hand as if to point to the fact that he didn't wear a ring. "No, I'm not married."

Knock knock; where the hell had the strong, determined and unromantic Dulcie gone?

"And before you ask, no, I don't have a … girlfriend either."

Holy Hades, this was getting more embarrassing by the second. And yes, Knight having a girlfriend had definitely crossed my mind. "I wasn't thinking that," I said, trying to save any sort of face. Well, at this point, I'd be happy just to save an eye, a nose or a mouth.

"I'm getting a little tired," Knight said and stretched his arms above his head with a yawn, as if to prove it.

"You really don't need to stay here. Trey and I will be fine," I said, forcing my attention away from Knight to the top of my cluttered desk. I started rattling papers and sorting through them as if I were a cleaning lady on an impatience potion.

"Not up for argument."

I stood up and tried to shake the annoyance that took hold of me even though, secretly, I was thrilled to have it back ... I knew the old Dulcie couldn't have been far. Ha, take that Knight and your perfect chest!

And as for an argument? Well, there was no use in debating—he was basically the boss of my boss. And that meant he was sleeping in my apartment. I stood up and shuffled to the linen closet in my dog slippers. Pulling out a sleeping bag, I tossed it to Knight. He caught it with a smile and headed for my bedroom.

"Where do you think you're going?" I asked, hands on my hips.

Knight jerked his thumb at Trey. "I can't sleep out here with him making that racket."

The hobgoblin was now flat on his back, his face aimed at the ceiling with his mouth gaping wide. What sounded like a lawnmower thundered from his throat as a clear line of drool coursed down his cheek and pooled onto the cushion. Maybe it was time for a new couch.

Knight took a few more steps toward my bedroom and then faced me. "Are you coming?"

"No, I want to get more writing done. I'll be in later. There's an extra pillow on my bed."

"Great," Knight said and with a wink, disappeared into my bedroom.

I stifled a yawn and returned to my desk, turning up the volume of the TV to drown out Trey's incessant snoring which sounded like a train derailing in my living room.

Rereading my opening paragraph for the nth time, I reached the conclusion I couldn't write anymore tonight. I yawned again, accepting the fact that I was tired. Not wanting to find Knight awake, I sat Indian style on the floor and flipped through the channels, hoping I could find something to occupy my thoughts for the next half hour or so. How long did it normally take someone to fall asleep? Well, since Knight was on the floor, it might take him a while.

I sighed and settled in for a cooking show where some cheery woman was making brownies covered in frosting and chocolate chips. I've never had a sweet tooth, but I could handle it for another half hour or so.

A choking followed by spluttering sounded from Trey, and that's when I decided I was going to bed. I turned the TV off and started for my bedroom. Turning the light off in the living room, I was surrounded by darkness, and it took my eyes a second to go into night mode. When they did, I opened my bedroom door and had to quash my temper as I realized

151

Knight was underneath my covers, in my bed. And the sleeping bag? It was laid out on the floor with one of my pillows above it.

The bastard!

There was no way in hell I was sleeping on the floor. I closed the door behind me and stormed up to Knight, hurling the covers off him. I was greeted with a long expanse of tan back and equally naked rear end! Shocked and mortified again, I threw the covers back over him.

"What the hell do you think you're doing?"

No response. I poked him in his incredibly tight bicep and still, no response.

"Wake up, damn you."

I shook him. Nothing.

Well, I wasn't going to sleep on the floor. I leaned against him and tried to push him out of the bed, but I might as well have been pushing a bus. He wasn't going anywhere. So now I had to decide—the floor or I could sleep next to Knight. I had a queen sized bed, and I was small enough that I could curl up on my side and avoid his nudity …

I wasn't sleeping on the floor.

My mind made up, I grabbed my pajamas and changed in the bathroom, brushing my teeth and hair before marching back out. I was careful to keep the covers tucked around Knight so I wouldn't get another flash of his tight ass.

"You're getting an earful tomorrow, you smug jerk."

I climbed in beside him and stayed as close to the edge of the bed as I could and shut my eyes. No sooner did my eyelashes touch my cheeks than Knight rolled over with a soft snore and wrapped his arm around me, pulling me against him.

I thought my heart would stop. I pushed him away furiously and catapulted myself from the bed. Then I crawled into the sleeping bag on the floor.

I tossed and turned a few times, then closed my eyes and hoped Morpheus would take me to the land of slumber soon enough.

Jack was in my bedroom.

"What are you doing here?" I demanded, my voice sounding just as raw as it had when he'd dumped me a year ago.

He sat on the corner of the bed and gave me a licentious smile, making my stomach clench. I glanced down at myself and realized I was naked under my bed covers. Pulling the sheet up to my chin, I continued glaring at him.

"Dulcie, don't tell me you haven't missed me, I know you have," he said.

I had missed him. I couldn't deny it.

"Is that why you haven't dated anyone else?" he continued.

I shook my head. "I haven't dated anyone because you gave me some real trust issues, asshole. It has nothing to do with missing you."

He leaned forward and put his hand on mine. I wanted to pull it away but I couldn't seem to summon up the will.

"Stand up and let me see you," he whispered.

I stood up in spite of myself, it was as if I'd swallowed a control potion and he was now calling the shots. The duvet dropped away from me, even though I still held it. Jack stood up and approached me, his eyes scanning me from head to toe. He stood so close, I could feel the heat of his breath on my forehead.

"I don't want to do this," I muttered, even as my traitorous body sung while he ran his hands down my breasts.

"He's your past, Dulcie." It was Knight.

I closed my eyes against the embarrassment that not only was Jack witnessing me naked but now Knight was too.

153

*When I opened them, Jack was still watching me through
those beautiful dark brown eyes I'd loved so much. Knight
stood behind him, his expression stoic.*

"Tell him he's your past," Knight demanded.

*I glanced at Jack again and he dropped his head,
capturing my lips. My eyelashes fluttered down until they
graced the tops of my cheeks.*

"Dulcie, let him go."

*I opened my eyes but didn't stop kissing Jack. Knight
grabbed Jack's shoulder and tore him away from me. I
glanced at Jack who didn't even react—he just watched me.*

"Tell him he's your past. Let him go."

*It was like slow motion as I faced Knight again. He ran
his fingers down one side of my face and bent my head as he
trailed steaming hot kisses down the length of my neck.*

"Say it," he demanded again.

*I focused on Jack who was standing there like the last
kid picked in PE. Anger and pain warred within my stomach
as I forced myself to gaze at the man who'd so royally
screwed me up.*

"You're my past," I said in a breathless voice.

*Knight chuckled and ran his fingers down my neck, past
my collarbone until he found one of my breasts. He took it in
his mouth as I watched Jack begin to fade, as if he were a
ghost.*

"Again," Knight demanded.

*But I didn't want to focus on Jack. I wanted to focus on
how amazing Knight's mouth felt on my breast. He pulled
away and glanced up at me.*

"Again," he growled.

I faced Jack. "I'm letting you go."

*Jack faded even more, until he was nothing but a fleck
of whitish steam.*

I gasped when I felt Knight's fingers between my thighs.

"Once more until he's gone."

154

I faced what was left of Jack and the words barely made it out of my mouth. "You're my past and I'm letting you go."

The steam disappeared and I woke up in a sleeping bag on my floor. I drew in my breath as I realized my own hand was pressed hard against my inner thighs. I quickly pulled it away and sat up, dazed.

Knight was an unmoving mound on my bed.

How freaking embarrassing that I'd been fondling myself with him in the same room! Humiliation heated my cheeks and increased tenfold as I wondered if Knight had involved himself in the dream—the same way he'd interrupted my pirate repose. Well, it wasn't like I was about to question him about it.

I rolled over and closed my eyes, praying the rest of my dreams would be rated PG.

FOURTEEN

Knight had been gone all day. Where, I had no idea, but after the first five hours of the day dragged on, my irritation with him sleeping naked in my bed had fizzled like a one hit wonder. Images of Knight licking my breast kept visiting me and it was all I could do to push them to the dark recesses of my mind. It was just too mortifying to even consider that maybe Knight had witnessed the incriminating dream. One thing that was clear, at least to my subconscious mind, was that I needed to get over my emotional baggage from Jack. If the dream wasn't a wakeup call, I didn't know what was.

Now, I was alone. And I reveled in every glorious minute of my solitude. Trey was still at Headquarters for another hour or two, and Bram was coming over as soon as the sun set.

I'd spent all day working on my Bram book and was now up to chapter seven. Even though I hadn't had a chance to interview Bram, I figured I could pepper the book with his stories later on. For now, I just wanted to get the bare bones finished.

Two strong knocks on the front door broke my concentration. I closed my file before approaching the door, palming the Op 6 at my side.

"Who is it?" I demanded, hoping it could only be the best looking man I'd seen in Splendor who also happened to be the most frustrating.

"Knight."

Ding ding, I won.

My hand hovered over the lock while a grin spread across my face.

"I'm sorry, I didn't hear you," I glanced through the peephole to find Knight laden with grocery bags. His brows pasted together in annoyance. Time to get him back for pulling the naked in my bed stunt.

"Dulcie, my arms are full, and I don't have the patience to play games with you," he snapped. "Open the door."

My grin broadened. Retribution is a beautiful thing. "Didn't you read the sign that says 'no solicitors'?" I eyed the peephole again, relishing every minute of his discomfort. The words: "don't get mad; get even" echoed through my head and inspired another grin on my lips.

Knight's sigh was long and loud enough to get through the door. "I'm giving you to the count of three, and then I'm taking the door down."

Hmm, apparently he was impatient and short-tempered.

"One."

He wouldn't dare.

I crossed my arms against my chest and continued watching him through the tiny hole in the door. His face was flushed red and dripping with irritation.

"Two."

Okay, maybe he would dare. He put the bags on the ground while I clutched the doorknob.

"Three."

I yanked the door open before he could do any permanent damage. "Knight, why didn't you say it was you?" I asked with a beaming smile.

Knight frowned and narrowed his eyes. "Very funny."

Then he dropped his gaze to the paper bags sitting on the ground beside him. "You wanna give me a hand with these?"

Making no motion to assist him, I glanced into one of the paper bags and noticed Captain Crunch cereal, a bag of apples and a bottle of Mrs. Butterworth's syrup.

"Groceries?" I asked, as if the idea that he'd gone to the store was completely foreign.

He grabbed four bags and carried them inside while the other two sat there idly, seemingly upset at having been left alone.

"You have no food in this place. And I'm a hungry man."

I shook my head. Knight going grocery shopping was one subject I'd never considered. I finally bent down and gathered the remaining bags into my arms, closing the door behind me with a kick of my heel. Watching him stroll through the living room, I tried to judge whether or not it seemed like he had any inkling about my dream. It didn't seem as though he did.

"Well, I don't cook," I said, retiring the bags on the kitchen counter. Knight was already unloading the ones he'd brought in. I took a seat at the kitchen table and watched him. Hey, he bought them, let him unload them.

Knight faced me with a broad smile. "You don't do anything domestic."

"Just because I'm a woman ..."

"Dulcie, I didn't mean it like that. It's just an observation. I like your modern Wonder Woman sensibilities."

Wonder Woman? What?

I shook my head and watched him pull open the vegetable bin of the refrigerator. He fished out a bag of rotten onions, holding just the tip of the plastic bag as if afraid the onion would crawl out and rub itself against his hand.

Casting me a look of disdain, he dropped them into the trashcan. "Any other surprises in here?"

"I guess you'll find out soon enough," I answered in a saccharin tone.

Knight chuckled and filled the vegetable bin with bags of carrots, onions and potatoes. Shaking his head, he turned his baby blues on me. "You take things way too seriously, Dulcie, you need to lighten up."

My lingering smile vanished. Who in Hades did he think he was? "I don't take things too seriously," I started but was interrupted by Knight's sarcastic expression. "I mean, I wouldn't describe myself as easy going ..."

"By any stretch of the imagination."

"Hey, what is this? Bash Dulcie day?" I knew I could be ... tough ... at times, but that's the type of personality a Regulator needed. What did he expect me to be? Some weakling who cried at the drop of a hat? Like Trey?

"See, taking me too seriously again."

I muttered something unintelligible even to my own ears before changing the subject. "So where were you all day?"

He held up a box of Hungry Jack pancake mix. "Isn't it obvious?"

"Going to the store takes maybe an hour or two at most. You've been gone all day, smart ass."

Hoisting a twenty-bottle pack of water, he placed it atop the counter and tore through the plastic, tossing a bottle to me as he grabbed another for himself. "Been keeping tabs on me, have you?"

Why weren't conversations with Knight ever easy? "No ... well, yes, I just wanted to tell you I didn't appreciate your little stunt last night."

Knight leaned against the counter and crossed his arms against his massive chest. "There was plenty of room on the bed. You seemed to fit alright."

I narrowed my eyes. "So you were awake even though you pretended to be asleep?"

He chuckled and grabbed the chair next to me and straddled it.

I took the cap off my bottle of water and sipped it, hoping it would give me time to come up with a good

response. "Well, I'm not sleeping on the floor again."
Apparently, it wasn't time enough.

He nodded. "That's fine."

"And you're not sleeping in my bed again."

He stood up and started collecting the clutter of paper bags littering my floor. When he faced me with raised brows, I pointed to the cupboard next to the stove, and he packed the bags in, closing the cupboard door behind him.

"I can't sleep on the floor," he said. "I have a bad back."

"Well, you should've thought about that before pulling your little naked stunt last night."

"Fine, I'll wear boxers." Knight chuckled. "Do we have a deal?"

I was just waiting for him to bring up the dream but he never did. Thank Hades. "Fine." I cleared my throat, not at all okay with the image of Knight's tight ass in boxers. "And about where you were for the rest of the day today ..."

"Confidential."

"You're impossible," I snapped and stood up from the kitchen chair so fast, I banged my naked ankle against the wooden leg. I yearned to grab it and hop around the kitchen in pain, since that's the only thing that seems to help. Instead, I just bit my lip and threw myself into the desk chair and reopened my word document.

I decided to ignore Knight for the rest of the evening.

The sound of the door opening startled me to attention, and I turned to observe Trey striding in, acting like he owned the place. "Hey, Dulce, whatcha doin?"

"Nothing," I grumbled.

Trey dropped his man-bag at the foot of the couch and started for the kitchen, his first pit stop whenever he returned from work. He ran headlong into Knight who kept him at arm's length.

"Hiya, Todd."

"Hi, Trey, how's it going?"

"Good. You guys eat dinner yet?"

I didn't bother responding but glanced back at the door, waiting to see if Quillan had followed Trey. After a few seconds, it looked like he hadn't. So because of the Knight-staying-with-me thing, he was avoiding me. Just great.

"I went to the store so help yourself," Knight said as he headed into the living room.

Trey nodded. "Word."

I sighed and returned to my computer while Trey rifled through the cabinets, apparently hell-bent on finding something to contribute to his weight problem.

"What's the plan for tonight?" Trey asked, while opening the box of Captain Crunch. He shoved his hand into it, throwing a handful of nuggets into his mouth. Note to self: *avoid Captain Crunch*. I glanced at Knight, who'd collapsed into the sofa and resumed his channel surfing.

"You guys are on your own," I said. "Bram's coming over."

Knight dropped his feet from the coffee table, and the sound of his boots hitting the floor was like a bowling ball falling from two stories up.

"I don't want to hear it," I started. "You can go ..." I glanced at Trey, who was riveted on the Captain Crunch box, reading the comics and snorting with laughter. "You can go ... drive around and ... look for a certain red-haired something." I hoped Knight got my gist.

"No point," he started, also glancing at Trey, who was still giggling at the box. "That certain something will have to make itself known. No use in me driving all over hell and back."

Trey carried the box of cereal into the living room, trailed by a blizzard of Captain Crunch and plopped onto the couch next to Knight, popping open a can of 7-Up. "Is Bram coming to babysit me?"

I shook my head and frowned, knowing Trey had no intention of cleaning up after himself. "No, he's coming to see me."

"Why's that?" Trey's cheeks filled with effervescence from the 7-Up which swelled his lips until he looked like a bloated toad mid burp.

"She's writing a book about vampires," Knight finished for me, in a crass tone.

"Oh, cool," Trey said with a nod. "There's a comic book I really like about vampires and werewolves, and they fight each other. Kind of like *Alien Versus Predator*. You ever seen that movie, Todd?"

"No," Knight answered.

"What about you, Dulce, you ever seen *Alien Versus Predator*?"

A knock sounding from the front door saved me from the need to respond, and I stood up, sending Knight a threatening scowl—warning him not to act anything but friendly to my vampire guest.

I pulled open the door and found Bram on my doorstep, a single, long-stem rose clutched in his hand. He eyed me from head to toe, and I felt like I was wearing a negligee under his lustful gaze.

"Sweet, wonderful to see you," he said and the accented words dripped English. Bram hadn't lived in England in at least one hundred fifty years (according to his A.N.C. bio), so I imagined the accent was put on—it wouldn't have lasted so long otherwise. Maybe he thought it enhanced his vampire persona. He definitely wouldn't be as intimidating or sexy if he talked like Trey.

He handed me the rose, and I took it with a frozen smile. "Hi, Bram," I said and stepped aside. He casually strolled in, but his grin dissolved when he noticed Trey and Knight on the couch. What, had he thought this was a date?

"Gentlemen," he said and gave them a slight inclination of his head in greeting.

"Hi, Bram, how's it goin'?" Trey asked, never pulling his eyes from the TV where Pamela Anderson strutted her red-bathing-suited self in a tired rerun of Baywatch.

162

Knight glared at Bram as his gaze traveled to the rose in my hand. His mouth was tight. "Hi," he said flatly.

I kicked the door shut and started for the kitchen, pulling out a chair for Bram. He took it with a smile and clapped his hands together like an excited kid. "How shall we proceed?" he asked and his eyes glinted with mischief, as if he were asking what position he should assume. Naked.

"Well, I thought I could ask you some questions, and then if you don't mind, I was going to record our conversation with this," I said and held up my black audio recorder.

The TV volume blared into the kitchen. Gritting my teeth, I craned my neck to see Knight holding the channel changer, a frown of what appeared to be annoyance marring his otherwise perfect face. Anger burned inside me as I turned to apologize to Bram, but he just smirked.

"Perhaps we are being a distraction, Sweet," he said and eyed me knowingly. "Shall we retire to your bedroom?"

My eyes found Knight's, and he immediately muted the sound on the television. "No need, you can stay out here," he grumbled. Hmm, was someone jealous?

Pulling out my notebook, I grabbed a pen and faced Bram. "Ready?"

He nodded and I pressed record, setting the palm-sized machine in between the two of us.

"Okay, please tell me where you were born and what year."

"I was born in 1709 in London."

I ticked off the first question on the pad of paper with a red "x." "Were you from a well-to-do family?"

He smiled. "Yes, Sweet, very well to do. My father was a prominent Tory and very respected."

"When were you turned into a vampire?"

"On my twentieth birthday, my dearest friend introduced me to a harlot named Meg."

Wait a second. "You're twenty?" I asked incredulously.

Bram chuckled. "No, Sweet, I'm soon to celebrate my three hundredth year."

"I meant, you were twenty when you were turned?" He nodded as I shook my head. "You just look much older than that ..."

He laughed again. "Times were different then, Sweet ... nutrition wasn't what it is today, and London was ... not what it is today."

I glanced up and found Trey lumbering toward us. He took a seat next to Bram and put his elbows on the table so they could cradle his enormous head. "Wow, twenty?" Trey asked, suddenly finding Bram more interesting than Pamela Anderson.

Bram arched a brow in my direction. "Next question, Sweet."

I glanced at Knight, who was also studying us. As soon as he caught my attention, he pretended to be absorbed in whatever show he hadn't been watching.

"Can you tell me what happened when you were changed?" I asked.

"Meg happened to be a vampire, and while I was taking full advantage of her body ..." He eyed me up and down, and I just shook my head, "she was lapping up my blood. Before I could realize what was happening, I was nearly drained. When I saw what she was, I made the decision not to go down without a fight. Weak as I felt, I managed to unsheathe a dagger I kept on my person, and I slit her wrist."

Trey's head nearly fell out of his hands. "Holy goblin's nuts. Did you kill her?"

Bram shook his head. "No, but I forced her wrist into my mouth and sealed my own destiny. Looking back on it, I did not force her to do anything—she was much stronger than I. She knew what she was doing."

Hmm, this Meg character sounded interesting. Interesting enough to be the heroine of my book? "This woman ..." I started. "What became of her?"

"She disappeared. I had heard she had been killed by another vampire, but I do not know for certain."

"So you wouldn't be able to answer particulars about her?"

He shook his head and frowned. "I thought your book was about me, Sweet?"

I nodded. "It is, but I thought she sounded interesting as a ... heroine."

Bram slowly smiled. "I prefer the idea of the fairy love interest."

A definite scoff came from Knight's direction, but I ignored it. "I never said there was going to be a fairy in it," I grumbled but ticked off the last question on my sheet.

Then I eyed the question I'd always wanted to ask Bram. "Okay, about your name," I started.

Bram sighed. "I was born long before the author of Dracula was even a thought," he said, sounding very put out. "For all I know, Mr. Stoker was named for me."

I laughed, thinking Bram's narcissism knew no bounds. "Well, that puts the lid on a mystery I'd wondered about since I met you."

The phone rang, and Trey grabbed it. Holy Hades, it was like he was my permanent roommate or something.

He handed the phone to me.

Before I could say hello, Dagan's voice interrupted me. "Gotta a little red filly here I think you want to meet."

Before I could reply, he hung up.

FIFTEEN

After promising Bram a favor, which I really didn't want to do, he agreed to stay with Trey as Knight and I headed for Dagan's. Trey probably would've been fine on his own, considering the creature was at Dagan's, but it's always better to be prepared, and who knew if whoever was controlling the creature might still be after Trey.

"Dulcie, whatever happens tonight, you need to go with it," Knight said in a hard voice.

"What's that supposed to mean?" I asked, being careful not to pull my attention from the road. Driving and arguing were not a good mix.

He shrugged and strained against the leather vest I'd created for him. I was sporting a red vinyl bodysuit that was confining as all hell. This costume stuff was really getting tiring.

"It just means that last time we went to Dagan's, you weren't a good actress. Put on a better show this time."

My fingers tightened around the steering wheel. "So what, if you try to have sex with me, I'm just supposed to let you?"

Knight chuckled. "Desperate times call for desperate measures."

"You're impossible."

The smirk dropped off his lips and imagining some serious topic was about to rear its unwanted head, I returned my attention to the red light before me.

"Just follow my lead," he said. "You know I don't want to put you in an uncomfortable situation, but you need to trust me."

I couldn't remember the last time I'd trusted anyone. Maybe Sam, but that was about it.

I sighed, long and hard.

"It's an order, Dulcie, let me handle this."

I inhaled deeply. One, breathe out. Two, breathe in. Three … I so missed Quillan's mode of management. Knight was more a dictator than a boss.

I pulled into Payne's parking lot and turned off the car, refusing to even glance at Knight. I opened the door and dropped to my feet. My five inch hooker heels clicked against the asphalt, sounding like someone chewing gum with a broken jaw.

Knight grabbed my arms and made me face him. I couldn't help the gasp that lodged in my throat. I forced my eyes to hold his which were roiling with excitement. So Knight enjoyed his work? I guess the same could be said for me. Though, I wasn't exactly climaxing to have to share the spotlight with him.

"Trust me, Dulcie, I don't want to see you hurt."

I just nodded, repressing the urge to battle him. His hands lingered on my arms a bit longer than necessary before I shrugged out of his embrace and started for the back door. Who the hell did he think he was? I could take care of myself.

I buzzed the speaker box.

"He's in room one," the voice announced, and the door opened.

Knight grabbed my hand and stepped in front of me, guiding me down the dark hallway. I swallowed a protest and steeled myself for the fact that I'd be taking orders tonight. Even if Knight was my boss's boss, I couldn't say it softened the fact.

Knight dropped my hand and weaved through the intricate passageways of Payne like he had a demon-locating compass. When we reached the first door, Knight hesitated, his hand clenching the doorknob. "Are you ready?" he whispered.

I nodded, and he opened the door. It was darker inside the room than it was in the hallway, and the smell of smoke trailed through the air, splashed by the scent of vanilla candle.

A moan interrupted the quiet, and Knight closed the door behind us.

"Ah, our guests have arrived," Dagan said, his voice coming from the farthest corner of the room.

There was a soft swoosh, and a flame appeared, brilliant in the dark. The orb of light cast shadows across Dagan's face, causing his usual scary looks to appear all the more menacing. With an eerie grin, he held the candle high.

"Dulcie, how good of you to come." He glanced at Knight. "And I see you've brought your bodyguard."

I inhaled, reminding myself I needed to be a good actress. "Dagan, sorry we're late."

He rested the candle in a silver holder and held a match up to it, the match igniting as soon as it kissed the flame. He brought the burning match to a candelabra, and lit the four remaining candles. Walking the candelabra closer to us, like a butler escorting us through a haunted house, he set it on a shelf next to me. It lit the entire room in a yellow glow that danced against the walls, like a myriad of undulating ghosts.

My eyes fell past Dagan and landed on the creature that lay sprawled against a velvet covered sofa, the candle wax cooling and hardening on her torso. She was completely naked except for a pair of high heels. Wiggling against the sofa, she acted as though the wax were tickling rather than burning her. Sensing my attention, she glanced up and smiled at me. Then she stood, and her exaggerated heels made her as tall as Knight.

The green-eyed monster known as Jealousy sunk its fangs into my otherwise sensible constitution, and I wanted to kick myself. She was beautiful. Her breasts were heavy and her waist tiny, flaring into broad hips with long, graceful legs. She looked like she'd just walked off a Victoria's Secret catwalk. I had to remind myself she'd eaten Fabian, Guy and Tad without a second thought.

Only inches from me, she paused and ran a long fingernail against my cheek as I shuddered internally. "You've brought the beautiful fairy for me to play with," she whispered to Dagan.

He just laughed, the bastard. The creature turned from me and let her gaze run down Knight's incredible body.

"Your lady is very," she glanced at me again, "sexy."

Knight's voice was low and controlled. "I know."

"Will you share her?" the creature asked, like I was a bag of M&Ms.

My eyes immediately found Knight's, and in their steel depths, they promised protection. I had to trust him. Much as I didn't want to, I had to.

"Will Dagan share you?" he asked, and my heart deflated as if it'd been stuck with a needle.

He's acting, Dulcie! I reprimanded myself. *It's all an act, you moron!*

The woman laughed a high and harmonious sound. My hands fisted. The incredible desire to arrest her right there nearly defeated my more sensible inclinations. If we were to arrest her, it would destroy any chance we had of finding her keeper. Whoever had called her from the Netherworld still owned her. Even if that meant death, she wouldn't reveal who her master was anytime soon. We'd have to do it the old-fashioned way and follow her. Which meant I was probably going to be here for a very long time.

So exactly how much acting would I need to do? And how far would it go? If this creature intended to bed one or both of us, could I go through with it? Could Knight? How much did I want to apprehend her master?

Dagan came up behind her. "Shall we give them a show?" he asked with a sibilant hiss.

She nodded, a slow, mysterious smile spreading over her face. I almost gasped when I felt Knight take my arm and pull me into the hard length of his chest. He grabbed my hair and shifted it over one side of my neck, his finger accidentally grazing my breast. My heart caught in my throat, and I swallowed hard. He wrapped his arm around me and pulled me against him, as if to remind me that I wasn't in this alone, that he was there with me.

Dagan pushed the creature back onto the sofa. With a leer, he turned to the corner of the room, opening what looked like a cupboard. Inside were paddles, whips, chains and other things I couldn't begin to categorize.

My heart started up again.

He approached her with a long piece of chain with clamps at both ends. The creature's breath caught, as she arched her back in excitement. Dagan ran the chain across her throat and over each of her breasts as she moaned. Then he pinched her nipples until they stood at attention. With a low chuckle, he clamped them.

Dagan eyed me over his shoulder and smiled. It was then that I realized he'd saved all of this for me. He could've easily done what he'd wanted with her and then called us. But no, he wanted me to suffer through it. He was probably enjoying my misery more than anything else. The fiery breath of anger cascaded over my skin, but I refused to grant it power.

Damn Dagan to Hades.

He jerked on the clamp chain, and the creature stumbled to her feet. Then he walked her to the cabinet and pulled out a paddle. He ran the paddle down her stomach. Grabbing her hair roughly, he yanked her head back and ran his tongue down her neck. With a vicious shove, he pushed her over the sofa, forcing her head into the pillows.

Then he turned to face me, and I wished he'd just finish his show. The creature moaned out as if to say she agreed with me.

170

"Shut up," Dagan growled, and a tremor of fear wound itself in my gut. His eyes were on me.

I leaned up against Knight, but I was already so close to him, I couldn't possibly get any closer. Dagan dropped the paddle on the sofa next to the creature and turned toward me. His eyes burned with delight.

"Dulcie, Dulcie," he whispered and caressed my jaw line with his finger, leaving my skin stinging in his wake. Knight grabbed my waist and tightened his grip as if to remind me I needed to trust him and more so, that I better not blow our cover.

Dagan only stopped advancing when his nose was millimeters from mine. His lower body pressed into me like we were Siamese twins. He brought both hands to my shoulders and never took his eyes from mine as he reached for my breasts. He plied them with his fingertips as I gritted my teeth to keep from throwing him off me.

He chuckled and brought one hand lower still, trailing from one side of my stomach to the other like a driver on a winding road. When it looked like he was going to push his fingers between my thighs, Knight's hand blocked his before I had the chance.

Dagan dropped his hand with a grin and returned to the creature who was impatiently awaiting him. He grabbed the paddle and whacked her four times. When he pulled the paddle away, her ass bore the red marks, but she was sighing as if he were pampering her, not beating her.

Bile filled my throat. I didn't know how much more of this I could take. But it appeared the night was young. There still hadn't been any sex. Hades be damned.

"Blood," the woman muttered and grabbed my attention.

Dagan smacked her with the paddle again, then dropped it on the sofa beside her and grabbed her hair, jerking her up. She turned to face him, and he crushed his mouth against hers. I dropped my eyes, wishing this night would end.

171

"Blood," the creature said again.

Dagan returned to the prop closet and produced a small dagger. At the sight of the weapon, I bucked. Knight held me against him until I felt like I was stuck in dried cement.

Dagan walked back to the creature and held the weapon just above her collar bone. With a slow sweep, he cut a straight line through her skin. The woman cried out in ecstasy as her blood poured from the wound, trailing down over her breasts to her stomach.

Knight shifted me to the side and approached them, his eyes riveted on the blood trailing down her body. Before I could even guess his intentions, he ran his hand through the red liquid.

My stomach churned. What the hell was he doing? I shivered in spite of myself and wondered if she had somehow bewitched him? But no, I would've felt her magic had she tried. Maybe Knight liked the sight of blood? It wasn't like I knew that much about him. Maybe he was as psychotic as they were.

The creature grabbed Knight's hand and held it to her breast, encouraging him to continue rubbing her. But he pulled away from her, the strangest of expressions on his face—like he'd been caught rubbing the blood of a brutal killer all over her breasts.

His eyes settled on mine, and he strode across the room, looking like a plundering Titan. I plastered myself against the wall, fighting the incredible need to vacate the room. Then it occurred to me, what if Knight was working with the creature?

Maybe Dagan was in on it too? If so, I was as good as dead. The more I thought about it, the more it made sense. My heart hammered in my chest until the creature's moans were drowned out by the blood throbbing in my ears.

I'd been such a fool, keeping all of this from Quillan, trusting Knight as blindly as a mole. And his A.N.C. ID? That had been real—there was no way it'd been a fake. So Knight

172

had the A.N.C. office tricked just as easily as he'd duped me. I guess we'd all fallen for his charismatic charm.

I shrunk against the wall. Knight's face was one of a statue, his eyes emotionless. Hades be damned, he was the creature's master, he had to be! It had been right under my nose all along and I'd been too distracted to see it.

With his clean hand, he pulled me against him. I shoved him aside, wanting nothing more than to let him know I'd figured out his little plan. But if I did that, I might not be leaving this room—alive anyway.

Knight resumed his place against the wall and positioned me in front of him. I'm sure he was getting miles out of forcing me to watch his little pet play with Dagan and after that, he'd probably order her to eat me. For now, I'd just play along. But when the opportunity arose, I'd be ready for them. I knew I could take the creature; my magic was strong enough. But Dagan and Knight?

I'd definitely be out-numbered and my magic out-powered.

"I need to taste you," the woman moaned to Dagan.

Before I could comprehend what the hell that meant, he grabbed the knife and handed it to her. She grasped it in her bloody hand and ripped a line across his muscular chest. Blood spurted out angrily, erupting into a volcano of red. She thrust her face into him, sucking and licking at the gash with uninhibited abandon.

That's when I snapped.

Demon blood is extremely potent and powerful. If humans drink it, it makes them stronger, faster and longer lived. If a creature of the Netherworld drank it ...

"What the fuck are you doing?" my voice blurted out before I could stop it.

Knight's vice-like grip around my waist didn't prevent me from attempting to attack Dagan, intent on doing any sort of bodily injury I could manage. But first, I'd have to wrench the creature from his chest.

173

I didn't get far before Knight grabbed me around the waist and pushed me back against the wall. He wrapped his hands around my throat, holding me immobile. Gritting my teeth, I raked my fingernails into the skin on his hands. He didn't even flinch.

Instead, a slow smile spread across his lips. "Don't mind her, she gets jealous."

The creature continued licking Dagan's chest, but Dagan was focused on me. His eyes threatened murder in no uncertain terms.

Okay, I'd basically just blown my cover and probably Dagan's and Knight's—if they were, in fact, not involved with the creature. But at this point, I couldn't say I cared. All I knew was Dagan was nurturing the creature with his blood which meant the job of taking her down was going to be a hell of a lot harder.

With renewed determination, I clawed at Knight's forearms. He glared at me with the promise of retribution.

He suddenly let go. I slumped back against the wall, sucking in a gulp of air. Knight didn't glance back, but continued to stare at me. "I'm sorry, but I think my little hell-cat here has had enough for the evening."

The creature laughed and continued sucking at Dagan. Meanwhile, Knight latched onto my arm and forced me out the door. He slammed it shut, and dragged me through the club as if I were a two-year-old having a tantrum.

"Let go!" I demanded and glared into his steely eyes, awaiting the detonation of his fury.

He gave me a shove out the back door and I tripped over my ridiculous heels, falling to the ground as embarrassment claimed my cheeks. It was bad enough Knight was fuming at me but I had to go and demonstrate the fact that I was less than accustomed to high-heeled footwear.

"Get in the car," he grumbled.

174

I stood up and shook off my embarrassment—it wouldn't do me any good. "I'm not going anywhere with you."

"Don't make me lose my temper."

"I've had enough of you and your orders," I snapped, wiping the asphalt crumbs from my palms.

Knight balled his hands into fists as he approached the Wrangler, pulling my keys from the exhaust pipe. I'd put them there since I had no pockets. He unlocked the driver's side door and pulled the seat back, slamming the door as he started the car.

"Where do you think you're going?" I asked, livid that he'd taken it upon himself to steal my car.

"Either get in now, or I'm leaving you here."

I stormed to the passenger door and threw myself into the moving car as he peeled into the street. "You have some nerve," I started.

Knight shook his head. "I don't have the patience to deal with you now. You just blew any chance we had of nabbing the creature." He glanced at me, and his eyes were filled with a rage I'd never seen before. It intimidated me a little.

"As if you have any interest in catching the creature," I snapped. He faced me and I continued railing at him. "I'm onto your little plan, Knight. I know you're the creature's real master."

He hit the brakes so hard, I banged my forehead on the dashboard. Not enjoying the feeling, I pushed myself back into the seat and put on my seat belt.

"What did you just say?" he said in a low, dismal tone.

Although it probably was going to be the last mystery I solved, I couldn't help but gloat. I'd figured out his little plan as easy as you please. I was no fool. "I know you're the keeper of the creature. I figured it out tonight."

He laughed, and it was a caustic sound. "You are an idiot."

175

"Don't pretend you aren't," I said, ignoring the "idiot" part. "And that incident with the creature's blood was really great, by the way. So let's get this over and done with. Stop the car."

He laughed again. "You want to fight me? You know where that got you last time."

"Well, I doubt you're going to just let me take you into custody, are you?"

He shook his head. "Nope, I'm not."

He took a left at the first street we encountered, and I faced a long alley of nothing but trees on one side and the county dump on the other. Perfect for our needs. He parked the car and opened the door, dropping the keys on the seat.

"Come on, then," he said.

I opened my door and exchanged my ridiculous heels for sneakers with just a thought and some fairy dust. Okay, so a red cat suit and white sneakers didn't exactly go together but what did I care? I'd probably be too dead to worry about it soon enough.

Knight had already made his way into a clearing between the trees, and he'd thrown his leather vest to the ground. He stood naked except for a pair of black jeans and a grimace.

"Come and get me, Dulcie."

I couldn't entirely rely on my physical abilities or I'd be dead, Knight being way stronger than I. And he couldn't be entirely immune to magic; otherwise, I couldn't have dressed him, right? Hopefully the answer was a resounding yes.

I braced myself in front of him and shaking my hand until a mound of fairy dust appeared, I imagined a pair of solid, silver handcuffs. When I felt the cold metal in my hand, I knew what I had to do. "It doesn't have to be like this, Knight. You can come willingly."

He laughed, and in a split second, was on me, pushing me into the ground. I tried to throw him off with a bolt of energy, but he acted like I'd just blown on him. He pushed on

176

my arms until they were immobilized against the dirt. Then he straddled me, holding my legs to the ground until I was as helpless as a turtle on its back.

"I'm not the creature's master, Dulcie."

I squirmed under him, outraged when I realized he wasn't going anywhere. I was a goner. "It all fits, Knight."

"It fits if you're looking for it to fit. Don't throw it on me because you're looking for a scapegoat."

"Then what was that part with you rubbing her blood?" I insisted. Remembering the obscenity, I glanced down at his hand which still bore the red stains. "Or was that just some sick, twisted fantasy of yours?"

He chuckled. "I needed her blood so Sam could do a tracking spell on her. I 'spose you could say I'd guessed the night might not work out exactly like I'd planned. Guess I'm getting to know you well."

Boil his brains for thinking of every possible angle. There was a reason he was such a big wig of the A.N.C. And he hadn't gotten there with his pretty face. Embarrassed though I might have been, I was also relieved to find Knight wasn't the creature's master because I had to face it—I sort of … liked him.

He chuckled, drawing my attention away from my inner monologue. "I believe we've been in exactly this position before. I'll have to ask you again, are you going to behave if I let you up?"

"And I'll have to again say yes," I snapped.

The smile disintegrated from his lips. "I prefer you underneath me anyway."

A thrilling tingle crawled up my spine and wedged itself in my stomach. I knew he was going to kiss me, and I wasn't about to stop him.

His lips were forceful and demanding, almost lacking in tenderness. I wrapped my arms around his neck and welcomed his tongue, meeting it with my own thrust for thrust. He pounded his pelvis against me and kissed me even harder. The fingers from one hand entangled themselves in my hair while his other hand tiptoed down my neck and chest until it found my breast. He teased the hardened flesh of my already erect nipple through the vinyl of my cat suit as I arched underneath him.

I palpated my fingers across his chest, reveling in the ridges of valleys and mountains of his abdomen. I paused above the scar that ran the length of his chest.

He pulled himself from me, and I licked my lips, savoring every last taste of him.

"I hope you killed whoever did this to you," I said as I traced the scar.

He chuckled and pushed his pelvis into me once more, as if trying to draw more attention to the bulge in his pants. He didn't need to. "Yes, Dulce, he's long gone."

He hovered above me, just watching me. I didn't know what to say or do. Anxiety welled within my stomach when it seemed he might kiss me again and I pushed myself out from underneath him, suddenly scared to death that we'd gone as far as we had.

Knight chuckled. "And where do you think you're going?"

I didn't know. All I did know was that I had to get away from him—I couldn't handle the anxiety pounding through my veins but I also didn't want him to know that.

"We shouldn't be doing this. What would the Relations Office think?" It was the only excuse I could think of.

"You're not my employee."

Damn. "I, uh, I'm just not …"

"You really know how to ruin a good moment, don't you?" he interrupted and stood up, starting for the Wrangler.

"You'll thank me later," I said, but Knight just shook his head and tossed me the keys.

SIXTEEN

Launching myself up my front stairwell, I opened the door to find Bram and Trey sitting side by side on the sofa, watching *Nosferatu*.

I couldn't find the wherewithal to come up with a snide remark.

"Sweet, you have returned," Bram said with a leer while his eyes traversed me from head to toe. "And what a sight you are."

He stood up and approached me, extending his hand as if he wanted to run it down the red vinyl covering my torso. I dismissed him with a wave. "Not now, Bram, I have work to do."

I grabbed the phone, about to dial Sam, then realized I really didn't want Bram hanging around for the rest of the evening. Not when it involved A.N.C. business. Neither, for that matter, would Knight. And he'd be way less polite about it.

"Bram, thanks for watching Trey, but I can take care of things from here."

He bowed, his fangs just cresting his lip as his eyes still danced with unabated lust. "I am happy to assist you, Sweet." He paused. "Do not forget the favor you owe me."

I nodded, knowing I wasn't about to forget it anytime soon. Hot Hades, it wasn't good to owe favors to anyone, let alone Bram. "Yeah, I won't forget."

"Well, I see you are busy." He motioned toward the door. "Shall I show myself out?"

"Yeah, thanks," I said as I dialed Sam's number.

"Bye, Bram, cool movie, man," Trey said, extending his bent knuckles like he thought he and Bram were gang brothers.

I didn't hear or see Bram's response, but I did notice the less-than-pleasant salutation offered by Knight and the equally less-than-polite response offered by Bram. Men ...

"Hello?" Sam said groggily.

"Sam, I need a big favor."

"Dulce, what time is it?"

I checked my watch. "Two in the morning. Can you come over? I need you to do a locating spell."

"Right now?" she squeaked in a hoarse voice.

"Yeah, Knight has the creature's blood on his hand, but he isn't sure how long it will last."

"Oh, wow," Sam's voice perked up. "Okay, give me a little time to get my stuff together."

"Thanks, Sam."

"Yeah, yeah."

I hung up and turning toward the living room, discovered Trey gawking with horror at Knight who stood in his black pants, the red blood staining his hand.

"What the heck happened to you guys?" Trey asked, fear trembling just beneath his bravado.

I shook my head. "It's a really long story."

An hour later, Sam arrived, carrying a brown leather satchel of potion ingredients. Her hair was in a ponytail, and she plodded into the house still wearing pajama pants and a sweatshirt. The expression on her face wasn't welcoming, rather, it screamed: *I want to get the hell back to sleep.*

"Hi, Sam," I said apologetically.

"Hi, Dulce." Then she glanced at Knight and Trey. "Guys."

They both said hello, and I followed Sam to the kitchen table where she unloaded her bag of tricks—a stone bowl, a wooden spoon and two vials of ... something.

"We'll need four people for the spell to work," Sam said.

"Then we'll have to use Trey," I answered, more to Knight than anyone else. He just nodded.

Sam faced him. "Where is the blood?"

He held up his hand.

She narrowed her eyes and frowned. "Might be too old, but we can try."

"Should we rinse it into a glass or something?" I asked.

Sam shook her head. "No, that will dilute the power of the blood, and the chlorine could kill any chance we have of making it work. Nope, the best thing is to see if we can scrape some of it off." She held his palm and rotated it, as if searching for the largest smear specimen on the top of his hand. "Looks like some is caught under your fingernails; that might be the best sample." Sam paused, then glanced at me. "Dulce, can you get a knife, and see if you can shave some of the blood off him?"

I frowned, that sounded painful. Thankfully it wasn't my hand. "Yeah, okay."

"Make sure you don't cut him. That'll ruin the spell, and we'll just end up tracking him."

I nodded and went for the smallest knife in my selection. When I approached Knight, I held it up with as wicked a smile as I could manage. He just shook his head.

"Hold his hand over the stone bowl, and try to get as many decent scrapings as you can. First, try under the fingernails."

Knight followed me to the kitchen table. He held his hand over the stone bowl, and I took hold of it, trying to ignore the feelings of pleasure that visited me at his warm touch.

"Proceed with caution," he said in a deep voice.

"What can I do?" Trey asked, moving forward. "And who are you trying to track?"

"Never mind," I answered.

Knight shook his head and whispered. "I'll take care of it later. You can tell him."

Thinking that sounded pretty ominous, I didn't respond, but Sam did.

"We're trying to track the creature, Trey. I'll need you in a second, but for now, just sit tight."

"Over and out," Trey said and returned to the couch, dropping himself into it as if all the bones in his body had just collapsed.

I rotated Knight's hand, trying to figure out the best way to get under his nails without slicing off the tip of his finger. After acquiring an adequate angle, I took the small paring knife and carved out whatever I could from beneath his nails. A few dark bits of blood drifted into the stone bowl. When I couldn't get any more, I turned his hand over to shave off the remaining blood.

"Use the back of the knife, not the blade," he said.

I glanced at him and grinned. "Why, are you scared?"

He paused a moment before returning the smile. "Yes."

I laughed and flipped the knife, shaving the dried stain with it. More crusty blood flaked into the stone bowl until it looked like a small mound of red dandruff.

"That's probably enough," Sam said as she inspected my work.

Knight pulled his hand from mine and started for the sink, washing his hands twice.

Sam grabbed the wooden spoon from the table top and a vial of something that looked like pink lemonade. She poured the entire contents of the vial into the blood bowl and began stirring, inspecting it for who knew what.

The stuff in the bowl didn't do anything—the blood just disappeared into the pink lemonade liquid and that was that.

"Dulce, there should be a pH test kit in the bag, can you get it for me?"

I shuffled through her bag until I found the rectangular sheets of paper.

"Just dip the end of one into the potion," Sam said.

I did as I was told, and the paper went from white to a deep purple.

"Flap it around like you're drying a Polaroid photo."

I obeyed and flapped it. It didn't change color.

"Great, now you just have to drink it," she said with a smirk.

"Drink it?" I repeated, my stomach churning at the thought.

"Sure, how do you think you're going to be able to find the creature without taking some of it into yourself?"

"Please tell me you're joking." I backed away, shaking my head. "I'm not drinking that."

Knight faced me. "It's either you or me."

That was easy. "You."

Sam's smile beamed wider. "Actually, you both have to drink it ... if you want it to work right. Besides, don't both of you want to be able to track the thing?"

I couldn't argue. Sam opened my cupboard and produced two juice glasses. There wasn't that much potion in the stone bowl, so we'd each just have a gulp, probably. Okay, I could handle that. Disgusting, yes, but doable all the same.

Sam ladled out two equal portions and placed the glasses before us. Then she turned to Trey, who was still riveted by *Nosferatu*. "Trey, I need you now."

He nodded, his attention still stuck on the screen, even as he made his way toward us. "What do I do?" he asked.

Sam took his arm and positioned him between Knight and me. She stood next to Knight so we were all surrounding the kitchen table like the wise men bringing gifts to baby Jesus. Only our gifts weren't gold, frankincense and myrrh, but nasty creature juice.

Just then, the phone rang. "Should I get it?" I asked Sam, not wanting to appear rude.

"Yeah, go ahead."

183

Wondering who the hell could be calling me at this hour, I lifted the phone. "Hello?"

"You have some nerve coming here and asking for my help and then nearly blowing the whole fucking thing!" Dagan roared.

I gulped down an acid response. "I already got an earful." I glanced at Knight—I'd gotten a lot more than an earful.

"You're lucky I don't come down there and show you what I really think of you."

"Is that a threat?" I asked, my temper thinning. Threatening a Regulator was not a good idea, even if I had royally screwed up.

"No, it'll be a promise if you ever embarrass me like that again. Luckily for you, I was able to convince my guest that you were just a silly, jealous idiot and not some incompetent cop."

I frowned. "Is that all you have to say?"

"Don't show your face around here for a while. I won't be held responsible for my actions if you do."

Yeah, I'd say that was a threat. "Speaking of being responsible, Dagan, why the hell did you let her drink your blood? And don't even start by telling me you don't know what a demon's blood will do to whoever drinks it."

He chuckled, long and hard. "There aren't any laws against me sharing my blood."

No, there weren't. He did it purely to make my job harder. "You asshole," I seethed. I slammed the phone down before he had the chance and turned to face the others, who regarded me with undisguised curiosity. I shrugged. "Dagan's just pissed off with me, that's all."

Sam nodded, like it wasn't news, and motioned for me to resume my place with a cock of her head. "Okay, now Knight, er Todd ..." she glanced at Knight sheepishly.

"It's okay," he said.

Trey didn't even notice.

"Okay," Sam started up again. "You and Dulcie need to drink the potion and then grab the hand of the person next to you as quickly as you can. Trey, you and I need to focus on containing them."

"What?" I asked, stiffening. "Containing us?"

"That's why we need four people. Well, really, we could've used more but four will do. When you take a creature into yourself, you adopt some of its mannerisms, and if it's a violent beast, then the same can be said for you."

I dropped her hand. "You mean to tell me that Knight might end up having some of the creature's ... tendencies in him?"

Sam nodded, a nervous smile on her lips.

I sighed. "So we might have a six-foot-four monster on our hands? Built like that?" I said, pointing at his chest. He just grinned. Bastard.

"Well, you might have a bad reaction, too," Sam said.

I shook my head, not concerned about myself—I'd be more like trying to contain an enraged mosquito; it was the potential Frankenstein in the corner that worried me. "Maybe this isn't such a good idea."

"It's the only chance we have," Knight interrupted. "I can control myself, and I can control you."

I frowned at that less than humble announcement and took Sam's hand again. "For Sam's and Trey's sakes, you'd better be right."

Knight disregarded me and faced Sam. "How long will this spell last?"

Sam was silent as she considered the question. "Well, if the creature does rub off on you, in terms of habits, those usually last maybe a day or so. As far as being able to track the creature, you'll probably have about two weeks."

"That should be plenty of time," Knight said. He picked up his glass of nasty libation and regarded me with a smile. I grasped mine and watched Sam take Trey's hand, hesitation in her eyes. Trey was eyeing the wretched juice as if he wanted some.

"Cheers!" Knight said and downed his. I was quick to follow. Then I plastered my hand into Sam's and Trey's. At first nothing happened. But then, I thought I was going to explode.

Searing pain shot through me, like someone was shredding my insides. Unable to continue standing up, I started to collapse to the floor but Sam and Trey fought to keep me upright. My blurry eyes found Knight's face. His eyes were shut tight against the pain as he leaned against the wall.

I wailed out against the agony as tears streamed down my face. Trying to tear my hands from Trey and Sam's tight grasp was next to impossible and finally, when I knew I couldn't handle anymore, it stopped.

I caved into the floor as soon as Trey and Sam released me.

Sam hovered over me, her expression pinched. "Well, now we know who can hold their potions."

I looked at Knight who seemed to regard me with amusement—a raised brow and broad grin. There didn't seem to be any sign of the creature in him. Just the same cocky bastard he always was. As for me, I couldn't say I felt any creature stirring within me either.

"Why didn't you tell me it would feel like that?" I demanded.

Sam held out her hand and helped me to my feet. "Because you never would have agreed to take it."

I frowned. "So how does this spell work anyway? I don't feel any different."

Sam shook her head. "You and Knight need to focus on wanting to track the creature. You have to awaken the spell for it to work."

"So what will we see?" I insisted.

Sam smirked. "Why don't you try it?"

"Okay, what do we do?"

"It helps if you're close together. Now focus on one another's eyes. Then inside your mind, call to the creature, make it show you where it is."

Knight stood before me, a slight smile playing with his lips. I faced him and gazed into his eyes, trying to call the creature, but the only image in my mind was how hard Knight had been when laying on me in the woods. I closed my eyes, hoping the darkness of my eyelids would dispatch memories of Knight and his erection.

Luckily, I saw the creature. And it wasn't the redhead at all. It was hideous in its natural state—oafish and bulky with red body hair that covered its entirety. Its face was flat, two huge, yellow and round eyes peered from its head. It didn't appear to have a nose, but its mouth was full of teeth that looked like they belonged to a tiger shark. It was hunched over, its back making a perfect half circle. It dug its teeth into the carcass of what looked like a rodent, macerating the small animal in the same way it must have done to Fabian, Tad and Guy. I was suddenly ill.

Victoria's Secret catwalk? Ha, not on your life.

"Where is it, Dulce?" Knight whispered.

I pulled my attention from the creature and noticed its surroundings. High ceilings and broken windows, cement floors with puddles of Hades only knew what. The whole place was dark and drafty. "The abandoned warehouse on Magnolia," I whispered, opening my eyes. "Let's go after it."

I started for the door, but Knight grabbed my arms, chuckling as he did so.

"It will be morning soon, Dulce, and shape-shifters are like vampires—they don't operate in the day. Its master isn't going to call it tonight. From here on out, we track it every evening."

I nodded, silently pleased I wouldn't have to do any more detective work tonight. Hey, I was tired.

Knight faced Sam. "Thank you, Sam, you are some witch." She beamed. "I hope you understand I'll have to swear you to secrecy, Relations Office orders."

I rolled my eyes. Damn, Knight and his Relations Office orders.

"I understand," Sam said simply.

"One more thing," Knight started before glancing at Trey, who'd returned to watching TV. "He can't remember what went on today."

"What the hell does that mean?" I insisted, thinking Knight was putting a hit out on Trey or something.

Sam smiled. "It means he wants me to give Trey a forgetting potion."

Oh, well that was better than killing him. Sam rummaged through her bag. "Dulce, do you have any chocolate syrup or anything?" she asked.

I shook my head. "I think Knight got some maple syrup but that's all we have."

Sam glanced at Trey and then nodded. "Yeah, he'll like that."

I grabbed the maple syrup and handed it to her. She fished inside her satchel and produced a vial of what looked like tea. "What's that?" I asked.

"Forget tea. It'll wash his short-term memories right out of his head."

"And you just carry that around with you?" I asked with a smirk.

"I came prepared." She laughed. "Can you boil some water?"

I grabbed a saucer. Filling it with water, I threw it on the stove and turned on the flame.

"Pour a little syrup in it. The tea can be tart."

I nodded and squeezed the syrup over the saucer until the liquid turned a caramel brown. Once it started boiling, Sam put the tea into a metal sifter and plopped it into the syrup water. After a few seconds, she removed it with a

196

spoon. Grabbing a mug, she poured the tea and handed it to me.

I carried it into the living room and presented it to Trey. "Drink this."

He willingly accepted it, blowing on it wetly before he brought it to his lips. "Mmm, takes like syrup."

I just smiled as I walked back to Sam, who was packing all her things into the grocery bag.

"Well, looks like my job here is done."

"Thanks, Sam." I said.

She started for the door, Knight and I right behind her. Her gaze drifted to Trey, who was sipping the tea like I'd told him. "He'll sleep like a baby tonight," she said with a little grin.

I shut and locked the door behind her. Then, crossing my arms against my chest, I thought about how tired I was. I sure as hell didn't need Knight's half naked body next to mine. I'd never be able to sleep. "Trey," I said as he glanced at me. "You're sleeping in my room tonight." Then I addressed the unimpressed Knight. "You get the couch."

SEVENTEEN

$\mathbf{K}$night was asleep on the couch, and Trey was at work. I was also working—on my Bram novel and getting closer to finishing it day by day. This Relations-Office-imposed hiatus was great for writing my novel, even if it was a bummer to no longer be on the team. And I missed Quillan, so what? I was disappointed he hadn't stopped over or called since discovering Knight was living with me.

I pushed thoughts of Quillan out of my mind. It wasn't my fault he was too proud or too whatever to continue our friendship. It was out of my control, and things out of your control should be left alone 'cause there isn't a damned thing you can do about them.

I finished chapter twelve with a smile and stretched my limbs, eyeing my outline. I had four more chapters to write, then I'd be finished.

The sound of Knight shifting on the sofa captured my attention, and I glanced over just as he threw a pen at me. It landed at my feet, with a tiny thud.

"Do you have to type so loud?" he muttered and crossed his arms behind his head. The blanket covering him shifted until it was only concealing his bottom half. A brown nipple appeared to be winking at me.

I threw the pen back, and it landed just beside his head. I wished I had better aim. "If you don't like it, go back to your hotel."

"You should be happy I'm forfeiting a comfortable hotel room to sleep on your uncomfortable couch to make sure you're safe," he said and shook his head. Sitting up, he threw me an unamused frown. The blanket dropped from around him, revealing his hunter-green boxers. With a groan, he hoisted himself to his feet and headed for my bedroom.

"I'm sleeping in here," he mumbled. "I don't care if you don't like it."

Actually, I did like it. Let him box himself up in my bedroom so I could actually get more work done. It was a hell of a lot better than having to feign disinterest in his half-clothed body.

I sighed, thinking I should be asleep, also, but I wasn't tired. Last night was the third night we'd spent camped outside the abandoned warehouse on Magnolia Street, or snooping outside Dagan's club—wherever the creature went, we went. But unfortunately, in those three nights, the creature hadn't been summoned by its master even once. And the spell's expiration date of two weeks loomed over us like a tornado.

I just shook my head and reread the notes Bram had left me when we'd put Trey under his less-than-thrilled but watchful eye. The notes were really three pages of anecdotes and stories from his life written in an impressive hand. I found myself admiring the curlicues and tendrils of what looked like calligraphy. Hmm, I wouldn't have thought Bram would have such nice writing. Then I remembered how ancient he was, and I found myself sorely wishing I could've learned eighteenth century graphology in grammar school.

The notes were so detailed, I didn't need any more interviews, which was great because it wasn't like I had lots of free time with Knight and Trey living with me.

I glanced at the postscript:

Perhaps these notes will suffice for the remainder of your book. I am not interested in watching the hobgoblin again.

Yours,
Bram

I smiled as I reread the note—at least he was honest. And I couldn't say I blamed him. I was getting mighty sick of guarding Trey, too. And you could throw Knight into that sentiment as well. I couldn't wait for my humble apartment to be mine again.

I shuffled through Bram's notes for at least the fifth time and thought about what a full life he'd led. Three hundred years … it seemed Bram had made good use of it, although I was convinced he'd exaggerated some of the accounts—the claim he was able to overcome two master vampires without suffering any injury to himself, being just one example. Oh, and there was also the amusing little account of his five-some at the Court of Queen Victoria with four of her ladies in waiting ... But other than those embellishments, I had to admit Bram was roguishly entertaining, and his liaisons would provide plenty of fodder for an interesting book. Well, at least I hoped they would.

"I can't sleep," Knight complained as he reappeared in my living room, rubbing his eyes. Apparently, modesty wasn't part of his vocabulary, and he strutted into my room practically naked.

"If you're looking for sympathy, you've come to the wrong person," I said snidely. "I've had less sleep than you."

He grimaced as he lumbered into the kitchen where he reached for a bag of ground Starbucks and poured some water into my Mr. Coffee—a cherished birthday present from Quillan. I decided to fight the urge to think of Quillan again and steered my attention back to Knight, who leaned against the counter, massaging the back of his neck as he waited for the coffee to run its course.

"And for Hades's sake, put on some damned clothes."

Knight chuckled as he performed isometrics on the edge of the counter until his muscles bulged, the show-off. "You appeared to enjoy rubbing your hands across my chest the other night."

He was never going to let me live that night down. This was the sixth time he'd brought it up in the course of three nights and four days. "You talk about it so often, I think you'd like a replay."

Knight grabbed a mug and poured his coffee. Not bothering with cream or sugar, he brought it to his lips and swallowed, the heat of the liquid apparently not bothering him. Hmm, another Loki trait? I felt like I should start keeping a log of all his abilities for future reference.

He nodded. "Just say when."

I grumbled something unintelligible but was interrupted.

"You must've thought about what it would be like," Knight continued and gave me a promising smile.

I laughed and shook my head, standing up. I suddenly found myself tremendously fatigued. In all truth, I was exhausted. Not only by my lack of sleep, but the constant banter with Knight was equally draining. I started for my bedroom, imagining myself in the arms of Morpheus, when it suddenly dawned on me why he was becoming so sexual.

I smirked and stopped in my tracks, turning to face him. "You do realize what's going on here?"

His eyebrows furrowed. "No."

I laughed, pleased to be the one still left untouched by the creature's blood. Apparently fairies were immune to *Kragengen* blood. But the same couldn't be said for Lokis. I took my time before explaining, enjoying every second of the fact that there was finally something I could hold over his head. "The creature is still in your veins, its ... interests haven't dissipated yet."

"Its interests?" he repeated.

My smile expanded. "It's sexual appetite."

He nodded and rubbed the stubble on his chin. "Could be." He shrugged. "I definitely don't feel myself."

"Yeah, no kidding," I chortled.

"What about you?" he interrupted, eyeing me lasciviously.

I shrugged, delighted with the conversation. In fact, I had to admit it was the best conversation Knight and I had ever had. "I feel just fine," I said with a confident grin.

"Oh, is that so?" he asked facetiously, apparently annoyed he was the only one feeling the sexual bug.

My eyes rested on his fingers tapping against the coffee mug. "Don't get any ideas. I saw what turns that fiend on, and I'm not into sadomasochism."

He smirked and placed the mug on the counter, closing in on me until I was backed up against the living room wall. "You should keep an open mind," he said in a subdued voice like he was telling me what the weather was like.

I tried to shake my head, but he kept coming. He stood less than an inch or so away—close enough to run his index finger down the center of my neck, dipping into the depression at the junction of my clavicle bones and down the center of my chest. I gripped his finger before it reached my breast.

"Trey is gone. It's just the two of us," he whispered, as if those words were incentive enough to jump his bewitched bones.

"You're not in the right frame of mind, Knight," I said with a counterfeit smile. "I'd be taking advantage of you."

"I want you to take advantage of me. I'm thinking chains and blindfolds …"

I squared my palms against his chest and thrust him away from me. "Don't push me, Knight, or I'll report you to the Relations Office … possessed as you are or not."

He frowned but his eyes continued to undress me, like he'd never seen a woman before. I glanced down at myself, trying to figure out what was so arresting, but couldn't find the answer. I was wearing a black tank top and short pajama shorts. Damn it all, I'd have to start wearing my winter jammies.

And Knight? He looked like a zombie determined to get my brains. But instead of a brain-besotted zombie, I had a horned out of his mind Loki on my hands. Sometimes life throws little surprises at you and this was definitely one I was going to get miles out of.

"Knight, pull yourself together! If we're going to work together, you've gotta snap out of it!"

Knight and I resumed our usual position of lying in wait on our stomachs, just outside the entrance the creature used to come and go through the warehouse. The cold bite in the air contrasted dramatically with the raw heat emanating from Knight's eyes.

It was midnight, and I'd had enough creature stalking to last me a lifetime. I hadn't slept well as I was afraid Knight was going to try to make a move on me again. Whatever he'd swallowed, his sexual appetite was getting more pronounced by the day, making him as fun to be around as a horny dog who refuses to let go of your leg. It was ironic to think I much preferred the staid, cocky and controlling Knight I'd come to know so well.

The feel of his palm smacking my ass was the last straw. "For Hades's sake, Knight, pay attention to the damned creature!"

"I can't help it!" he groaned and rolled closer to me.

I pushed him away and when he ventured a hand near me again, I smacked it away.

"Hit me again please," he whispered. "Harder."

This was going to be a long night.

I wrenched my eyes from his lusty gaze back to the creature who was in its natural hairy state in the midst of devouring what appeared to be a road kill carcass. From the corner of my eye, I could see Knight still watching me, paying zero attention to the creature. I handed him the binoculars, hoping it would give him something to do.

He held them up and feigned interest in the creature before dropping them to the ground and returning his insistent gaze to me. "You're much nicer to look at," he whispered.

Why the hell did I have to put up with this? "Watch the creature."

"We have time, Dulce, it's not going anywhere," he said, wrapping his arm around me. I pinched it hard and he moaned out. "Again, Dulce, do it again."

Instead, I crawled away from him. "Knight, lay off me. You're going to be very humiliated when you come out of this." I glanced at him with a smile. "And you can bet your ass I'm never going to let you forget it."

I grabbed the binoculars, figuring one of us needed to pay attention to the creature. Refocusing on our subject, I suddenly noticed the creature wasn't in the warehouse.

"Goddammit!" I seethed. "The creature left. Get up, get up."

I got to my feet and sped down the alley, Knight directly behind me. Turning the corner, I nearly lost my footing in some loose gravel and pushed myself against the wall of the warehouse to regain my balance, motioning Knight to do the same.

I peered around the corner and watched the creature, now in its feminine shape, stepping into a dark Ford Explorer. I spotted the Wrangler which was parked maybe forty feet up the street, hidden behind a dumpster.

Once the Ford started down the alley, I bolted for the Wrangler, pulling my keys from my jeans pocket as I did so. Knight was quick behind me. I beeped the alarm off and threw open the door, not waiting to see if Knight was seated. I didn't have time.

I turned the key in the ignition, put it into drive and peeled into the street, madly searching for the black Ford. At the base of the alley, red taillights disappeared over the crest of the hill on Magnolia Street, heading onto Periwinkle Street. Craning my head to the left, there was nothing in sight. Hoping the taillights belonged to the Ford, I followed them.

I caught the Ford at a stop light and suddenly worried the creature might glance behind and recognize us. "Knight, drop down so it can't see you."

He did as I told him, thank God.

I was careful to keep at least two cars between the Ford and myself as we drove down Periwinkle Street and headed for Splendor's city center. When the Ford reached Main Street, it took a left, and I did the same.

The Ford continued down Main Street, approaching Headquarters. When it was about thirty feet from Headquarters, it slowed down and made a left into the parking lot.

"Why the hell are they going to Headquarters?" I asked as I drove past them, not wanting to leave any clues that they were being tailed. Instead, I took the first left onto Penelope Street, and then took another left into the alley that bordered Headquarters. I drove slowly as I navigated around the potholes and trash.

Suddenly, it occurred to me why they might be at Headquarters. The illegal potions that were being stored in the vault. Maybe they hadn't been destroyed on purpose? Maybe these bastards were going after them? The only thing I could wonder is how they would've gotten access. Maybe it was an insider job? But who within the A.N.C had access to the vault? It was basically top secret.

I glanced at Knight. "Hey, who has access to the vault?"

His eyes were closed, his arm out straight as he repeatedly pinched it, writhing in what looked like bliss.

"For Hades's sake, Knight!"

He threw open his eyes and glared at me. "Why do you want to know?"

I shook my head, wanting to keep my reasons to myself. I mean, I didn't have the whole picture yet so no need to fill him on every little detail. "Just curious."

He shrugged. "Anyone management level and above."

"So that means Quillan and you and who else?"

"About a handful of people in the Relations Office."

I turned the headlights off and pulled up to a break in the wall separating the parking lot from the alley. Turning the car off, so as not to attract any attention, I watched the Ford sit idly in the parking lot, but my mind was still on the connection with the A.N.C.

If a handful of people from the A.N.C had access to the vault, maybe one of them was involved? And only Quillan had access within our branch? Hmmm … No, it couldn't be Quillan—I'd worked with him too long and knew him too well. There was no way he was involved. And as far as anyone from the Relations Office in the Netherworld? Well, I'd never met any of them and it's not like the potions went back to the Netherworld—they were destroyed on Headquarters premises.

That left just one person.

Course, I'd thought he was guilty once before and that had resulted in my total humiliation so I wasn't exactly thrilled with playing that card again.

Knight got out of the car, so I followed suit and forced my attention from the facts that seemed to be pointing the finger at Knight to the Ford which was still idling in the parking lot.

No one got out. No one got in. Maybe that killed my theory about the illegal potions and the link with Headquarters? Maybe Headquarters was just backlogged on destroying the street potions? I mean, who knew how reliable the cauldron delivery system was. Maybe my imagination was running away with me … Good thing I hadn't said anything.

198

"Why the hell would they come here?" I whispered, now at a complete loss.

"Because it's the one place where no one would imagine they would," Knight started, looking pained. He crossed his arms against his chest like he was restraining himself. From what, I had to wonder.

I glanced at him and nodded, wondering if he were the criminal in question. "I guess so."

He took a deep breath. "That's exactly why they chose to come here. Because it's safe."

The breath caught in my throat as I watched another car enter the Headquarters lot. This one was a silver Lincoln Town Car. It pulled up behind the Ford and a man I didn't recognize stepped out. I grabbed the binoculars.

Holding them to my eyes, I watched the man. He was stout and short with a mustache and a sinister air about him. He waddled up to the driver's side of the Ford and had a conversation with the driver. I returned my attention to the Town Car when I glimpsed movement in the back seat. There was someone sitting back there but they were covered by the cloak of night.

The stout man inspected the surroundings of the parking lot, as if alerted that someone might be watching them. I instinctively shrunk back, even though there was no way he or anyone else could see Knight and me. We were completely hidden in the alley. The man shook his head and returned to the Town Car. The Ford started for the parking lot exit, the Town Car behind it. Both disappeared into the lamp-less darkness of Main Street.

"Get in the car," I said as I went for the driver's side. I started the car and gunned it until we were out of the alley and following the creature and its master.

EIGHTEEN

I'd managed not to lose the Ford or the Town Car, and Knight and I were now following them out of the city center and toward the town of Estuary on Highway One. The farther we ventured from Splendor, the fewer cars on the road and the more I worried the Ford and Town Car would notice us.

"This creature juice is giving me a serious upset stomach," Knight said through gritted teeth. He dug his fingers into the armrests and shuddered.

I didn't glance at him, entirely too focused on not losing sight of the two vehicles, which wasn't hard considering they were the only other vehicles on the road.

At least his issues were going from erectile to merely gastrointestinal. Gastrointestinal I could handle. His erectile issues were just getting downright annoying.

"Pull over, I feel like I'm going to be sick," he said and sounded like a junkie going through withdrawals.

"I'm not interested in you or your issues right now, Knight. We've got more important stuff to deal with. Just breathe deeply until the feeling goes away."

I had a mind to call Sam and find out what the hell went wrong. But I knew what the answer would be—it wasn't her; it was Knight.

"I feel sick to my stomach," he hissed.

I laughed. "That's called blue balls."

Knight just grumbled.

The Ford took a right on an unpaved road with no sign. The only distinguishing landmark happened to be an old defunct mill, looming in the shadows like a nightmare. The

Town Car turned onto the road, following the Ford, but I stayed on Highway One, not wanting to draw any attention to myself. Soon both vehicles disappeared down the road, trailed by a cloud of red-tinted dust from their taillights. I pulled a U-turn and started back after them.

"Oh, God," Knight groaned as he rolled his head back and forth.

"Just don't throw up in my car." I gave him a meaningful glance. "I'll kill you if you do."

Not waiting for a response, I pulled onto the dirt road and put the Wrangler into four-wheel-drive. With the potholes and the incline, I was surprised the Town Car made it up at all.

"Where are we?" Knight asked, finally pulling his attention away from that which makes him male.

"Some dirt road. I think we're in the city limits of Estuary but I'm not sure." I paused to glance at him and noticed his erection raring against his khaki pants like a demon wanting out of Pandora's Box. Course, in this case, Knight's demon wanted in.

I shook my head. Once this case was done, and if we were lucky enough to survive, a new type of torture awaited Knight—and that torture included me reminding him in vivid detail of every sexual notion to come out of his mouth.

"Do you think you're going to puke?" I asked, wondering if I should just leave him in the car and handle the arrests myself.

"I'm not going to be sick," he groaned and glanced outside. "You should turn off your headlights—otherwise, the lights are going to blow any chance we have at getting these guys."

The word "guys" struck me, being plural. "There are at least, what, four of them including the creature? And there are two of us," I said, sounding like I was setting up the foundation for a math problem.

"I'm easily as strong as three men," my nymphomaniac passenger said calmly.

"You were. Now I'm afraid you'll just toss your cookies on them." I fished inside the cubby hole below my CD player for my cell phone. "I think we need backup."

"No, no backup. We can handle it," Knight insisted.

I grabbed my phone and flipped it open. "Knight, we'd be stupid to go in there without anyone covering our asses."

I started to dial.

"Hang up the phone, Dulcie, that's an order." The steel set to his jaw was warning enough and I flipped the phone closed and dropped it back into its designated slot. "We can handle this," he continued. "I can feel my strength returning."

"Well, for our sakes, I hope you aren't exaggerating."

I turned the headlights off and struggled to locate the dirt road in the darkness. Luckily, the moon broke from the clouds every so often to highlight my path. If I thought I'd been driving slowly before, now I was proceeding at a snail's pace.

Then I noticed the tire marks leading to a dirt driveway. At the top of the driveway was what looked like a house—a one-story, modest house that stood out like a blemish against the otherwise barren landscape. Parked in the driveway were the Town Car and the Ford.

I stopped the Wrangler and reached for the binoculars in Knight's lap. I grazed his anxious unit and when he grabbed my hand, I realized I'd reawakened his libido. Damn it all.

I pulled against him but he held me rigidly. "Knight, for Hades's sake, go stand behind the bushes and wank!"

His eyes blinked open as they settled on me. "That won't help."

I sighed, knowing I was fighting a losing battle. I reached around with my other hand, grabbed hold of the binoculars and bashed them against the back of his head.

He let go of my hand. "What the hell did you do that for?" he yelled and grabbed his head.

Hmm, he didn't seem to have enjoyed getting hit upside the head so maybe he was coming back to himself. "To knock some sense into you."

Knight continued to rub his head, glaring at me while I brought the binoculars to my eyes. No one was in the front, and it didn't appear anyone was in the back either. They must have already gone inside. Not wanting to make a drastic mistake, I continued watching the Town Car and the Ford for any sign of occupancy. After another five minutes, I was convinced they were empty.

I dropped the binoculars into my lap, and put the Wrangler into drive so I could pull off the road. The engine groaned as it ascended the small hill. A grove of pepper trees looked perfect for hiding the car so I pulled behind them.

"Knight, are you ready to go after them?" I asked, seriously suspecting he wasn't.

He nodded, undid his seatbelt, and as he was reaching for the door, I grabbed the lapel of his shirt, wanting to prove how serious I was.

"You need to focus or you could get us both killed."

"You don't need to warn me."

I laughed at the irony in that, and grabbing the binoculars, opened the door and jumped to the ground. My sneakers barely made a sound as I ventured to the back of the Wrangler and pulled my Op 6 from inside the spare tire. It was always good policy to keep an extra weapon hidden. Knight caught the flash of the gun in the moonlight and grinned his approval.

"What are you armed with?" I asked.

He pulled the waistline of his pants forward and revealed the butt of his weapon. I shook my head. "You know, one of these days, that's going to misfire and you'll be a eunuch."

He just chuckled and we started down the hill. At the foot of the hill, I crouched down and motioned for him to do the same. "I think I should go for the front of the house, and you go for the back," I said.

Knight motioned for the binoculars. I handed them over, and he positioned them on top of his aquiline nose. "Looks like you've got your choice of two windows toward the east end of the house. I think those are your best bet."

I motioned for the binoculars to double check, and decided he was right.

"How are you going to get in?" he asked.

I shrugged. "Break the window. I'll use my magic so it won't make a sound."

Knight nodded, apparently satisfied. "I'll take the back and meet you in the middle. Try to keep them in the living room—easier to contain that way."

"Good luck."

Hopefully he'd have the stamina to do his job. I could just imagine him finding some secret spot to tiddle his widdle and where the hell would that leave me?

"Knight, you aren't going to get ... sidetracked are you?"

He frowned when he got my meaning. "No, I won't."

"Okay, just wanted to check."

"Shoot to kill and ask questions later," he said.

I knew the real Knight was in there somewhere.

"Understood." I started forward but Knight's hand on my arm prohibited me. I turned to face him.

"Be careful, Dulce."

I nodded with a smile. "Ditto."

Then I started forward and ran for the windows at the east end of the house. Reaching the windows, I tucked the Op 6 into my jeans and peered into the dirty bedroom window. It boasted nothing but an old mattress and a pair of even older sneakers. This looked like the best way in.

Now, how to break the glass. I could bust it with my arm (wrap said arm in my sweatshirt first) and magic out the sound but that required a lot of energy. So I decided to use magic entirely. Summoning a palm of fairy dust, I blew the dust at the window and focused on the pane of glass. I imagined it slicing down the middle and opening out like French doors. The glass obliged. Grabbing hold of the window pane, I hoisted myself up to the ledge, being careful not to make a sound as I dropped onto the stained carpet below.

Facing the window again, I imagined the separated glass melding back together and smiled at my handiwork. Not bad.

Pulling the Op 6 from my jeans, I cocked the gun and held it at eye level, starting for the hallway. The only light in the small house emanated from the living room where I could hear voices. Three were deep and one was a high-pitched, grating tone I knew only too well.

Zara, the hooker.

"Please let me go," she said in an uneven voice, fraught with tears. "This ain't none of my business. I swear I won't tell a soul."

"Shut her up," someone grumbled, followed by the sound of a slap and Zara's pronounced sobbing.

I threw my back against the wall and sidled down the hall until I reached the threshold of the living room, but was still hidden by the darkness of the corridor.

"Don't feed me to that thing!" Zara said in a voice made tight by tears, but her tone held an angry edge. I could only imagine the "thing" in question was the creature. So they were planning on using her as a snack? Hmm, who knew what grisly chore they were designing for the creature in return.

"It's hungry," a deep voice said. "What would you have us feed it?"

I'd heard enough.

Hoping the deep voice was someone in charge, I honed in on it until I figured it was coming to the left of me, on the opposite side of the wall I was leaning against. Holding the gun out before me, I pivoted and stepped out of the darkness. I immediately held my Op 6 against the temple of the perpetrator much to the shock of the other living room guests. He'd been exactly where I'd thought he was. Yay me.

"Nobody move a finger," I demanded as I wrapped my arm around the flabby guy's chest and secured the barrel of the gun against him. He was a human—I could smell his sweat.

"Dulcie," Zara said, gazing at me like I'd just ridden in on a white horse and was sporting the latest in shining armor.

I returned my attention to the two men in front of me. One was a vamp—tall, skinny and had the general look of someone who hadn't eaten food in centuries and the other a gnome—small and angry. The vamp would be the harder to take down. He held a leash to the creature who was half in its human state and half ... not. The upper part of its face was human, that of the red-headed siren, and the bottom part was hairy with those razor sharp teeth I'd come to know so well. Its body was covered in hair but its forearms and hands were human. It looked like someone hadn't separated their humans from their monsters in the wash cycle.

Its eyes fastened on Zara who sat on the floor in front of it, mascara and red lipstick smudged across her face.

"Zara, get out of here," I snapped, resisting the urge to take my gun away from the human's head in order to put a bullet between the creature's eyes. If I so much as flinched, the vamp would be on me. "Nobody touches her, got it?"

They sullenly nodded, although I noted the twitchy composure of the vamp. He wouldn't stay immobile for long. Luckily, it seemed the human was the one in charge, otherwise they would've let me kill him by now and they'd both be working on putting my wick out.

Zara didn't waste any time in flying for the door.

"Hey, Vampy, throw her the keys to the Explorer," I said, realizing it wasn't like she could get a bus out of here. He hesitated so I rammed the barrel of the gun further into Pudgy's head. "Pronto!"

The vamp fumbled inside his pants pocket and tossed the keys to Zara who took them eagerly. The creature eyed her longingly, as if its peanut butter and jelly sandwich was about to escape with its glass of milk.

"Zara, go find Quillan and tell him to get his ass out here ASAP," I said, no longer concerned about Knight's insistence on confidentiality. Quillan was a great cop and as far as I was concerned, we needed him. I needed him.

"Quillan?" Zara questioned like her brain had decided to take a vacation ... and at the most inopportune moment, I might add.

The vamp grabbed hold of her arm, and she screamed out against him in a terrified panic.

I didn't get a chance to respond.

"Already here, Dulce." Quillan's familiar voice came from directly behind me and my entire body relaxed. I didn't have any time to figure out how he'd gotten here or when or where the hell he'd been hiding. I was too overcome with the pleasure of having him at my back, knowing how much easier it would be to take these miscreants down.

He took a few steps forward until he was parallel with me, and I could smell his Tommy Bahama aftershave. Holy Hades, I'd missed him.

"Let Zara go," he said in his "don't screw with me" voice.

The vamp looked like he'd enjoy sinking his fangs into Quillan's neck but he released Zara's arm. Zara didn't need another clue that she'd nearly been the beast's main entrée and turned on her stiletto heel, the sound of the door slamming behind her like music to my ears. The Ford started up and screeched from the driveway.

Zara was safe. And Quillan was here. The night was looking up.

"It's good to see you, Quill," I offered, keeping my gaze trained on the vamp. "Can you keep the vamp and the gnome occupied while I cuff Pudgy?"

He didn't answer so I glanced behind me and found Quillan's Op 7 aimed directly between my eyes.

"Sorry, Dulce, but no."

NINETEEN

With Quillan's gun pointed between my eyes, I really wanted to believe he just had bad aim. But, unfortunately, the facts in this case were starting to align like the planets. The potions in the vault at Headquarters hadn't been destroyed because Quillan was selling them to these idiots. All this time Quillan had been the in. How freaking stupid had I been? Well, if I managed to live through this, one thing I knew for sure was that I wouldn't doubt myself again. It was a lesson I'd much rather have learned from an after-school special.

"Quillan?" I asked, my voice trembling.

"Drop your weapon, Dulcie."

Though I sensed a slight quake in his voice, the steel set of his eyes warned me not to argue or even try and pull a fast one on him. He knew me well enough to know the gamut of emotions running through my mind.

I didn't drop my Op 6, but Pudgy took it upon himself to step out from underneath the barrel of the gun with a satisfied smile, and I begrudgingly allowed him to. Then his smile turned ugly, and his eyes pinched at the ends as amusement fled his expression, giving way to anger.

He slammed his fist into my lower abdomen. Pain seared through me as though he'd shredded my intestines rather than just sucker-punched me. I reeled back, hitting the wall and gripped my stomach. The pain became too intense, and I succumbed, sliding down the wall to the ground.

Where the hell was Knight?

Pudgy pulled his leg back like he was about to lay his boot in my stomach, where he'd just introduced his fist, but Quillan grabbed him. "You lay one more finger on her, and I'll kill you myself," he said, the truth of his words echoed in the ire of his eyes.

Pudgy hesitated, his boot issuing plenty of warning of its own as it hovered beside my still upset stomach. But then he backed away, apparently wanting no quarrel with Quillan and started for the opposite side of the room. I sat up and leaned against the wall, cradling my bruised gut as I took deep breaths. The bastard had landed a good shot.

"Dulcie, get up," Quillan said, and I glanced up to find his gun still aimed at me. Any relief I'd encountered fled like a thief in the night as soon as I remembered I still had Quillan to deal with. I took one last deep breath and forced myself to my feet even though my stomach roiled against the insult.

"Kill her now," the vamp said.

I glared daggers at him, but they just bounced off him like water on a freshly waxed car. Now that he was in a position of power, his true surliness was coming through. I'd figured he'd be a difficult one. Bastard.

"The *Kragengen* needs to feed," the gnome said, raising his chin in my direction as if to say I should assume the role of first course.

I eyed the creature, and it began drooling at the mention of its next feeding. I couldn't help but imagine its multiple teeth grating away at my flesh. I glanced back at Quillan. "You better kill me first."

"No one is feeding you to the *Kragengen*," Quillan snapped, then eyed the others as if to reiterate his point. "I'm taking her into the bedroom so you three hang tight." They chuckled at the mention of the bedroom. Quillan started forward then paused, turning to face them again. "I mean it. No one leaves this room."

"Save a little for us," the gnome called out.

I flipped him off before Quillan grabbed me by the scruff of my neck and pushed me down the hall, unceremoniously thrusting me into the bedroom and closing the door behind him.

"Goddammit, Dulcie," he admonished. "Talk about nearly blowing my cover."

"Your cover?" I repeated angrily; how freaking dumb did he think I was?

A small smile skipped across his lips and he shook his head, apparently at my stupidity. "You didn't actually think I was guilty, did you?"

Um, yeah I had and I still thought he was guilty, but the A.N.C motto was innocent until proven guilty. Guess I could give him the chance to explain.

"Okay, so what the hell are you doing working undercover on a case like this by yourself? Have you lost your mind?"

He kept his eyes on the door but that smile wouldn't leave his lips. "This was a tough case to break, Dulce, so I did what I thought best." He paused and then brought his attention to the window behind me. "Climb out the window and I'll think of something to tell them."

"I'm not leaving you here to tackle this alone. I'm staying," I said, knowing the time for mindlessly believing in Quillan was long gone.

He shook his head. "It's too dangerous."

I was quiet as I reasoned with myself not to let my anger get the best of me. No, I would be level-headed and calm, cool and collected. "Quillan, look at me," I said in a small voice. If I was a terrible liar, Quillan was just as bad. This would be the test that would tell the Hades-honest truth.

When he turned to face me, it was like he was moving in slow motion. And when his eyes met mine, his pupils were wide.

"Are you lying to me?"

He didn't need to answer. The slight twitch in his left eye was answer enough. I lashed out and smacked him across the face with the palm of my hand.

"I thought I was your friend, Quillan."

He gritted his teeth, but I didn't think his frustration or anger had anything to do with the fact that I'd just slapped him. He kept his gun trained on my forehead, and the red of my slap burned an imprint on his cheek. His jaw was tight. "I like to think we had more than a friendship, Dulcie."

I wouldn't admit anything. Not when whatever I'd thought we had was as fragile as a balloon and Quillan was playing the role of the needle. "Whatever we had, Quillan, it's long gone now," I said in a small voice. I swallowed against the tears that suddenly threatened my eyes.

I would not cry.

I would focus on the facts of this case and figure the damned thing out. It was all I had left. "So all those illegal potions I found in the vault at Headquarters … you never intended to destroy them because you were selling them all along."

"How did you get in there? How did you know about …"

"Never mind that now," I interrupted, holding up my hand to silence him. I stared at the black stains on the beige carpet, questions swarming through my mind like flies on a carcass.

"How are you involved in this?" For now, the personal part had to be shelved. All that remained were the dry, dirty facts. And as a good Regulator, I lived for those facts.

"Dulcie, please believe I never wanted anything to happen to you." He dropped his eyes. "My feelings for you haven't changed."

"Well, in that case, why don't we forget about the fact that because of you, Fabian, Guy and Tad are dead, and let's go get married," I said, my eyes constricted. "Holy Hades, Quillan, you screwed up … royally."

Quillan nodded, and the emotion in his eyes dissipated, replaced by cold stone—as if he'd just had the misfortune of glancing at Medusa. He pointed to the mattress, his jaw even tighter than it had been before. "Sit down. I'm in charge and I'll ask the questions."

I took one look at the filthy mattress before returning my less-than-thrilled gaze back to Quillan. "I'm not getting anywhere near that thing. I don't care if you shoot me or not."

He sighed. "Sit wherever. I don't have time to screw around with you right now, Dulce. In case you haven't noticed, we're in a grave situation."

I sat down in the corner of the room and leaned my back up against the wall, exhaling with exhaustion. "Don't call me Dulce." It was all I could think to say. Quillan wasn't my friend and truly, never had been. Only friends could call me by my nickname.

"How did you get here?" he asked.

"I never stopped working the case," I started. "I guess you can say I'm good at my job. I just figured it out, and here I am." I purposely omitted any references to Knight. Speaking of, where the hell was he? If he wanted to show up any time now, that'd be great. Damn men.

"Who helped you?"

Hmm, Dagan, Knight, even Bram a little. Trey, Sam ... the list went on. "You should know better than to ask me that question." He knew the rules ... I'd been trained not to give up names—even under duress.

Quillan smiled. "I should never have expected less of you."

I didn't return the smile. "Now, how about you answer some questions for me?"

He shook his head. "The less you know, the safer you are."

I gave him a courtesy laugh. "You really don't think I'm just going to walk away from here? That vamp out there is dying to kill me. No pun intended. And if he doesn't get to do the job, the gnome looked pretty thrilled about taking it on himself and the human ..."

"No one will hurt you," he interrupted, the pained expression on his face suggesting how much he disliked the thought of my death by anyone's hand. Touching ... but I didn't have time for this.

"I'll say you escaped." He paused, as if deep in thought. "Dulcie, do the smart thing and pretend like you never came here tonight."

"And what? Continue working with you? Knowing you're a criminal?" I could feel the anger simmering through me and burning my eyes. "We'll just continue going to lunch and making fun of Trey and acting like everything's hunky dory?"

"I'm done with Headquarters. Obviously, I can't go back."

If I had anything to do with it, he would be going back to Headquarters, all right, but occupying a cell until the Netherworld figured out what to do with him. Even though I knew it had to be done, it wasn't a thought that brought me any sort of joy. "I want answers, Quillan. I'm not giving up on this." I was probably signing my own death warrant, but it was too late for regrets. Guess I have a big mouth.

"Stand up," Quillan said. "I'm going to break the window, and I want you to climb down and run out of here as fast as you can. Don't look back."

I shook my head. "You should know me better than that."

I wouldn't run away. I couldn't run away.

"Dulcie, for once don't be so pig-headed. I'm trying to buy your life. I don't want you getting hurt."

He made the mistake of looking away, so I shot to my feet and jumped on him, knowing he couldn't shoot me ... well, hoping he couldn't shoot me. I pushed him into the wall, and we clamored against one another, me straining for the gun and him trying to hang onto it. Not wanting to alert the three stooges in the living room, I buffered our little tiff with a magic cloud so they couldn't hear a thing.

With a growl, Quillan flipped me over his shoulder. I hit the floor square on my back but not before trying to stabilize myself against the wall. Searing pain shot through the palm of my right hand. Glancing down, I saw the tell-tale signs of gold and glimpsed a rusty nail jutting from the line where the carpet met the wall. Damn, that was the hand I used to create fairy dust. Looked like I couldn't rely on my magic for the rest of the night. Hades be damned!

Before I could roll out of the way, Quillan pinned me to the carpet. "Damn it, Dulce, listen to reason. I'm trying to save your ass."

But I wasn't interested in him saving my ass. I was more interested in overpowering him. Even though he had me pinned, fairies are faster than elves. In a split second, I bucked him off and wrenched the gun from his grasp, trying to ignore the searing pain as the gun made contact with my ripped palm. Even if it hurt like a son of a bitch, at least I could close my hand around it. The night was looking up.

"Back off me," I hissed and thrust the gun into his sternum.

Quillan must have been more afraid of me shooting him than I was of him shooting me, because his eyes widened as he pushed away from me. Then his gaze found the drops of gold falling from my palm like Rumpelstiltskin's wet dream.

"You're hurt."

I pushed aside his concern with a shake of my head. "I want to know how long you've been working with these creeps."

He swallowed, the mental conflict of whether to tell me or not playing out on his features like a classic movie. I had a feeling the barrel of the gun pointed at his face might influence his decision.

"A little over a year."

"And tell me if I'm right—you killed Fabian and Guy because they were infringing on your turf?"

He shook his head and stood up. "No, I had nothing to do with their deaths."

"And how did you feel about the fact that even if you didn't kill him directly, because of your involvement, Tad is dead? A kid, Quillan, he was just a kid."

He dropped his head. "I didn't want any of them dead. This whole situation went too far. The six of us were working together distributing illegal potions but Frank, the human, got greedy and decided to dust Fabian and Guy."

"So why kill Tad? He wasn't selling anything."

"They killed him behind my back. He'd been at Guy's when they'd put the hit out on Guy and Tad had seen Frank."

I promised myself I'd see Frank dead. If it was the last thing I did, I would see him dead. I owed that much to Tad. "So Frank called the creature to kill all three of them?"

Quillan shook his head. "The vamp did—he has connections directly to the Netherworld. This all happened against my will, Dulcie, you have to believe me. I never wanted it to go this far."

I wanted to believe him, but look where my trust had gotten me so far. "Looks like you got in way over your head," I said and he nodded. "That's why you shouldn't have trusted them in the first place. God, Quillan, I never picked you for the dumb type."

He swallowed, his face downcast, and disregarded my comment. "I never wanted anyone killed, Dulcie, and I never would've summoned the creature."

"So why get involved in the first place, Quillan?"

"I've regretted it since the day I decided to do something with those potions. It was the biggest mistake I've ever made."

I wasn't interested in a regretful Quillan. I needed to get the details of the case more than anything else. "So you put the spell on Trey and you used an illegal ingredient so it would take us longer to crack it."

He nodded. "I had to. The gnome is a sensitive so he was able to tell every time Trey had a vision. Frank wanted to put a hit out on Trey, but of course, I couldn't allow that. To keep Trey safe, I put him under the sleeping spell and told Frank I'd taken care of him. When the gnome didn't get any more hints that Trey was having visions, I guess they believed me."

"And Frank put the hit out on me then that day in the woods outside my apartment?"

Quillan bobbed his head. "I had to tell him I was pretending to investigate the case with you. I guess he got scared and decided it was better to have you out of the picture."

I remembered that night—how frightened I'd been, how Quillan had seemed so nonchalant, so unconcerned about what had been out there. Then I remembered the gremlins. "You ordered the gremlins?"

"Yes, when the Relations Office said you were on hiatus, I suggested they send gremlins to further protect you. I thought it would be a good idea." Then he paused. "How did the Relations Office happen to know you were involved in this?"

I shrugged, feigning innocence. "I have no idea. That was my next question for you." Ha, my acting was getting better and better.

"No idea."

I sighed, figuring I knew as much as I needed to. Then I remembered Knight telling me to keep everyone in the living room and figured I should start corralling them. I waved the gun in a motion of "get up" and Quillan did as he was told. "We're going back into the living room. You walk in front of me and don't try anything because I won't hesitate to shoot you."

He nodded solemnly. "There's no way I can talk you out of this, is there?"

I shook my head. "Eight ball's sources say no."

He laughed quietly but it was a sad sound. "I will miss you, Dulcie. Whatever happens, I'm going to miss you."

I didn't care to think about what exactly he thought might happen or how ominous his words sounded. Whatever I'd felt for Quillan was in the process of being blocked up by an impervious wall, never to see the light of my emotions again.

"Okay, out you go," I said, my voice hoarse with fatigue.

Just as soon as the words left my mouth, the lights twitched like they were blinking and then died, leaving us in total darkness. I grabbed Quillan's collar and pressed the cold nose of the gun into the back of his neck. "Don't do anything stupid."

Seconds later, the sound of crashing glass shattered the still of the night, followed by scuffling, and I figured Knight had finally arrived. And it was about damned time.

I pushed Quillan forward, the gun still threatening his lower neck just as two gunshots rang out. My heart in my throat, I continued pushing Quillan into the hallway and down the long corridor. It seemed like it took years to get out of the hallway and emerge into the living room.

In the darkness, I could just make out the shapes of two large lumps on the floor. It took my fairy vision a second to kick in, but once it did, I realized the gnome and the human were dead, a single bullet wound in each of their heads. Two points for Knight. Then I suddenly realized Knight, the creature and the vamp were nowhere to be found.

"Who's with you?" Quillan asked.

"No one you need to concern yourself with."

Thinking Knight had gone outside to battle against them, I pushed Quillan toward the door, imagining I could walk him to the Wrangler and hogtie him with some horsehair rope in my trunk. The rope would keep him from using his magic to escape—horses' hair being one of the few substances immune to magic.

"You and I are going to go for a quick walk," I said.

Quillan didn't say anything but stepped over the shards of broken glass that used to be the living room doors and jumped onto the dirt below. I was directly behind him. When we hit the ground, he started walking a bit too fast for my comfort. "Slow the hell down."

He didn't slow down but, instead, took off running. I had the split-second thought to shoot him in the leg but the dragon blood bullets in his gun would kill him as soon as they made contact with his blood. And I definitely didn't want to kill him, so I started after him, running full bore. There weren't any fences or anything else that might slow Quillan down—just a hill with a clear path to the highway below, and a few pepper trees dotting the landscape.

"Quillan, I WILL shoot you," I yelled.

Surprisingly, he stopped and held his hands up, turning around to face me. If I thought he was surrendering, the little smile pulling at his lips made me think otherwise. I was prohibited from any other thoughts as a maniacal laugh pierced the air. Quillan and I glanced at each other, question marks clearly emanating from each of our eyes.

"Goddammit!"

Knight.

Knight's voice was followed by the sound of someone landing on the ground ... hard. I could only hope it wasn't him.

"Let me go, Dulcie. It sounds like your friend is in over his head."

Maybe Knight was in over his head. I tightened my grip around the gun, ignoring the thundering pain in my hand. But if Knight wasn't in over his head, I'd be making a crucial mistake.

"I'm not letting you go," I said, hoping Knight could take care of himself. He had said he was as strong as three men. But that hadn't included a vamp and they were renowned for their physical strength. And the creature wasn't anything to scoff at either.

Quillan started walking backward. "Let me go, Dulcie, it's a lot easier than killing me."

I kept the Op 7 aimed on him but he continued to back away. I wasn't sure why he didn't just resort to using magic—he could've escaped me a lot easier by surrounding me in a thick fog or just becoming invisible. Instead, he was playing by the rules. Admirable. "Stop walking now."

"Dulcie, you know if you take me into custody, the Netherworld will order me dead. I can't have that. I'd hope you wouldn't want it either."

Damn him to hell. Of course I didn't want his blood on my hands. But I had to let justice run its course. "Stop walking, Quillan."

He didn't, and I squeezed the trigger ever so slightly. He was within range. If I hit him, I'd definitely kill him. And it was at that moment I realized I couldn't do it. As much as I hated admitting it, I still cared for Quillan and I couldn't kill him. The sound of grunting and fists meeting flesh assaulted my ears. I had to make my choice. Either go after Quillan or help Knight.

The choice was already made. I lowered the gun and Quillan smiled gratefully.

"I'll make it up to you, Dulce."

"I don't ever want to see your face again. You were lucky this time; you won't be lucky next time."

He didn't respond but turned away and started down the hill, disappearing into the distance. Fighting the soreness in my gut, I prepared to confront a more important subject—Knight.

TWENTY

I didn't have time to regret letting Quillan go.

Another loud grunt sliced the tranquility of the evening air, pulling my attention to the fact that Knight might be in trouble. I took a deep breath and cocking Quillan's Op 7, started in the direction of the muffled sounds.

More grunts and swearing, then the definite sound of fists pounding flesh led me to the grisly scene. Blood splattered the ground, the moonlight reflecting on it like spilled oil. Knight was caught between the vamp and the *Kragengen* shifter, doing his best to keep them both at arm's length.

The vamp lashed his dagger-like fingernails out, but Knight ducked, the blades just missing his throat. The rise and fall of Knight's chest bore witness to the fact that they'd been at this for a while—this pattern of thrust and parry.

Using the girth of a nearby pepper tree, I managed to hide my body and regroup, wiping my still bleeding palm on my jeans. I needed a plan—I couldn't just charge in or I'd be done ... that or Knight would be. Okay, second idea: maybe I could get off a good shot and nail the creature. The dragon blood bullets would kill it. And the vampire? Before jumping to extremes, I examined the bullets in the chamber. They weren't dragon blood bullets, but just standard lead ones. And those wouldn't kill a vampire or a shape-shifter—they'd just piss them off. Goddammit!

But bullets would stun them and buy me some precious seconds; maybe enough to give Knight the upper hand? I really hoped so.

Knight pushed against the vamp, barreling him into a tree. The vamp hissed out and sliced his cheek with a rake of his claws. Blood immediately began coursing down the harsh planes of Knight's face. The creature just paced along the sidelines and watched.

Much though I wanted to take out the vamp, I couldn't get a clear shot at him without the possibility of hitting Knight and those were odds I wasn't about to take. Double goddammit.

So instead, I watched idly—waiting for an opportunity to strike. The *Kragengen*, apparently unsatisfied with just being a spectator, lurched at Knight. It raised a clawed paw as if to strike. But he deflected the attack and with a push, catapulted the creature toward my pepper tree.

It hit the trunk with a resounding thud then plopped onto the ground, shaking its head. It got up on all fours almost immediately. I sprang from behind the tree, my gun aimed at its temple. I squeezed the trigger and the *Kragengen*'s body shook as it landed on the ground. It was still. Well, dragon blood bullets or not, a bullet to the head should've been enough to seriously incapacitate it. Eyeing it, I unloaded another two bullets into its head. Hey, I wasn't taking any chances.

"That's enough!" I yelled at the vamp. "Step away from my partner."

The vamp smirked and spat a bloody clot, revealing a tooth. Ew.

"Dulcie, get the hell away from the ..." Knight started before the vamp took advantage of Knight's shift in attention and sucker-punched the side of his head, sending him flying three feet into the air. Knight hit the ground with a grunt but rolled back onto his feet.

I aimed the Op 7 at the vampire's head and was about to squeeze off a shot when something smashed into me, sending me flying. I dropped the gun. When I hit the ground, I had to force myself upright. But I was too late. The

Kragengen straddled me. I pushed against its chest, trying to keep its mouth from my throat. The tear in my palm burned as the gold of my blood stained the creature's coat.

Without my magic, this was hopeless. I didn't have the strength to keep it from tearing me apart. Feeling my arms weaken, I heaved against the beast, and using the quickness inherent in my species, rolled out of the *Kragengen's* grasp.

I stood up and faced the creature, panting as drops of blood coursed down my open palm.

"Face me as a woman," I screamed, thinking any chance I had of taking it would require it to be in human form. "Woman to woman."

The creature seemed to smile—its teeth reflecting the moonlight. It stood before me on all fours and like a great, rumbling bear, stood up on its hind legs until it towered over me.

"Dulcie!" It was Knight but I couldn't spare him a glance.

"Fight me like a woman," I repeated, this time softer.

The *Kragengen* just stood there, staring at me. It took me a second to realize it was shifting—the crude hair on its body began to recede back into its skin, leaving nothing but a smooth palate of porcelain. Its rib cage seemed to fold in on itself until it had a definite waist flanked by large breasts on one side and generous hips on the other.

As the creature shifted into its human counterpart, it dropped in height. Its shark-like teeth recessed into the cavity of its mouth until only a set of human teeth smiled out at me. When it was finished metamorphosing, the beautiful redhead beamed at me ... naked.

Okay, so I'd never had to fight a naked person before. I guess there's always a first.

The creature's attention fell to my dripping palm. "You don't have your magic."

I didn't feel the need to agree and instead, turned to the fact that, human form or not, her strength easily out powered mine.

I was done.

As if to prove my point, she lurched for me and with a push, sent me careening into the tree behind me. I hit my head against the bark and had to shake my vision free of stars. That's when I was able to glance at Knight who was on his back, the vampire sucking at his throat.

"Knight!" I screamed.

There wasn't an answer.

Tears threatened my eyes but I blinked them away. I couldn't focus on the loss of someone I now considered a friend. I had to face the fact that I was next and I had to do something about it.

I pulled my attention back to the *Kragengen* just as it pounced. It threw its full weight into me and smashed my head against the bark. Holding my neck against the tree with its forearm, I could smell flesh on its breath. Its eyes found the pulse in my neck and it stood transfixed. That's when I realized that in its human form or not, there was nothing even remotely human about this creature. It was wild.

Its eyes found mine as its mouth opened and its teeth elongated. Without any warning, it buried its face into my lower neck. The feel of its teeth perforating my skin was nothing compared to the agony as it bit through my collarbone.

I screamed and it released me.

I sunk down the line of the tree and collapsed against the ground.

This was it. I was going to die.

I glanced up at Knight and found him still lying prostrate against the ground, his throat open and gaping. The vamp was no longer feeding from him though. Instead, it was making its way toward me.

I didn't flinch as the vamp grasped my head and pulled it back, revealing my neck. He was on me instantly, tearing through my flesh like a kid ripping through wrapping paper on Christmas morning. The creature joined the feast with renewed energy and buried its face into my side, its teeth gnashing my flesh.

This was not the way I'd planned to go.

I fisted my hand and prayed my magic would work even with a ripped palm. I shook it and focused hard, focused on those little specks of fairy magic that would see me through this. I reopened my palm and noted nothing but the gold of my blood.

Dulcie.

It was Knight's voice in my head. I glanced over at the heap of inanimate pile that was Knight.

So now I was losing so much blood, I was losing my mind.

I'm going to heal you. You have to let me into your mind like you did in your dreams.

But you're dead, I thought.

No, I'm not. Let me inside your head, Dulcie. Once your palm is healed, I want you to envision a stake and aim it over the vamp's heart. Can you do that?

Yeah.

I closed my eyes, thinking it might help.

And then I felt him. It was like liquid heat rising up through my body. Every appendage stung with what felt like electricity. I opened my eyes, thinking the vamp and the creature must have felt it too but they were both too busy feeding on me to notice. I glanced at my palm and the wound was gone.

I closed my eyes again and shook my fist, imagining a wooden stake. Dust flowed between my fingers and I wanted to cry. It had worked! Somehow it had worked.

I rotated the stake in my hand and moving slowly, so as not to alert the vamp, I held the stake directly before his chest.

It's there, I thought, hoping Knight was still listening.

I opened my eyes and watched Knight sit up, his neck no longer a gaping wound, but smooth as if it had never suffered the insult in the first place. He moved quickly until he was directly behind the vamp. With a smile at me, he shoved the vamp from behind until the stake buried itself deep into the vamp's chest. The vamp's eyes widened as they met mine and then he merely collapsed onto the ground beside me.

His eyes went vapid, the life slipping out of them as his body and face rapidly aged, decades going by in mere seconds. When his body stopped morphing, an old man lay before me.

The *Kragengen* gave a cry of alarm and turned away from me, facing Knight.

I stood up, feeling slightly woozy and watched Knight turn to face the creature.

"No, this is my fight," I said.

Knight smiled and backed away from the creature who faced me with renewed interest.

"Come here, you ugly bitch," I seethed.

The *Kragengen* started to shift back to its true state, wiry fur unfolding down its body. It doubled in size and waved its paws through the air as massive claws sprouted from them like bulbs breaking through soil.

I fisted my palm and shook it. Then I blew the glittery particles toward the creature, imagining a roaring inferno. Once the particles hit the creature's fur, they erupted into flames of orange.

Knight backed away as the creature began to howl and dance around in a circle, fueling the intensity of the flames. In only a few more minutes, it was an incendiary and a couple minutes later, it toppled to the ground and the flames went out.

"Nicely done," Knight said with an appreciative grin.

I just nodded and fell back against the tree.

Knight was beside me momentarily. "I wasn't able to completely heal you."

I collapsed into his outstretched arms.

"Let me inside your head again."

I closed my eyes and welcomed the heat as it poured through my body. The stinging, electrical sensation seemed to focus on my collarbone and side.

"That's about all I can do. You'll need to sleep well and eat lots of protein for the next few weeks to get all your strength back."

I opened my eyes and offered him a smile. "I hope you know I'm keeping track of all your many abilities."

Knight chuckled. "What do you say we get the hell out of here?"

He didn't wait for a response but scooped me into his arms and stood.

"What about the bodies?" I asked.

"I'll call for backup."

At the mention of backup, of calling Headquarters, the fact that I'd let Quillan escape came back to haunt me. I could tell it was going to keep on haunting me. I shouldn't have been so soft. I should've taken him in. Shoulda woulda coulda.

"That reminds me," I started before taking a breather. I definitely wasn't feeling myself. "All this talk about confidentiality and getting me dropped off the team at Headquarters …"

Knight raised an eyebrow like he had no idea where my questions were leading.

"You knew all along that someone from Headquarters was involved, didn't you?"

He grinned. "Confidential."

I couldn't help my laugh, weak though it was.

Knight glanced at me. "What happened to Quillan?"

I gulped down my own sense of failed responsibility. "He got away."

Two days later, as I ambled into Headquarters, I might as well have been the Virgin Queen of England for all the whispering and knowing looks I aroused. I'd never liked being the center of attention so I hurried to my desk until I got too winded and walked the rest of the way.

Trey was at his desk but I didn't acknowledge him, just dropped my backpack on the floor and started up my computer, relaxing into my chair.

"You okay, Dulce?"

I glanced at him and nodded although I still wasn't feeling myself. "Yeah, I'm fine."

"If you need to … talk to anyone, I'm always free."

I smiled, thinking Trey had definitely turned out to be a better coworker than I'd thought he would. "Thanks, Trey, I might take you up on that."

The unmistakable sound of Sam's heels tapping down the corridor heralded her arrival. I glanced at her with an encouraging smile and a wave of my hands.

"I'm fine, I'm fine."

Sam's eyes were wide and her mouth twitching—something she always did when she was nervous. She hesitated only momentarily before throwing her arms around me. "God, I was so worried. I wanted to come see you—why didn't you answer your phone?"

I sighed. "I guess I just needed some alone time."

Sam nodded. "I can't believe Quillan! I can't believe he lied to us all!"

I still couldn't believe it myself. The truth of the matter was that I hadn't been able to sleep, remorse plaguing my every thought. I shouldn't have let him go—that's what it came down to. I was, before anything else, a Regulator. And as a Regulator, my first and foremost duty was to apprehend criminals, but I'd let Quillan slip through my fingers.

I stopped berating myself as Elsie's voice interrupted.

"Guys, the chief of the Relations Office is here!"

I glanced at Trey and Sam, who stared vacantly back at me.

"He wants us all to meet in the conference room," Elsie insisted and clapped her hands together as if to tell us to hurry when none of us made any motion to do anything.

I followed Trey and Sam into the conference room where I was ushered to a seat at the end of the conference table. Trey tried to take the seat and Elsie shooed him out of it, beaming at me instead.

I wasn't a hero and I didn't want to be treated like one.

Nonetheless, I took the seat with a lukewarm smile as if to say "thanks" and turned to the sound of the door opening. Knight strolled in, dressed in black, as beautiful as he ever was. Damn, the man was sexy as sin!

Then I noticed the smaller man next to him—maybe five feet eight inches, fifty years old or close to it, receding hairline, and thick glasses. So this was the Chief of the Relations Office, come from the Netherworld? Rhetorical question.

Knight eyed me and gave me a grin; I was embarrassed and looked away. I didn't want anyone to think I was getting preferential treatment. I was just another Regulator and that was that. Knight took the seat next to me and the Chief assumed the seat at the head of the table. Elsie fluttered about offering coffee.

"Well, let's get started," the Chief said. "For those of you who haven't met me," none of us had, "I'm Chief Sterno and I run the Relations Office in Hildoff, Netherworld. It's my pleasure to be here today to meet all of you."

He glanced at every one of us while we murmured our "happy to see you toos" and I felt like it was my first day at school.

"I'm sure you've heard of the unfortunate situation involving the previous Chief of Headquarters so I won't get into that," Sterno continued. "I do want you to know we are doing our best to find a replacement."

There were a round of nods and sighs.

"In the meantime, Knightley Vander will be substituting, just until we find a permanent replacement," the Chief finished.

"Please call me Knight," the Loki clarified.

I glanced around and noticed all the females openly admiring him. Ugh.

"Knightley?" Trey whispered, elbowing me in the ribs.

"Watch it," I grumbled, wondering if my poor side would ever heal.

"His name isn't Todd?"

"No," I whispered back, frowning. I hadn't wanted to lie to Trey and hopefully he wouldn't take our mis-truth as a slight. "We didn't want to put you in harm's way so we had to withhold his true identity."

"He really wasn't your friend at all?" His expression was crestfallen.

"No, he forced me to secrecy, Trey." When all else fails, blame someone else.

Trey just nodded. Meanwhile, the fact that Knight was going to be my boss, if only temporarily, was starting to sink in. I couldn't say I liked it. In fact, I didn't like it at all. I'd gotten a taste of Knight's mode of leadership, and it wasn't one I wished to repeat.

"So please welcome Knight," the Chief finished.

Everyone clapped.

Knight smiled and raised his hands as if to quiet the room. "I'm Knight, as the Chief said, and it's great to meet all of you."

A few sighs from the ladies in the room. I just shook my head.

"Today is not only about introductions, though," Knight continued. "I also have a bit of good news." He paused and glancing at me, pasted a huge grin on his face.

"I'm not sure if you are all aware, but Dulcie O'Neil worked with me on this case." There were a round of oohs and aahs. I didn't like the direction of the conversation but there wasn't a damned thing I could do about it.

"And because of her courage, we were both able to escape. I just wanted to announce that I'm promoting Dulcie O'Neil to the position of Head Regulator."

Another round of claps, and I felt as if I'd been slapped. Surprise overtook me, and when I met Knight's grin, I resisted the urge to walk out. No one in the room should've been congratulating me. I didn't deserve a promotion. As far as I was concerned, I'd failed miserably.

"Thank you," I said in a small voice, trying to pretend that nothing was the matter, that I was as thrilled as everyone else. It was a hard order and I'm not sure I succeeded.

Sam hugged me, and Trey looked like he was biting back tears. Holy Hades.

After the meeting disbanded, and I'd had about all the pats on the back I could take, I followed Knight into Quillan's old office. Quillan's name plate still hung on the door, and I had to drop my eyes. It made me feel oddly sad.

Knight took a seat in the large, brown leather chair and cracked his knuckles. "How's your side?"

"It's fine."

He nodded. "Dulce, what can I do for you?"

I didn't know how to say it, so I just reached inside my pocket and handed him the envelope.

He took it with a smile but the smile soon disappeared as soon as he started reading. "What is this?" he demanded and dropped the letter onto the desk as if it had just bitten him.

I sighed. "My letter of resignation."

TWENTY-ONE

"Resignation?" Knight repeated, his eyes fixed on the surface of his desk ... Quillan's desk.

"You shouldn't have promoted me," I said and collapsed into the large leather chair across from Knight's. Eyeing Quillan's office fern, I rubbed the fronds between my fingers as a wave of sadness coursed over me.

Knight chuckled. "Usually people are thrilled to get promoted." He leaned forward, propping his chin on his fist. "You deserved it and more."

I shook my head and sighed. I'd have to tell him sooner or later. "Quillan didn't escape."

Knight's eyebrows furrowed and his mouth twitched as his eyes searched mine like a hawk's. This wasn't going to be fun.

"Go on."

I inhaled. "I let him go."

Knight reclined in the leather chair again, and bobbed back and forth, the chair groaning in protest underneath him. Surprisingly, he didn't look angry—he didn't look anything at all, really. "As far as I see it, you didn't have a choice. It was him or me."

I nodded—that was fair enough.

"And you chose me." He stopped rocking. "And I will forever be grateful to you. Although I'm aware you don't want to hear it, Dulcie, you were a hero that night."

"You don't understand, Knight." I paused, fumbling to find the right words, trying to justify my own cowardice. "I just ... just couldn't shoot him."

Knight shrugged. "No one blames you for that." He paused, distractedly picking up a pen and started doodling on Quillan's desk calendar.

"You should blame me for that," I said.

"Quillan must've known you wouldn't shoot him, or he wouldn't have left it as your only option."

Okay, he had another point there. I stood up and started pacing the room, hating the fact that the air still smelled of Quillan's aftershave, that everything in this office reminded me of Quillan and made me miss him. I stopped pacing to find Knight smiling with amusement.

"Either way, Knight, I don't deserve the promotion. I failed in my duties and ... I'm sorry but I'm resigning my post." I crossed my arms against my chest.

Knight stood up, his intimate gaze never breaking from mine, and approached me. I backed away.

"I won't let you quit."

I laughed involuntarily. "You don't have a choice."

I dropped myself back into the visitor's chair, and he braced himself against the edge of Quillan's desk, still fidgeting with the pen. "You're the best person on my team. I can't afford to lose you."

"I'm sorry, but ..." I shook my head. "I've made up my mind."

He ran an agitated hand through his hair and dropped the pen against the desk. "What are you going to do for work then?"

I hadn't thought that far ahead. "I don't know."

He arched a brow. "Not a very good plan, Dulce."

I sighed, annoyed with myself. "I guess I could go back to waiting tables for a while—just until I find something better."

He nodded, but the concerned lines in his forehead said he was anything but optimistic. "And what would that something better be?" he asked.

I just shrugged.

"You belong in law enforcement, Dulce, it's in your blood. I've seen you out there and you love it ... just as much as I do. You'll never be happy doing anything else."

Okay, it's super annoying when someone claims to know you better than you know yourself. Although I had enjoyed my job, there were a myriad of other things I liked better—writing being the first and foremost. But I didn't want to admit that to him.

"Well, I won't be happy here either. Maybe I'll move from Splendor and live somewhere else."

"Don't you realize you can't run away from things? No matter where you go, they'll eventually find you until you confront them."

My hands started to contract into fists. Since when had Knight become Dr. Phil? "Are you done? I want to go now."

Knight was quiet for a few moments, and his silence unsettled me more than his cockiness. Finally, he sighed and stood up, gazing out the window that overlooked Splendor Park. "I can't change your mind?"

"No."

He turned to face me again, his hands seeking solace in his pockets. "Then, I want you to work as a consultant."

"What?"

"When I need you for a particularly difficult case, I want to be able to call on you. You won't have to come to the office but you'll be on call should I need you."

I started to adamantly shake my head.

"Please, Dulce, just until I can find your replacement. If you don't want to do it for me, do it for the team."

I bit my lip. *Do it for the team*; what a great line. Damn him. "You're a real bastard, you know?"

He smiled. "It's gotten me this far."

I gulped down my protest and laughed, but it was a courtesy laugh. I should've known Knight would force the issue. "Okay, okay. Can I go now?"

"Not just yet." He was silent as a smirk curled his lips. "One more thing ..."

I frowned. "What?"

His eyes searched the ceiling as the smile on his lips broadened. "Now that we aren't officially working together and you're no longer my subordinate ..."

As if I ever was his subordinate! Holy Hades, the man was narcissistic.

"Yes, what?" I impatiently demanded.

"I want to ask you out to dinner."

My mouth gaped in astonishment. "Like a date?"

He chuckled. "Yeah, a date. I imagine I wasn't the only one of us to feel ... a connection?"

A connection wasn't exactly what I'd call it. And that reminded me ... a moment I'd been looking forward to had arrived at last. The wheels of my brain began spinning with delight. "That's right, I haven't made true on my promise to torture you yet, have I?"

"Torture me?" he chuckled.

"Hmm," I tapped my chin, wondering where to start. "Yeah, don't you remember your little reaction to the creature juice?"

He studied me with a bewildered expression. "What are you talking about?"

"Ah, of course you don't remember. How convenient. You turned into quite the horn dog after Sam made us swallow that potion."

Knight dropped his stare, but a smile crested over his lips. Oh, he remembered all right. "Yeah, um, about that ..."

"'Chains and blindfolds' is a direct quote," I continued, savoring this as much as I promised myself I would.

"Let me make it up to you," he said, his eyes begging me to stop.

I stood up. Even though Knight was gorgeous, he was one cocky bastard. "Thanks for the invitation, but I'm going to pass."

He couldn't keep the surprise from registering on his face. So Knight wasn't used to rejection? Even better then that he should get it from me.

I started for the door, valuing the expression on his face as priceless. I paused with my hand on the doorknob and turned to face him for the last time. "Give me a call when you get a tough case."

Then I opened the door and walked out.

One month later, I'd finished my Bram book. Now it was time to try and recruit an agent. If I said I wasn't excited about going through the process again, it would be an understatement. But unfortunately, I had to do what I had to do.

After finishing my query letter and a five-page synopsis, I compiled the list of agent names and e-mail addresses and began the task of e-mailing my queries. After an hour, I'd managed to get through the entire list and sat back in my chair, heaving an exhausted sigh.

I was proud of this book—I'd put a lot of time and effort into it. And Bram ... well, without him, I wouldn't have had a book at all. Thinking I should probably let him know I'd finished it and was now trying to find an agent to represent it, I called No Regrets.

Angela answered the phone and was quick to connect me with Bram.

"Sweet," he said, with genuine surprise.

"Hi, Bram, I wanted to let you know I finished the book."

"Ah, did you? That is very good news. What is next?"

"Well, I'm trying to get an agent to represent it and if I find one, he or she will pitch it to the publishing houses."

"I wish you much luck, Sweet." He paused. "Regarding that favor you owe me ..."

237

I knew that favor would yield its ugly head sooner or later. "Yes?"

"I would like to escort you to dinner tomorrow evening, if that suits you."

"You want to take me on a date?" I laughed. "Really, Bram, I would've thought owing you a favor would turn out to be a much bigger pain in my ass than that!"

Bram chuckled. "Well, I am flattered to think you regard a date with me as not a ... pain in your posterior. Are you free tomorrow evening?"

"Yes."

"Then I shall pick you up at nine p.m. Please dress with elegance."

"Okay, Bram, I'll see you tomorrow."

He hung up and it suddenly dawned on me that Sam might not find this arrangement especially pleasing. Ugh, I hadn't even considered her feelings before I'd agreed. Dammit. I dialed her number.

"Hello?"

"Sam, it's Dulcie."

"Hey, girl, what's going on?"

I gulped down my guilt. "Nothing. I just got off the phone with Bram, and he invited me to dinner to celebrate my finishing the book." I paused. "I just wanted to make sure you were okay with it? If not, I won't go."

She was quiet for a few seconds. "Yeah, I'm fine. I always knew he had the hots for you anyway ..."

"No, it's not like that, Sam."

She laughed. "Whatever you're convincing yourself, it is like that and no, I'm not bothered by it at all. I'm over Bram." She paused. "Actually, I'm thrilled to hear you'll be going on a date. This will be your first in what?"

"A year," I grumbled.

"Wow. Yes, go and enjoy yourself! And don't worry about me."

I sighed in relief. "Okay, thanks. How are things with you?"

"Good, everything at work is good." She started to laugh. "All the women are in love with Knight."

I smiled, figuring such would be the case. I was sure Knight was in hog heaven, the bastard. "Well, I'm glad to hear everything is fine with you."

"Yeah, it is." She paused. "I miss Quill."

Quill.

Just the mention of his name caused an indescribable sorrow that I felt deep in my gut. "I do too."

###

For my evening with Bram, I'd chosen to wear a mid-thigh length, black cocktail dress with black beading that reflected the lights and sparkled like a prism. It was really tight and I'd only worn it two times in the four years I'd owned it. Guess I didn't get out much. I'd finished it off with three-inch black leather stiletto boots and magicked a little curl into my hair, which of course, I wore down. Some pink lipstick, a touch of blush and a few strokes of mascara completed the look.

It felt good to be going out on a date, even if I didn't think Bram and I would ever be a couple. But I was now convinced that I needed to defeat my trust issues and what better way than to throw myself back into the dating game?

When we arrived at The Chateaus, Bram pulled out my chair from the table, and I could feel the shudder of his gaze as it traveled over me with quiet appreciation.

"I have never seen you look so enchanting, Sweet. I am honored you chose to appear in such a way for me."

I smiled, not exactly comfortable with this date stuff. I watched Bram assume his seat, and then I let my eyes wander over the restaurant. The Chateaus was in nearby Sanctity. It was the nicest place to eat and I had to admit I was pretty flattered.

Candle glow illuminated the otherwise dark interior and contrasted against the pristine white of the table linens and chairs in flickering shadows.

"This place looks just like your office," I said with a smirk.

Bram chuckled. "It is just missing some red."

I returned my gaze to his. "What's up with your accent, Bram? You haven't been to England in over a century."

His grin deepened, the tips of his fangs just protruding over his bottom lip. "I was wondering when the Sweet I knew so well would surface." Apparently, not wanting to enlighten me on the particulars of his counterfeit accent, he changed the subject. "Any more word on the book?"

I shook my head. "Nothing yet. Any word on the Chinese massage parlor?"

"Yes, I've purchased it. I plan to open a restaurant to top even this one."

"Big ambitions."

He nodded. "Of course, Sweet, of course."

"So Dagan was never after your massage parlor?"

Bram tapped his long fingers along the stem of his wine glass, reminding me that vampires didn't eat. They had no problem with liquids, but food wasn't something they were capable of digesting. Guess I'd be dining alone tonight. Strange that Bram would've invited me out to dinner in the first place. Hmm, he must've really wanted to get into my pants.

"I believe Dagan was after it, but I beat him to the punch. He is in the process of purchasing the dark arts store."

I nearly choked on my water. "Fabian's?"

"Yes, Sweet, the very same."

I'm not sure why but Dagan owning Fabian's just seemed … wrong. Not that I'd been fond of the cretin Fabian at all.

"Sweet, No Regrets is throwing a party in honor of my birthday at the end of the month. I do hope you will attend?"

I'd forgotten about his three hundredth birthday. I smiled. "I'd be happy to."

The uneven grin on Bram's lips hinted to his unspoken thoughts. "It would please me greatly if you ... attended as my date."

Hmm, another date with Bram? It would be beneficial to remain on his good side, especially in light of the fact that his three hundredth birthday would see him as much more powerful than he now was. And furthermore, he was nice to look at ... and I was trying to work on dating more. "I'd be happy to," I repeated.

An hour later, I'd finished a third of my steak, declined dessert, and now Bram and I stood outside my apartment.

"I had a lovely time, Sweet," Bram said. "I hope you will allow me to take you out again?"

"Maybe." I guess I was feeling magnanimous. I actually had enjoyed myself, and Bram's company had been agreeable. Hmm, why the hell not go out with him again?

"I suppose a maybe is better than a no," Bram said with a twinkle in his eye.

I just smiled. "Thanks, Bram, I had a good time."

"My pleasure, Sweet," he said and stepped closer until maybe an inch of air separated us. He wanted to kiss me; I could see it in his eyes. And I couldn't say the idea was such a bad one.

He tilted his head and caught my lips softly, his arms wrapping around me as I opened my mouth. He was a good kisser—gentle and slow. But one kiss was enough for me. I pulled away from him with a little smile.

He stepped away, and his eyes burned with passion. "I have wanted to do that for a long while."

It was the same thing Quillan had said after he'd kissed me. Great—another memory to depress me. Trying to shake the thoughts of Quillan from my head, I pried myself from

Bram's embrace, and started for my apartment. "Have a good night, Bram."

"I will call you soon," he said, and I knew he meant it.

What I thought about it? I wasn't sure. Not something I had to worry about now, though.

I unlocked my door, walking into the house. When I went to close it behind me, I found him still standing in the same position, just watching me. I gave him a little wave and locked the door.

Throwing my purse onto the couch, I unzipped my boots and tossed them carelessly onto the floor. I plodded over to the computer and turned it on, deciding to check my e-mail.

I had one new message. It was from Great Fiction Agency. My heart started jack hammering in my chest as I clicked the e-mail open and dropped myself into the desk chair.

Dear Ms. O'Neil,

I would be happy to read the first three chapters of your paranormal romance, A Vampire and A Gentleman. Please send it as an e-mail attachment.

Kind Regards,
Barbara Mandley
Great Fiction Agency

Finally, someone was showing interest ... it was about damned time.

TWENTY-TWO

It was seven p.m., and I wasn't expecting any visitors, so when a knock sounded on the door, I was understandably taken by surprise. Peering through the peephole, I found Knight standing on my doorstep.

With an exasperated sigh, I opened the door.

A smile lit up his face. If I'd thought our month's separation would make him any less handsome, I was sorely mistaken. Holy Hades—the man should've been a model.

I eyed him suspiciously. "This is a surprise." It was a surprise and even though I didn't want to admit it to myself, it was a nice surprise. There was definitely a part of me that really liked Knight.

"I was in the neighborhood and thought I'd drop by and see how you're doing," he said with an embarrassed smile. Clearly he hadn't been in the neighborhood.

"Is that so?" I arched a brow but opened the door wide and he stepped inside. He smelled of soap—a clean, fresh fragrance.

"How are you?" he asked, still acting a bit awkward. It was a role I'd never seen him assume and one I liked.

"I'm fine. How are you?"

He nodded and rubbed the back of his neck. "Good, I'm good." He was quiet for a second as his gaze roamed my living room before settling back on me. "Are you busy tonight?"

I guess I felt sorry for him because I shook my head. Any nervousness in Knight fled as soon as I did so and was replaced with a beaming smile.

"I'll be your entertainment for the evening then." He clapped his hands together as if the entertainment had already begun.

"Entertainment?" I asked, sounding less than thrilled as I locked the door behind me.

"Have you had dinner yet?"

I shook my head. "Nope."

"Great, can I take you to dinner?"

I laughed at the eagerness in his voice. "I thought I already told you I wasn't interested in going on a date with you?"

"Well, this isn't a date."

"Oh, then what is it?"

He smiled that charming smile of his, and I knew something interesting was about to come out of his mouth. "Think of it as networking," Knight continued as I started for the kitchen and he followed me. I poured myself a glass of water and watched him pull out a chair and straddle it.

"Networking?"

He laughed, and a stray tendril of hair that had a tendency to drop in front of his eyes, did exactly that. I had to suppress the nagging urge to secure it behind his ear.

"I have a job for you," he said simply. Then standing up, eyed me from head to toe with a definite smirk.

"What?" I asked, nonplussed.

"Go change. I want to take you somewhere nice."

Figuring I didn't have a choice, I headed for my bedroom with a long and dramatic sigh. If Knight noticed, he didn't comment. Closing the door behind me, I sorted through my less than impressive closet and settled on a short, flouncy black skirt and a long-sleeved red blouse. Not wanting to take the time to do my makeup, I just magicked myself some red lipstick, eye liner and mascara and throwing on my black leather jacket and high heels, headed for the living room.

A huge smile lit Knight's lips upon seeing me, and I could feel my cheeks burning with a visible blush. So much for trying to act nonchalant.

"You look great." He paused, as if not able to check me out and talk at the same time.

"Thanks," I shrugged. "So about this job?"

"Let's talk about it in the car."

I grinned and opened the door, immediately spotting the brand new, silver BMW parked in front of my apartment. It was the nicest car on the street.

"Yours?" I asked, motioning to the car with a tilt of my chin as I locked the front door behind us.

A boyish grin spread over his lips as he stood gazing at the vehicle. Men and their cars.

"Just got it last week. What do you think?"

"Pretty posh." At the expression of pride on his face, I begrudgingly forced myself to show more interest. "What model?"

"BMW M3 Coupe." He said it like a proud father.

He unlocked the BMW with his remote and hurried down the steps before me, showing me to the passenger seat with a great sweep of his arm. I was just waiting for him to break into song and dance.

"Yeah, I always wanted a BMW, and I figured I might be here for a while," he finished as I pulled my legs into the passenger seat and buckled myself in.

His eyes lingered on my legs, and I self consciously smoothed my skirt down. Then he seemed to remember himself and started for his side of the car. He got in and settled himself comfortably into the driver's seat.

"I thought you were just here until they find someone to replace you?" I asked as he put the car in drive and blasted loud techno music from the speakers. He turned it down with an apologetic smile. I'm not sure why, but I hadn't expected Knight to be the techno sort.

He peeled into the street so fast, I felt as if I were in the midst of a tornado. He changed gears, double-clutching and revving the engine as he did so, a small grin on his lips. Hot Hades, he was such a kid.

"Well, according to the Chief, he wasn't sure how long it would take to find a replacement, and in Chief talk, that could mean years."

I nodded, silently pleased to hear it. Then I chided myself; I shouldn't care where the hell he went or what the hell he did. "So are you looking for a place to live, too? Or sticking it out at the Marriott?"

"No, looking for a place now, as a matter of fact. Looking in the heart of the city."

I held onto my seat as Knight took the turn at the base of my hill a little too fast and the car's tires screamed in protest. I should've figured him a speed demon. A speed Loki.

"So where are you taking me?" I asked, trying to keep my voice steady.

"Only the nicest restaurant in this area. The Chateaus."

Again? Just my luck. I wasn't sure if I was up for The Chateaus again but better to be polite, I guessed. "I was just there the other night. They have great food."

Knight braked a little too abruptly at the stop sign. "You were already there?"

I shrugged. "Yeah, it was good—you'll like it."

He frowned. "With who?"

"That would be with whom," I corrected him, then smiled and feigned interest in my fingernails for a few seconds. "Bram took me."

Knight did an abrupt U-Turn. He was a ticket waiting to happen.

"What are you doing?"

His lips were tight, his jaw even tighter. "Going back to your place. We can order in."

I laughed. So I enjoyed his discomfort—call me a sadist. "I liked The Chateaus."

"Well, I'm not taking you there if the vampire did," he snapped, driving up my hill faster than he'd driven down.

I frowned, still clutching the gray leather seat as if my life depended on it. I glanced at the dash to make sure there were air bags. There were. Phew. "So I got all dressed up for no reason."

Knight kept his attention trained on the road, a slight twitching in his jaw. "I'm not no reason."

Ha, so he was jealous, the bastard! I'm not sure why, but provoking Knight was one of the few things in life that brought me great pleasure. "Why are you so bothered by Bram taking me out?"

"I'm not bothered," he growled and came to an abrupt stop as the light turned red. He tapped his fingers against his lips impatiently and refused to look at me. His other hand massaged the gearshift, as if itching to resume his illegal speeds.

I cleared my throat. "Um, then what would you call it? Jealousy?" I shrugged. "That works too."

"I'm not jealous." He cast me a scowl, and put the car into gear as the light turned green, launching us forward. "I just don't think you should be dating him."

I laughed. "Who said I was dating him?"

"Well, you agreed to go out with him, so I just figured," he snapped.

"I agreed to go out with you; am I dating you?"

The anger simmered out of his expression, and he turned to give me a big smirk. "Not yet."

He pulled up to the curb and put the car in park, turning off the engine as he unbuckled his seatbelt and glanced over at me. "Why'd you agree to go out with Bram? I didn't think he was your type?"

I sighed. "I finished my book, and he took me out in honor of it. That, and I owed him a favor, so he chose that as his favor."

Knight chuckled. "He couldn't get you to go out with him any other way so he basically bribed you? That's tasteful."

"Well, it's not like you gave me much of a choice in going out with you tonight either."

He frowned but didn't respond. Instead, he opened the door and stepped out of the car. I opened my door as he locked it behind me, offering his arm as we took the flight of stairs. When I refused it, he appeared embarrassed—clearing his throat and glancing in my opposite direction. "Congratulations on finishing your book," he said.

"Thanks." I fished inside my purse for my keys and unlocked the front door. "So what's this job you were talking about?"

Knight strode in behind me and eyeing the yellow pages sitting beneath the coffee table, started for it. He dropped himself onto the couch and opened the book, sorting through it for delivery options.

"Let's decide what we want to eat first. How's Italian sound?"

I locked the door behind me. "Fine. I like eggplant parmesan."

I threw my jacket on the sofa arm and stepped out of my heels, leaving them beside the couch. I tossed my purse onto the kitchen table as Knight dialed and placed our order. When he finished, he returned the phone book and stretched his long legs out before him, crossing them at the ankles as he stretched his arms behind his head.

"There's been a murder in Sanctity. We know it's a werewolf, but we haven't been able to track him down."

I studied him and took a seat at the table. "Sounds pretty standard. Anyone at Headquarters should be able to solve that with their eyes closed."

He leaned forward and shook his head. "Yeah, it's not standard." He paused. "Will you help me?"

The offer didn't look so bad, and I needed the money. I'd already dipped into my savings to pay the rent for this month, and it wasn't something I wanted to repeat. "It depends. What are the particulars?"

He leaned back against the couch smiling. "I'll pay you whatever you think the job's worth, and I'll pay you weekly." He paused. "If you can solve the case within a month, I'll pay you an extra thirty percent commission on top."

Hmm, that didn't sound half bad. "I name my own price?"

"Yeah, whatever you want, it's yours."

"I was supposed to get my review sometime soon which would've been at least a ten percent increase."

He shook his head. "I don't care what your raise should've been. I could get the information on what you made, but I don't care about it. Just decide what you think is fair and we'll go from there." That same cheeky smile returned to his lips. "And don't short yourself. Now that you're a consultant, the work won't be reliable, so make it worth your while."

"Sounds like you're teaching me how to be a good businesswoman?" I laughed, appreciating the fact he wasn't trying to screw me over.

"Well, if I had it my way, you'd be coming back to the force."

I started to shake my head, still not at all okay with the fact that I'd let Quillan go. I didn't imagine I ever would be. "I haven't changed my mind about that."

He nodded. "I didn't think you would have."

"Besides, Sam told me about all the women in the office chasing you. You wouldn't want me in the way of that." I threw him a smile.

He stood up with an elevated brow. "Who says you'd get in the way of that?"

I feigned indignation. Knight just chuckled as a knock sounded on the door, announcing the arrival of our food. Knight paid the delivery boy and carried the plastic bags to the kitchen. "Do you have anything to drink?"

"There's beer in the fridge and I have a bottle of wine on the counter." The wine had been a going away gift from Sam.

"Wine sounds great. You want a glass?"

"Sure." I pointed to the glass cabinet and Knight reached for two dusty glasses, throwing me a rolled eye look as he rinsed them out.

"Looks like I just rinsed away a few resident spiders."

"I forgive you."

I watched him pour two glasses of red wine, and he handed one to me. Holding his own in the air, apparently he was going to make a toast. "To our new relationship," he said with a lascivious smile and an equally lascivious wink.

"To our new work relationship," I corrected him, and we both took a sip. I unpacked the contents of each bag as Knight watched me. "Ready to eat?" I asked.

He nodded and sat down while I started in on my eggplant. Knight had ordered stuffed shells. We were pretty quiet as we devoured our dinners and twenty minutes later, I'd had enough. I pushed the food away and downed my glass of wine.

"Good?" Knight asked.

"Great."

Knight took his last bite, and I saran-wrapped the remainder of the eggplant, tossing it into the fridge as Knight gathered the rest of our mess and deposited it in the trashcan.

He refilled my wine glass.

"Okay, no more talking about work," he started and extended his hand. I took it, and he led me into the living room, motioning for me to take a seat on the couch. I did so and he dropped down beside me, resting his hand on my thigh. I didn't move it.

"What do you want to talk about?" I asked, setting my wine glass on the coffee table.

He shrugged and taking another sip of his wine, set it beside mine. "Let's talk about you."

"Me?" I asked, as if talking about myself were the last thing I intended to do.

"Let's talk about the fact that I haven't been able to stop thinking about you since that night I kissed you."

His hand massaged my thigh and nervousness agitated my stomach. I'd kissed and been kissed before—there was no reason for my anxiety.

"Oh, is that so?" I whispered. "I haven't thought of it since."

"Liar," Knight said as his lips met mine.

His lips were full, and when he ran his hand through my hair, I opened my mouth and he thrust his tongue inside. He pushed me down against the couch and moved his body on top of mine as he continued kissing me, his body gyrating against mine just like he'd done when I'd tried to arrest him.

I wrapped my arms around his neck, and he continued undulating above me, making the blood in my veins burn. He pulled his mouth from mine and gave me a smirk as he tilted my head back and planted a few tender kisses down the length of my neck. I arched up against him as he dug his pelvis into me, and I could feel the obvious stirring of his attraction for me.

"Should we move to the bedroom?" he asked.

Call me old school, but I wanted to be in a relationship if sex was on the horizon. That, and I was just starting to date again. I pushed away from him. "Um, I think that's a bad idea."

He chuckled. "Dulcie, you think about everything too much."

"Well, one of us has to," I said with a smile and stood up, offering my hand.

251

He took it and stood, running his fingers through his hair. "Sending me home with blue balls again," he said with a laugh.

I shrugged. "Looks that way."

He reached for his keys on the coffee table. "I'm going to take you out on a real date one of these days."

"You say it like it's a threat."

"Just a warning."

I shook my head and followed him to the door. "You definitely are eager."

He nodded. "You're a hard woman to stop thinking about."

He reached down and circled my waist with his arms, pulling me into the hard length of him and planted a chaste kiss on my lips. "Goodnight, Dulcie."

He turned around and started for his car.

"Night Knight," I said with a laugh.

I closed the door and went back into my living room. So more dates with Bram and Knight. Wisps of what felt like panic started in my stomach but I forced myself to ignore them. Dates were not a big deal. It wasn't like I was getting into a relationship with either one, I thought to myself, hoping to subdue my trust issues.

Glancing at my computer, I noticed I had a new e-mail. I took a seat and opened my inbox. On further inspection, the e-mail was from Dr. Goodman. I clicked it open and read:

Dear Ms. O'Neil,

Please let us know if you would like to set up an appointment for your ear augmentation.

Regards,

The office of Dr. Goodman

I leaned back in my chair. I hadn't thought about the ear augmentation in over a month. Running a finger over the points of my ears, I remembered Quillan telling me not to go through with it. I'm not sure if his words had made up my mind but something had.

I deleted the e-mail, a new sense of overwhelming pride suffusing me.

The phone rang, interrupting my moment of epiphany. "Hello?"

"Check your front door."

It was Quillan.

I checked the caller ID but the number was unlisted.

"Quillan?" I demanded, but the dial tone resonated through my ear. I hung up.

"Dammit!"

Running to my front door, I tore it open, hoping to find Quillan even though I knew better. He was a wanted man; he wouldn't just show up on my doorstep. Just as I'd suspected … nothing. Looking down, I found a box about as high as my knee and maybe two feet wide, wrapped in white paper and a bright red bow. I grabbed the card on top and tore into it.

Dulce,

He's cuter than a gremlin.

Q.

Not wanting to guess what was in the box, I ripped open the wrapping paper and tearing off a piece of tape binding the box together, I found a yellow Lab puppy gazing up at me. I reached inside and picked him up, his puppy breath tickling my cheek.

He was the most adorable thing I'd ever seen.

"Hello, boy," I whispered, wondering what in the hell Quillan was up to.

Noticing his red collar and the silver name tag, I rotated the tag around until I read his name "Blue."

I shook my head unable to suppress the happy smile that beamed across my face.

Holding the puppy up against my chest, the sound of a car starting caught our attention. It was parked across the street—some sort of white sports car. The driver's chuckle floated up to me as he started down the street. The windows were too tinted for me to make out who it was.

But I knew.
Quillan.

A TALE OF TWO GOBLINS

Book 2 of the Dulcie O'Neil series

AVAILABLE NOW!

Flip to the next page to read the first chapter of
A Tale of Two Goblins!

ONE

I yawned but forced the desire to crawl back into bed out of my mind. Exercise was important in my line of work, and although it was only five in the morning, it was my favorite hour to jog. I grabbed my iPod and glanced down at Blue as he pawed my toes, only to lean back on his haunches and stretch. Guess it was early for him too.

Pushing an earpiece into my ear, I opened the front door of my crappy apartment and inhaled the cold Splendor air. The chirping of insects was as loud as the finale of any symphony and I shivered as a cold wind assaulted me. I wasn't a big fan of November in California—give me hot, sunny weather all year long and I'd be as happy as a pixie on a bliss potion.

I leaned over and grabbed my ankles, stretching my quads and stood up, pulling my arms over my head and stretched my triceps. One should never exercise with cold muscles. Blue started groaning and circled me as if to say "hurry up already." Feeling limber enough, I stepped outside, locked the door and started my jog while Katy Perry sang "Teenage Dream" into my head.

Maybe five minutes into our run, Blue slowed and cocked his head to the side, but I didn't need his canine sixth sense to know someone was following us. I swallowed the anxiety in my throat and went into autopilot or auto cop, as the case may be. Turning the volume down on my iPod, I didn't remove the ear buds, not wanting to alert my visitor to the fact that I knew he was there. Rolling my arms in tight circles, I waited—well figuratively, I was still jogging, still giving the illusion of everything being hunky dory in the life of Dulcie the fairy.

Before I had the chance to think, a shadow flickered from between the trees. My breath caught in my throat, and I paused, bending over to pretend to tie my shoelace. Even though I was doing my damndest not to give anything away, Blue wasn't quite so stealthy. Instead, he stood as if in rigor mortis, his hackles raised and his lips curling back to reveal an impressive set of sharp teeth. His growl interrupted the otherwise still night, and I glanced back at the tree line, watching and waiting for whatever was out there to make itself known. When it did, I'd be ready to take it down with a palm full of fairy dust—my weapon extraordinaire. I stood up and braced myself, feet shoulder width apart.

I didn't have to wait long. My assailant made himself known, jumping out at me with a huge ... smile?

"Knight!" I leaned onto my knees, breathing out the angst that just seconds ago would have dictated I use my fairy powers to take him out. "You bastard," I breathed, refusing to look at him.

Blue wasn't as polite. His growl sounded like a large truck driving over rocks. The dog must have thought growling wasn't threatening enough because he then broke into a deep and angry bark. I petted his head and tried to calm him with "it's okay, boy" but the dog wouldn't back down. Instead, he lunged for Knight and much as I was annoyed with Knight myself, he didn't deserve to get bitten. Not that I thought Blue would bite him, but better to be safe than stuck in the emergency room. So I grabbed Blue's collar and held him back with a none too subtle "No!"

"Nice dog," Knight scoffed as Blue continued to growl. Hmm, maybe I hadn't socialized him well enough. Come to think of it, I hadn't socialized him at all, which shouldn't have been much of a surprise as I wasn't a very social person myself.

"What do you want?" I demanded.

"Morning, Dulce," Knight said, completely disregarding my less than friendly greeting. Unable to avoid looking at him for more than a few seconds, I finally brought my attention to his face.

Knight Vander was a *Loki*, a creature from the Netherworld who also happened to be an investigator working for the Association of Netherworld Creatures otherwise known as the ANC. And he also happened to be the hottest thing in Splendor.

"What the hell are you doing outside my apartment at five a.m.?" I insisted, and patted Blue's head so he'd stop growling. He finally obeyed and sat silently at my feet, wearing a happy dog smile.

"Technically I'm not outside your apartment," Knight said and flashed me a beautiful smile. Holy Hades, the man was sexy.

"So, we're going to play word games?" Rather than waiting for an answer, I started jogging again. Not that I disliked Knight but he was a cocky SOB and there wasn't any room in my life for cockiness or SOBs or, for that matter, Knight. "So, what, you just hang around my house waiting for me to come out?"

"I needed to get in touch with you," he said in his baritone voice, as rich as a piece of dark chocolate cake.

The moon was still in full effect, and the milky rays glowed against Knight's white tee shirt. His shorts ended just below his knees, and I couldn't help but notice how muscular his calves were, muscular and evenly covered with black hair. Realizing I was checking his legs out and very obviously, I brought my attention to the road and tried to increase my pace. Knight easily kept up with me which wasn't hard considering I was five-one and he was at least six-two, maybe six-three. To me, he looked like a giant.

"Have you heard of this pretty cool invention called the phone?" I asked, keeping my attention straight ahead. "Through a series of wires and electrodes, my voice travels to you and you never have to leave your house! Imagine that!"

"Haha, Dulce, I've called you countless times over the last two months, and I've lost track of how many messages I've left." He didn't sound angry, merely conversational.

Okay, so I was guilty about not calling him back, so what? "I've been … busy," I said, though it was farthest from the truth. Having recently given Knight my letter of resignation (he'd been my boss), I now had lots of free time but not a whole lot to fill it with. Course, Knight didn't need to know that.

"Busy?" he repeated, his tone just as dubious as his smile. "I see you've got a dog but other than that, what's been occupying your time?"

The sound of our footfalls against the pavement echoed my shallow breathing. I hadn't been on a jog in at least a week and it was making itself known in every section of my body.

"Writing," I answered succinctly. And it was the truth. I'd been spending all my time working on a book, the second in a series. I had aspirations to be a full-time writer, and it seemed those aspirations might actually be headed somewhere—recently a literary agent had requested the full manuscript of my book, "A Vampire and a Gentleman."

Knight just nodded, and I felt my breath becoming more and more shallow. It wasn't easy to run and talk at the same time. I glanced at my companion, the *Loki*, and found he didn't seem to be huffing or puffing. Instead, he just wore an amused smile and looked me up and down appreciatively. I frowned and glanced back at the road, feeling the need to slow my pace. But I wouldn't give in—not yet.

"Where'd you get the dog?" he asked, eyeing the subject all the while.

"He was a gift," I answered and felt like I was going to pass out with the effort.

"Who from?"

Hmm, this was a question that wouldn't get an honest answer, or at least not a full honest answer. Blue had been given to me by my ex boss (the one before Knight), Quillan, who was now a wanted potions smuggler. Quillan … just his name left a bad taste in my mouth—he'd been my boss, yes, but also my friend, and I'd sort of lusted after him … just a little. But when it came down to apprehending him, when I was still a cop, aka Regulator working for the Netherworld,

I'd failed. And so far, I hadn't been able to forgive myself for failing, for allowing my emotions to get in the way of my position as Regulator. It had been a sign that I wasn't the Regulator I'd thought I was or needed to be. So I'd resigned.

I didn't like to think about Quillan, and I really didn't like to talk about him.

"Just a friend." I made the mistake of glancing up at Knight. The cock-eyed expression he wore made me look away quickly. He seemed to always know when there was more to a story. Course, I was also a terrible liar.

"A friend?" he inquired.

Not able to continue on, I stopped jogging and faced him, irritation seeping into my gut as I fought to catch my breath. "Didn't your mother ever tell you it's rude to put your nose in other people's business?"

Knight also stopped jogging, that same smile still hanging from his lips. "Can't recall that she did."

I crossed my arms against my chest, trying to ward off the cold night air and wished I'd worn something over my sports bra. Maybe my annoyance with Knight would be enough to keep me warm. "Let's cut the crap, Knight, what are you doing here?"

"I need your help."

That could mean many things but due to the fact that I'd promised Knight I'd be available to work as a consultant whenever he had a tough Netherworld case, the playing field was narrowed. "What do you need my help for?" I asked, watching Blue arch his back and pee against a bush. He still hadn't mastered the art of lifting one leg but I wasn't sure how I was supposed to teach him.

"There's a case that's been baffling us all."

Before I decided to hear anymore, I turned around and started walking back toward my apartment, rolling my arms in big circles. No use in discussing ANC business while we were standing in the middle of the road. Knight was beside me momentarily and threw me another disarmingly handsome smile. With his black hair, blue eyes and tan complexion, immense height and broad build, he looked like a God. And, boy, wouldn't he have loved to know that.

"Let's talk about it in my apartment," I started.

"I was hoping you'd say that."

"Don't get any ideas," I grumbled, watching Blue scout the bushes and trees before us. I never took him on a leash because we never met anyone on our 5:00 a.m. excursions. Guess I couldn't say that anymore.

"Dulce, I've been getting ideas where you're concerned since we met," Knight said, his voice heavy.

"Well, keep them to yourself," I snapped. I'd already made up my mind not to get involved with Knight.

"Why do you fight your attraction to me?" His tone wasn't clipped or otherwise pointing to a hurt self-esteem. Course, he was never anything other than sure, and his infallible confidence was one of his character traits that bothered me the most. I mean, didn't everyone succumb to self-doubt once in a while? Ha, not if you were a *Loki* who answered to the name of Knight.

"Who said I'm attracted to you?" I insisted, wishing I could wipe the cocky and proud smile right off his mouth.

"No point in denying it; I'm fully aware of your real feelings for me."

I laughed, but it was an acidic sound because I was suddenly worried that he could sense it. Even though I'd pledged never to develop feelings for him, I couldn't deny the fact that I was attracted to Knight and always had been. But I tempered that attraction by keeping him at arm's length.

As a rule, I didn't get involved with men. Now, before you question that statement—I also didn't get involved with women—I just didn't get involved period. After a pretty crappy breakup two years earlier, my heart still hadn't fully mended and Knight was the type of man who would break it again, into tiny little shards that would be impossible to glue back together. If he ever got the chance, that is.

"Hmm ..." I started, really not knowing what else to say. Even though, as a fairy, I had the innate ability to detect creatures just by looking at them, Knight had thrown me for a loop from day one. Course, the reason had been that I'd never come into contact with one of his kind before—a *Loki*. Furthermore, the unfortunate thing about Knight's being a

Loki was I had no clue what his powers were. Unlike my ability to create magic from fairy dust, Knight's abilities weren't quite so straight forward. I'd actually been keeping a list of the types of powers he'd demonstrated so far. Guess I could add attraction detector to the mix. Unless he was full of it ...

"You just know?" I asked doubtfully. "What, is that another of your *Loki* character traits?"

"Nope," he said in a self-satisfied sort of way. "It's just Vander instinct, one hundred percent."

"Well, your Vander instinct is confused by your Vander cockiness," I snapped.

He laughed, but his eyes were hot, hungry and I felt consumed just by his wolfish stare. I dropped my attention to the ground and mumbled something under my breath, trying to keep Knight from noticing the red flush currently overtaking my cheeks. We reached my apartment and could now talk about ANC business and not the fact that I was lusting after Knight and, furthermore, that he knew it.

I jammed the key into the lock and nearly lost my focus when I felt the heat of Knight's body just behind me. The iciness of the air seemed doubly cold in front of me while Knight's heat penetrated my back. I closed my eyes at the feel of his hands massaging my forearms. Thank Hades my back was to him and he couldn't see my reaction. Course, the goose bumps on my arms could be compared to a big arrow sign pointing at me with the words: "she's hot for you" emblazoned on it.

"You have goose flesh," he whispered and caused a seizure in my stomach.

"I, uh, it's ... it's cold out here."

He chuckled and lifted the heavy curtain of my honey blond hair over one shoulder, trailing the back of my neck with his index finger. I couldn't help the shudder that raced through me.

"I haven't stopped thinking about you, Dulcie." His voice was a mere breath whispering against my skin, and I closed my eyes, reveling in the feel of him. The touch of his lips against my neck brought a hiss of air from my mouth, and before I lost all sense of reason right there, Blue walked over and pawed my toes, as if reminding me I'd been attempting to unlock the door and, more so, that I was acting like an idiot.

I opened my eyes and silently praised the dog for bringing me back to my senses. Cranking the key to the left, I pushed the door open with such strength, I nearly lost my footing. But I was inside and away from Knight ... things were looking up.

Turning on the light, I flung myself into my computer desk chair, making sure to sit somewhere Knight couldn't sit beside me. I wheeled around and faced him, finding the air in my tiny apartment considerably stuffy. Knight closed the door behind him and lumbered into my living room, seating himself on my couch.

"One of these days, Dulce, you aren't going to be able to deny there is something between us."

Irritation bled through me. I didn't like people telling me what I could and couldn't do. "Regardless of what you think, I'm not interested."

Knight cocked a brow and chuckled, but said nothing.

"So let's talk about the reason you're here," I said.

"There have been quite a few cases recently of comatose victims, both here in Splendor but also in Estuary and Moon." His tone was suddenly all business, and I breathed an inward sigh of relief. All business Knight I could handle.

Estuary was in our district—we provided police work for Splendor, Estuary and Haven. Moon, though, was out of our district and had its own ANC force. But back to the comatose victims ... "So why should I be concerned?"

Knight shrugged. "All victims were otherwise healthy, according to their friends and family. Then one night they go to sleep and never wake up the next morning."

I nodded, feeling a cramp building in my calf. I propped one leg over my knee, leaned forward and started my after exercise stretch routine. "Has anyone died?"

"One death."

Stretching my calf, I winced against the pain.

"Cramp?" Knight asked. "I can do wonders on sore muscles."

"I'm fine," I started and, not wanting to appear so out of sorts, added: "Thanks."

Knight, apparently not used to hearing no for an answer, stood up and approached me. "Lay with your back on the floor and I'll show you a good one for leg cramps and for stretching your quads."

The cramp in my calf suddenly started pounding as if it wanted nothing more than to be massaged by the incredibly handsome *Loki*, and before I knew it, I was lying on the floor, looking up at him. He reached for my right leg and cradled it against his thigh as he massaged my calf, kneading my sore muscles with his large hands. Little by little, the cramp stopped throbbing and eventually went away. Hmm, another Knight Vander *Loki* ability?

"When did these comas start?" I asked quickly, trying to pull my attention from his hands. He worked up my thigh and then took my foot in his hand and bent my leg at the knee, pushing my knee up into my stomach.

"How does that feel?" Knight asked.

"Good," I managed. He pulled my leg straight and put it back on the floor, reaching for the other one. A massage of my other thigh followed, and although I didn't want to admit it to myself, I was getting incredibly turned on.

"We've been noticing these sudden comas popping up for over two months," he said. Hmm, hence his repeated calls to me over the last couple of months. He didn't say it but it was there in his eyes. I felt a little bit guilty, but quickly banished the feeling. If Knight had really needed to get in touch with me, he would have invaded my happy little jog months earlier.

"So I guess you want me to review the files?" I asked, thinking I could use some consultant work. My savings account had been dwindling recently, but I just hadn't been able to bring myself to call Knight for work—it wasn't that I was avoiding jobs, I was avoiding Knight.

"If you feel so inclined," he answered with a grin and brought my foot back to the ground, offering his hands. I took them, and he pulled me up.

"Any ideas on what could be causing all the comas?" I asked.

He made his way back to the couch and sunk into it, stretching his arms above his head and clasped them behind his neck. I was convinced he liked showing off his chest and huge biceps. "Healthy victim one day, comatose the next."

"*Toad Wallow*?" *Toad Wallow* was a potion—one drop and you'd be dead to the world for a week at the most, then you'd wake up with one raging headache, but at least you'd wake up. Course, it didn't seem the same could be said for these victims.

Knight shook his head. "None of the patients have reflexes, and their EKGs come back inactive."

"*Somnogobelinus*," I whispered. "A sleep goblin, a *Dreamstalker*."

Knight nodded. "All roads lead to Rome, or a *Dreamstalker* in this case."

I shook my head. "There are only two registered *Dreamstalkers* in the ANC files: one has been locked away in a Netherworld prison for centuries and …"

"The second was locked away five years ago," Knight finished for me, with an approving smile.

"Ah, so you have done your homework." Apprehending Druiva, the *Dreamstalker* in question, had been one of the most difficult cases Splendor ANC had ever seen. I'd been a junior Regulator at the time and hadn't really been involved, but it was one of those legendary cases that was still discussed, even now.

"I have."

"And are they still locked away?" I demanded, thinking we'd found our solution if the answer was "no."

"Yes, as of yesterday, they are both doing time in Banshee Prison from here until eternity, both under extra security."

"How can this be then?" I asked, and slunk back into the computer chair, suddenly irritated by the fact that I'd let

Knight touch me. I was like mush in his hands—if I was going to keep my distance, I needed to avoid him. Damn it all, I'd been doing a pretty good job before he'd just waltzed back into my life as pretty as he pleased.

Knight shook his head and dropped his arms, thank Hades. A chest that broad should have been illegal. "We're baffled, which is why I wanted to bring you into the case." He stood up and approached me, causing me to shrink back into my chair. "Will you help me, Dulce?"

I just nodded before the vision of his lips against my neck slapped me back into reality. Knight needed to know this arrangement would be purely professional, purely business. "Yes, on a few conditions."

Knight sighed and started pacing my living room. "Name them."

"One, you have to be professional."

He faced me, his mouth open in mock offense. "I'm always …"

"No flirting, no accidental touches, no running your fingers down my neck, no lips on my shoulders …"

He chuckled. "You enjoyed that; don't deny it."

I had enjoyed it and couldn't deny it, so I merely ignored him. "No double-entendres, no gifts …"

"Okay, I get it," he said none too happily. "Is that all?"

"No sex jokes, no invading my personal space, no comments on my appearance, no lustful glances and absolutely no winking."

Knight threw himself back into the couch and faced me with a perturbed expression. "I should have found someone else to help with the case."

I laughed. "Don't be a spoil sport. You know I'm the best."

He offered me a boyish grin. "Yes, you are."

Inwardly, I breathed a sigh of relief. Maybe this would be easier than I'd assumed. As long as Knight kept his distance, I could keep my guard up. "Good, now that we've reached an understanding, let's meet up again tomorrow night. Bring the files with you."

"What about tonight?"

"Tonight's not good; I have plans." And plans I wasn't thrilled about. I had a date with a vampire. Well, I didn't exactly think of it as a date—more like two people accompanying one another to a party.

"Plans?" Knight asked, warily.

"Yes," I started before interrupting myself. "Add that to the list of rules: no being nosy and definitely no being jealous."

He dropped his pinched lip expression and exchanged it for one of detached indifference. "I'm not jealous."

"No use in lying," I said with a broad smile. "I know you are—call it my instincts, one hundred percent pure Dulcie O'Neil."

With a chuckle, Knight stood and approached the door, the sunlight of morning just peeking through my windows, basking him in a yellow glow until he looked like an angel. Ha, Knight was no angel.

"Until tomorrow night then," he said and reached for the doorknob.

"Yes."

He smiled. "It's a date." Then he opened the door, winked and walked into the daylight.

Men.

As I mentioned earlier, Bram was a vampire and it just happened to be his three hundredth birthday. Every hundred year birthday found a vampire stronger, quicker, more powerful and in Bram's case, he'd even gotten better looking. His day old stubble was still in full effect but that wasn't something he'd ever be able to do anything about, seeing as how he'd had it when he'd been turned. But there was something about him that was just more attractive—maybe it wasn't so much his features that had improved but more his control over what other people thought of him.

"Ah, sweet, you are ravishing," Bram said in his lofty English accent and kissed my hand as his eyes devoured every inch of me.

I smiled my thanks and accepted his arm as he escorted me down my front walkway and into the leather plushness of a black stretch Hummer. Our driver, a were, doffed his head politely as I pulled myself into the stretch limo. Bram was just behind me and once he'd taken his seat across from mine, eyed me with undisguised admiration.

"Dulcie, these many months of separation have been difficult on my memory. I do not recall you appearing quite so beautiful."

I sighed and tried to smile. I was just not good at accepting compliments. Was Bram sincere? Yeah, I thought so. Did he want to get into my pants? Yeppers and always had. But regardless of Bram's intentions, I had to admit I did feel … pretty.

I'd worn a knee-length, strapless black evening gown in a diaphanous material that graced my skin like a whisper. Even though the gossamer material hinted at the curves of my body, it was just that—a hint. My lace thong panties were my only undergarments, the dress not lending itself to a bra. Not exactly comfortable exposing so much skin, I'd covered the dress with a fitted black leather jacket. And to finish off my evening attire, I'd worn the highest heels I owned—four-inch Jimmy Choos with so many straps, they would have pleased any dominatrix. I wore my hair down which wasn't a surprise since I wasn't exactly thrilled with showing off my ears. As a fairy, my ears came to points at the top and they were my least favorite of my physical attributes. I'd considered getting an ear reduction but threw the idea out because it was just too risky. Fairies didn't do well with human sedatives. That and my old boss, Quillan, had said I didn't need it, that I was beautiful just as I was.

A sadness descended on me at the thought of Quillan, so I brushed it aside and focused on my handsome vampire date. Over six-four, he had the physique of a swimmer—broad shoulders tapering to a trim waist with a pair of legs that seemed to be as long as I was tall (not that I was tall). His black hair was on the longish side, just curling over his ears. His licentious smile was … sexy. But like my relationship with Knight or lack thereof, I wanted to keep things strictly platonic with Bram. Although I had started dating more recently, I still wasn't completely comfortable with it and rather than running for cover with my tail between my legs, I just decided to take it one step at a time. The fact that I was even out tonight was a step in and of itself.

"Thanks for the compliment," I said with a small smile.

He returned the smile and appeared to be studying me. Feeling entirely too uncomfortable under his libidinous stare, I fought to find something to say. "So are you feeling any different on your birthday?"

He nodded but didn't expound.

I cocked my head and considered him. "And? What's different?"

"I'm faster."

"Faster?" I started but Bram had suddenly … disappeared. Just dissolved into the air as if he'd never been, as if I'd been imagining him all along. As a vamp, he'd always been fast—moving like a blur from point A to point B but as a blur, that's exactly what you'd been able to see. This was different.

"Bram?" I repeated, shifting my gaze from one end of the limo to the other. Just like that, I felt an icy cold penetrating my back. I whipped around to find Bram sitting beside me, smiling smugly. "What was that?" I demanded, shock straining my voice. "You can disappear now?"

He shook his head. "No."

"But …"

"I merely moved too quickly for you to follow with your naked eye."

"Bullshit," I bit out, wondering if he was going to backpedal and try to talk his way out of it. It would do no good. I knew what I'd seen … or hadn't seen in this case.

He laughed. "Your mind tricked you, Dulce. I have been sitting here all along but you were relying on the incorrect sense."

"Incorrect sense?" I asked dubiously and crossed my arms against my chest as I regarded him coolly.

He leaned into me until his icy breath fanned across my naked collarbone and brought goose bumps to my skin. But I held my ground and didn't move away.

"Close your eyes," he whispered.

"You'd better not try anything," I started, eyeing him suspiciously.

"I know you too well, Sweet, to attempt anything. You would have me flat on my back with a stake over my heart before I could blink."

He did know me well. I closed my eyes and then I heard him. It was the tiniest, most insignificant disturbance in the otherwise still air. I opened my eyes and glanced to my right and there he was.

"You see?" he asked.

I nodded and watched him disappear as if the air had swallowed him—right there in front of me. I didn't have enough time to think to rely on my other senses rather than my eyesight and suddenly felt myself falling, pushed backward by unseen hands. The leather of the seat met the back of my head, and I inhaled sharply as adrenaline pounded through my veins. My dress slinked up my thighs but I wasn't concerned with propriety at the moment. What I was concerned with was the fact that Bram had materialized and was now on top of me.

"Back the hell off me," I hissed and pushed against his chest, suddenly angry with myself that I'd ever agreed to be his date in the first place. I could never truly trust Bram. Sure, he'd helped me with certain cases when I'd been a Regulator but he definitely wasn't a law-abiding citizen. If he had one hand in the morally upstanding cookie jar, the other hand was in the process of stealing all the cookies.

His fangs descended, and he was panting. His eyes, though, were far more scary. There was a depth to them I'd never seen before, something wiser and older. If I hadn't been a fairy with my level of magical ability, I'd now be under the vampire's spell, allowing him to do whatever he wanted to with me. As it was, I was finding it difficult to fight. "Bram, I'm giving you three seconds to back the fuck off me."

Bram suddenly sat up and adjusted the tie at his neck while his fangs retracted. "Apologies."

I pushed myself aside and pulled my dress down, throwing him an angry glare. "What the hell is wrong with you? Are you trying to make me hate you?"

"I was curious to learn if my increased age could make you submit to me," he answered tersely, casually, as if he hadn't just attacked me. But somewhere in his comment was disappointment. He'd been hoping I was weak enough to submit to him. But to what end?

"You're lucky I didn't taser you, bastard!" I retorted, although it was an empty threat. I hadn't brought a taser with me. But Bram didn't need to know that.

"I would not have injured you, Sweet," Bram said and pasted an artificial smile on his handsome face. "It was merely a test."

"Well, I don't like tests so don't do it again," I snapped, feeling the pounding of my heartbeat start to slow. Maybe it *had* merely been a test and not something more sinister. "If we're going to be friends …"

"I do so enjoy our friendship," he interrupted.

"Then don't screw it up." My eyes narrowed as I reconsidered his earlier statement. "If your powers of persuasion had worked, what would you have done?"

"Kissed you, Sweet, as I am still dying to do." He leaned forward like he thought he'd give it a try.

"Keep away from me," I said angrily. To reinforce the comment, I quickly moved to the seat across from him. I crossed my arms against my chest and wondered how I'd get through the evening.

"I apologize for offending you. I seem to lose my wits where you are concerned."

I was spared the need to respond as the limo came to a halt and moments later, our driver opened the door. I hopped down and glanced up at the restaurant before us, The Chateaus. It was the same place Bram had taken me when I'd agreed to a first "date" with him. I had half a mind to leave him at the curb and walk inside without him but forced myself not to. This was Bram's big night, and I didn't want to embarrass him. Granted, he'd just tried to molest me but hopefully he'd learned his lesson. And I'd learned my lesson to pack heat no matter where I was going or who I was seeing—you never knew when some jackass vampire was going to try to nibble your goodies.

The jackass vampire in question was beside me momentarily and offered his arm as he leaned down and whispered. "I apologize, Sweet, I will never impose myself on you again. Do you accept my apology?"

"Yes," I grumbled and took his arm as we started up the marble walkway of the grand restaurant. A doorman greeted Bram by name and pulled open the ornate ten-foot-high mahogany door, revealing the crowd within. That was when I realized we must have been pretty late. Not that it was a surprise—Bram definitely labored under the misguided notion of his own self-importance. Of course he'd be late to his own party.

As we entered the overcrowded room, I felt like I was on exhibit—"Bram's date, who can she be?" going through everyone's minds. I dropped my attention to the click of my heels against the black marble floors. When I could still feel the flush of anxiety on my cheeks, I forced myself to take in the dark red of the walls, the open ceiling, warehouse like with its rows of exposed metal piping. Candelabras topped with slender red candles stood proudly at the center of each table, throwing a yellow glow against the plates, soup bowls and the silver of utensils that decorated each table. My eyes fell to one table, dead center in the room, separated from the other tables by a girth of about two to three feet all the way around. And guess whose table that was? I swallowed down my anxiety and allowed Bram to lead me to the small table currently playing the part of island. There were only two chairs. Holy Hades …

As soon as we reached the table, Bram's posse descended on us, smiling and offering congratulations. Many of his female acquaintances embraced him, there were even some kisses, from which he quickly pulled away and eyed me speculatively. I just shook my head and took a seat at the table, pretending extreme interest in the cutlery.

"Looks like you've got the best seat in the house."

I glanced up into Knight's smiling face and felt my stomach drop.

 **H. P. Mallory** is the author of the Jolie Wilkins series as well as the Dulcie O'Neil series.

She began her writing career as a self-published author and after reaching a tremendous amount of success, decided to become a traditionally published author and hasn't looked back since.

H. P. Mallory lives in Southern California with her husband and son, where she is at work on her next book.

If you are interested in receiving emails when she releases new books, please sign up for her email distribution list by visiting her website and clicking the "contact" tab: www.hpmallory.com

Be sure to join HP's online Facebook community where you will find pictures of the characters from both series and lots of other fun stuff including an online book club!

Facebook:
https://www.facebook.com/profile.php?id=100001249643765

Find H.P. Mallory Online:
www.hpmallory.com
http://twitter.com/hpmallory
https://www.facebook.com/profile.php?id=100001249643765